'The Underground Village: Short Stories by Kang Kyeong-ae *anthologizes the major short fictions by Kang Kyeong-ae, one of the most innovative writers of colonial Korea, rendering them into natural and graceful English. Kang's stories of poverty and hardship, often featuring female protagonists and set in Japanese-occupied Manchuria, cross multiple borders, those of race, gender, geography, culture, ideologies, and literary schools, thus forcing us to reconsider our notions of feminism, Marxism, modernism, socialist realism, and "Korea".'*

—JIN-KYUNG LEE
Associate Professor of Korean and Comparative Literature,
University of California San Diego

'Kang is an important representative of Korean women during the Japanese colonial era; a rare reflection of lower-class women's voices. Moreover, Kang brilliantly captured the zeitgeist as a writer who witnessed participants in armed struggles against the Japanese, testifying to their suffering and validity, and she was able to convey all of this to colonial Korea directly under Japanese rule.'

—SANG-KYUNG LEE
Co-editor of *Rat Fire: Korean Stories from the Japanese Empire*

THE UNDERGROUND VILLAGE

SHORT STORIES BY KANG KYEONG-AE

Translated by ANTON HUR
Introduced by SANG-KYUNG LEE

HONFORD STAR

This translation first published by Honford Star 2018
honfordstar.com
Translation copyright © Anton Hur 2018
Introduction copyright © Sang-kyung Lee 2018
All rights reserved
The moral right of the translator and editors has been asserted.

ISBN (paperback): 978-1-9997912-6-1
ISBN (ebook): 978-1-9997912-7-8
A catalogue record for this book is available from the British Library.
Cover illustration by Dal Sang
Book cover and interior design by Jon Gomez

Printed and bound by TJ International

This book is published with the support of the
Literature Translation Institute of Korea (LTI Korea).

  Supported using public funding by

ARTS COUNCIL
ENGLAND

This book has been selected to receive financial assistance from English PEN's
"PEN Translates" programme, supported by Arts Council England. English
PEN exists to promote literature and our understanding of it, to uphold writers'
freedoms around the world, to campaign against the persecution and imprisonment
of writers for stating their views, and to promote the friendly co-operation of
writers and the free exchange of ideas. www.englishpen.org

CONTENTS

INTRODUCTION

One of the things which makes Kang Kyeong-ae (1906-1944) unique among Korean women writers of the era, most of whom lived in the cultural hub of Seoul, is that all her prose fiction was written in Jiandao in Manchuria, China. Although it was on the periphery of Korean literature, Jiandao was at the time the centre of an armed struggle to overthrow the Japanese colonial rule of Korea (1910-1945). This meant that while most other authors in Seoul also worked as reporters for magazines or newspapers and were central members of literary circles, Kang had vastly different preoccupations. Living in Manchuria and devoting herself to literary creation imbued Kang with an artistic and political tension which enabled her to make a greater artistic achievement than any of her contemporaries.

*

Kang Kyeong-ae was born to impoverished peasants on 20 April 1906 in Songhwa County, Hwanghae Province, in what is now North Korea. However, following her father's death and her mother's remarriage, Kang grew up in Jangyeon county, also in Hwanghae Province. Although her stepfather had money, he was an elderly, disabled man, and Kang's mother is said to have been a veritable servant to him. At around the age of seven, Kang taught herself to read *hangul*, the Korean alphabet, from a copy of the classic Korean novel *Tale of Chunhyang* (*Chunhyangjeon*) that happened to be in the house. She went on to read other traditional prose fiction in *hangul*, and elderly neighbours vied with each other to take her home to have her read similar works out loud, buying her sweets as recompense. The girl was thus given the epithet 'Acorn Storyteller' in her neighbourhood.

As a result of her mother's pleas to her husband, Kang was able to enter primary school in 1915, already past the age of ten. The family was unable to pay expenses such as tuition fees and money for stationery, and Kang had to study while feeling ill at ease, even fantasizing about stealing her classmates' money and possessions. In 1921, with help from her brother-in-law, Kang entered Soongeui Girls' School (present-day Soongeui Girls' Middle and High Schools) in Pyongyang. A Christian institution, this school was dubbed 'Pyongyang Prison No. 2' due to its strict dormitory regulations. In October 1923, during Kang's third year, the students staged a class boycott in protest against both the strict dormitory life and the American principal who had banned 'superstitious' visits to ancestral graves during *Chuseok*, the mid-autumn full moon festival. Kang was expelled due to this incident, and she reportedly went to Seoul where she studied for one year at Dongduk Girls' School (present-day Dongduk Girls' Middle and High Schools).

While a student in Seoul in May 1924, Kang published a poem titled 'Autumn' (*'Ga-eul'*) under the pen name of 'Kang Gama' in the literary magazine *Venus* (*Geumseong*). However, Kang soon withdrew from Dongduk Girls' School and returned to her hometown of Jangyeon in September 1924. Back home, Kang found her mother impoverished and was tormented by the silent criticism that an intelligent student had come back without any accomplishments. As a result, Kang went to China and worked as a teacher for two years in Hailin, northern Manchuria.

Hailin in 1927-1928, during Kang's sojourn, saw the Manchurian Bureau of the Communist Party of Korea (*Manju Chongguk Joseon Gongsandang*) expand their power after colliding with ethnic Korean nationalists represented by the New People's Government (*Sinminbu*), and Kang would have directly witnessed the serious ideological and physical conflicts between the two groups. Life in Manchuria at this time was particularly ruthless due to the secret 'Mitsuya Agreement' between Manchurian warlord Zhang Zuolin and Mitsuya Miyamatsu, the head of the Bureau of Police Affairs in the colonial Government-General of Korea. This agreement promised monetary reward for those reporting ethnic Koreans who possessed weapons or were involved in anti-Japanese activism, and resulted in both Manchurian warlords and Japanese imperialists expelling or arresting ethnic Korean independence activists – nationalists and communists alike. Additionally, under the perception that imperial Japan was invading the area with ethnic Korean peasants as spies, Manchurian warlords persecuted ethnic Koreans, demanding they pay money and become naturalized citizens of China. In such a situation, ethnic Korean nationalists and communists often suspected and even killed each other, and the lives of many ethnic Korean peasants who had settled in the area were destroyed. It is in this context that Kang came to harbour communist sympathies and to maintain the belief that for poor Korean peasants there was no difference between compatriot landlords back in Korea and non-Korean landlords in Manchuria.

Leaving Hailin in 1928 and returning to her hometown of Jangyeon, Kang played a key role in the establishment of the local branch of the Society of the Friends of the Rose of Sharon (*Geun-uhoe*) in 1929, and she founded Heongpung Night School, an academy for children from impoverished families where she taught classes on literature and started writing fiction in earnest. This period was also when she met future-husband Jang Ha-il, a graduate of the Suwon College of Agriculture and Forestry who had been appointed to the Jangyeon County Office. Living far away from his wife, whom he had been made to marry at an early age, Jang had come to Jangyeon together with his mother and lived in Kang's house as a tenant.

As a writer who was involved indirectly with KAPF (*Korea Artista Proleta Federacio*; Korean Proletarian Artists Federation), Kang would have been influenced by the 'December 1928 Resolution' – the decision adopted by the Communist International on the reorganization of the Communist

Party of Korea. This document argued that the party must discard intellectual-centred organization methods, organize labourers and indigent peasants by infiltrating factories and agrarian villages, and isolate ethnic reformists. While many Korean writers criticized these methods and the document, Kang did not and was consistent in her political attitude.

Therefore, the essays that Kang published after her return to Korea from teaching in Hailin in northern Manchuria and after the 'December 1928 Resolution' exhibit a level of awareness completely different from that in the short sketch-like poems that she had published earlier. For example, in October 1929 Kang published a criticism of the popular author Yeom Sang-seop, who was dubbed a 'centrist' at the time, and in February 1931 Kang published a rebuttal of Yang Ju-dong, a self-styled 'syncretist'.

As the romance between Kang and Jang progressed, the couple invited friends to a simple wedding ceremony before relocating to Longjing in Jiandao around June 1931. In Jiandao, Jang worked as a teacher at Dongxing Middle School (present-day Longjing Senior High School) and Kang started to publish her fiction while taking care of their home. Jang was a good reader, understanding Kang's literary world, always being the first one to read her works, engaging in discussions, and providing advice. Indeed, he was a devoted husband who did his utmost to treat Kang's chronic illnesses.

Jiandao in the early 1930s was a land of war. While the Chinese people engaged in a fierce movement against both feudal landlords and warlords, Japanese imperialists incited the Mukden (or Manchurian) Incident in September 1931 and established the puppet state of Manchukuo in March 1932, before proceeding with mass-scale operations to eradicate ethnic Korean independence fighters. In the process, many people lost their homes, families, and lives. To flee such chaos, Kang left Jiandao and returned to Jangyeon around June 1932, then went back to Jiandao around September 1933. Although she did travel to Seoul and Jangyeon from time to time, from this point she lived in Jiandao, maintaining the household while steadily publishing her fiction.

In 1939, Kang returned to Jangyeon for the final time because her health had started to worsen in the previous year. In the end, she died on 26 April 1944 due to aggravated illness aged thirty-eight.

*

The class consciousness that Kang embraced in Hailin and the atrocities and popular resistance that she witnessed in Jiandao became archetypal experiences for Kang's literary activity. Though she produced nearly all her writing in Manchuria, she never mentioned the Japanese puppet state's specious propaganda, for example slogans such as 'concord among five ethnic groups' (Han Chinese, Manchurians, Mongols, Koreans, and Japanese) and 'paradise under royal government' (rule by the puppet emperor of Manchuria). Kang's works are instead infused with the desolation in people's lives caused by the creation of the Japanese puppet state of Manchukuo, the ruthless reality of being ruled by soldiers, and the strenuous efforts required to protect one's individual and social life against such forces.

Kang's early fiction gives insight into the lives of Korean peasants living in Jiandao who had moved to Manchuria because life in their home villages had become unsustainable, and how compatriot landlords back in colonial Korea and non-Korean landlords in Manchuria were equally oppressive. For example, 'Break the Strings' (*Pa-geum*; 1931) recounts how a young ethnic Korean couple tormented by family and romantic problems comes to devote themselves to the armed anti-Japanese struggle in Manchuria, and 'The Authoress' (*Geu Yeo-ja*; 1932) clearly exhibits a class consciousness that transcends nationalism. Thus, the starting point of Kang's literary career clearly displays a criticism of the Korean bourgeoisie which continues throughout her writing. This is also shown in the character of Sin-cheol in her sole novel *The Human Problem* (*In-gan Munje*; 1934. Published in 2009 by Feminist Press as *From Wonso Pond*); an untrustworthy university student who finally joins the anti-labour camp after wavering between peasants/labourers and landlords/capitalists.

Kang thus established class problems rather than ethnic problems as the main conflicts in her fiction overall and, based on them, penned many works reflecting proletarian internationalism. In the case of 'Vegetable Patch' (*Chae-jeon*; 1933), all personages are Chinese and class problems among the Chinese are addressed. While 'Salt' (*So-geum*; 1934) and 'Opium' (*Mayak*; 1937) likewise feature Chinese landlords and capitalists, their evil deeds do not take on particularly ethnic characteristics. In other words, these figures oppress Bongyeom's mother ('Salt') and Bodeuk's mother ('Opium') economically and sexually not because they are Chinese but because they are wealthy males. Continuing with the theme of class, Kang published 'Cape Changsan' (*Changsan-got*; 1936), a Japanese-language short story not included in this volume that focused on proletarian internationalism more clearly and specifically than any other proletarian literary work by other KAPF writers. Although internationalism first emerged among KAPF writers around 1927 and was highlighted again before and after 1931, it led to no noticeable achievements. In contrast, 'Cape Changsan' is a significant demonstration of Kang's resolute maintenance of internationalism even in 1936.

Kang strove to depict the lives of impoverished ethnic Koreans living in Jiandao, the oppressors making such lives unbearable, and the anti-Japanese activists fighting against these forces, so changes in the situation in the area had a strong effect on her writings. Works such as 'Mother and Son' (*Moja*; 1935), 'Anguish' (*Beonnoe*; 1935), and 'Darkness' (*Eo-dum*; 1937) portray the gradual defeat and retreat of ethnic Koreans' armed anti-Japanese organizations in Jiandao following their fierce resistance in the early 1930s. These stories also display the struggles and undaunted spirit of the families left behind, and the ethnic Korean betrayers who treated them with hostility. At this time, under increasing militarism by the Japanese rulers, writers in colonial Korea swerved from earlier topics of ethnicity and class and began to sensitively portray poverty and emotions in everyday life. Kang's works, too, reflected such a tendency. Her 'The Underground Village' (*Jihachon*; 1936) depicts extreme states of poverty in exhausting detail, making it impossible for readers to disregard the harsh reality despite a possible desire to do so. In addition, Kang ceaselessly produced writings that focused on and reminded readers of the fates of anti-Japanese independence activists in Jiandao. A representative work in this vein, 'Darkness' (1937) presents the younger sister of a young Korean man executed by the Japanese authorities for his involvement in a political incident, about which everyone in colonial Korea maintains silence. In addition to such doses of reality, Kang also published 'Manuscript Money' (*Won-go-ryo I-baeg-won*; 1935), which directs criticism against intellectuals such as herself.

*

For a woman to become a writer in the Korean colonial era, she needed the economic means to receive at least a secondary education and a network through which she could publish her writings. In this respect, Kang's formative background differed from other female authors. An unhappy home environment and extreme poverty gave Kang a different perspective. Male writers with such backgrounds were not hard to find, but in the case of women, opportunities to overcome such poverty and to establish themselves in the literary scene were extremely rare. In impoverished environments, most women were not provided with any education nor could they possess the time to establish their identities and the time and space to produce writing. Consequently, they were unable to leave lasting records. In this respect, Kang is an important representative of Korean women during the Japanese colonial era; a rare reflection of lower-class women's voices. Moreover, Kang brilliantly captured the zeitgeist as a writer who witnessed participants in armed struggles against the Japanese, testifying to their suffering and validity, and she was able to convey all of this to colonial Korea directly under Japanese rule.

Sang-kyung Lee
Professor of Modern Korean Literature
Korea Advanced Institute of Science and Technology

THE UNDERGROUND VILLAGE

MANUSCRIPT MONEY

My dear little K,

I received and read your last letter with gladness. I'm happy to learn that you have strengthened somewhat since I last heard from you. What can be worth more than good health?

Dearest K, you write that with the prospect of graduation, you feel dread rather than joy, hopelessness rather than hope. I understand. With everything that is going on in the country, of course you feel that way. But you must also seek a new awakening amidst the dread and despair. You must discover a new path that burns with joy and hope.

Dearest K, I feel that I still lack the knowledge to express in simple sentences, as you have asked me to, my philosophy on love and marriage. But I shall write down the whole of what is going on in my life and the whole of what I feel from that life in my rough and unlearned sentences. You're a wise soul, so please discard what you don't need and use what you can.

Dearest K, I don't know if you're aware of it, but for serializing a novel in the newspaper D, I've been paid two hundred won in manuscript money. This is the largest sum I've ever had in my life. The sudden headiness that came from it made me imagine all sorts of things.

Dearest K, I'm sure you've already realized this about me ... I grew up in an insolvent household, and things did not get better as an adult. My brother-in-law helped me obtain what mouse's portion of learning that I do have. As a child, I never got to own a new dress with colours dyed into it. Instead of rice, I only had boiled millet to eat. I never had proper school supplies when I was going to school. At the beginning of the school year, I would cry and cry because I could not afford any textbooks. I could only manage to get a hold of some old ones, and oh how my lack of paper or pen made my small heart tremble!

Dearest K, I still remember it all very well. I was in the first grade. We were taking final exams the next day, but I had nothing to write with. In my desperation, I stole some implements from the classmate sitting next to me, and can you imagine the scolding I received from my teacher? And the taunts from my classmates: 'Dirty thief! Dirty thief!' My teacher, with his terrifying stare, detained me in class instead of letting me go out for recess. I had to keep my arms raised and stand silently by the window. Outside, my classmates were busy making a snowman in the playground, their hands clapping with joy. Even as I stood there in punishment, the sight of the snowman's mouth and eyes were so funny that I would go back and forth between giggles and tears.

Dearest K, the innocent child that I used to be was fool-hardy enough to think of taking someone else's things, but once I reached middle school I could not bring myself to do so, no matter how desperate I felt. With the money coming from my brother-in-law, I could just barely cover food and my monthly tuition. Sometimes there wasn't enough for my tuition either, and I could not look my teachers in the eye or ask questions about things I didn't understand in class. Naturally,

I became listless and stupid. It followed that I couldn't make a single friend. I was so lonely that I came to depend on God, and every night I would go into the dormitory chapel and cry as I prayed. The suffering, however, did not disappear, and it only grew by the day and month.

Meanwhile, my classmates had parasols, new skirts and jackets, knitted scarves and cardigans, and watches. It all seems so silly now, but I envied them so much that tears would come to my eyes. Whenever I saw a classmate knitting a scarf with soft, fluffy yarn, I would wrap the thread between my fingers and my vision would cloud with tears. What that feeling of yarn was like to a schoolgirl! Whenever my husband would ask, 'How is it you can't even knit a cardigan?' and glare at me, I would think back to my schoolgirl days and feel the same jolt to my belly that I felt back then as I touched my classmate's yarn.

Dearest K, let me tell you about one summer long ago. My classmates were busy shopping in preparation for their return home. In my day there were no synthetic fibres, and everyone prepared ramie skirts and jackets that were as light as dragonfly wings, and they each bought a white or black parasol. I was beside myself and didn't know what to do. More than anything else, I ached for a parasol. Nowadays, even the salt seller's wife has a parasol, but back then you couldn't call yourself a schoolgirl if you didn't have one of those things. It was as if the parasol were a wordless, exclusive symbol for female students. The silly girl that I was, I simply couldn't face returning home without a parasol. I ended up crying over it all the time. My roommate must have caught on and wanted to mock me; she managed to procure for me an old, broken parasol from somewhere. I was overjoyed. But I couldn't find it in my heart to jump up and take it. As I sat there in my awkwardness, my roommate cackled and left the room. As soon as she left, I grabbed the parasol and opened it, but it was broken and ripped in every way. An inexplicable rage and sadness seemed to rise up and seize my throat. But I could not throw that parasol away!

Dearest K, I seem to have wandered too far off the path. That ought to have been enough to give you an idea of what my past was like ... I've rustled up these old memories, which I hate dwelling on, because I wanted to talk about my present. But you see, even before I received the manuscript money that I mentioned before, I would lie awake for a long time at night thinking about what I would do with the money. It embarrasses me to think about it now, but I thought, *First of all, because it's winter I'll get a fur coat, a scarf, and shoes ... The gap between my teeth is too wide, so I'll get a thin gold filling, I'll get a thin gold ring, maybe a watch ... No, my husband will have something to say about that. But it's money I made on my own, what objection could he possibly make? If I don't get anything now, I'll never get to own a gold watch. Just grit your teeth and do it. And get your husband a new suit; his old one is falling apart.* My husband wouldn't approve, but I decided I was going to put my foot down. Then the day came when I held my manuscript money in my hand.

Dearest K, my husband and I were so happy we didn't know what to do with ourselves. Gazing into the lamplight that seemed especially bright that night, I asked him, 'What should we do with the money?' just to hear what he'd say. My husband sat silent for a moment and spoke as if to himself: 'Funny how for people like us, having money is more agitating than not having it ... Well, as long as we have it, we should spend it. The most urgent thing would be to get Comrade Eungho a doctor ...'

These unexpected words darkened my sight. I was silent. The face of my husband, who was looking at me, suddenly seemed that of a dog and his eyes that of a bull.

'And then Hongsik's wife. It's up to us to take care of them this winter. What else can we give?'

I did not want to hear what he had to say. I turned my

head and stared at the wall. Of course I pitied his Comrade Eungho and his friend Hongsik's wife, and before this money had come to us I had wanted to help them as much as we were able to, but once the two hundred won was in my hand, those thoughts disappeared without a trace. I couldn't help feeling that way.

My husband, who had noticed my expression, glared at me for a while and said in a rough voice, 'So how would you rather spend the money?'

This question forced out my suppressed tears. I found my stubborn husband more frustrating and pathetic than I had ever known him. More than anything else, he had never given me so much as a simple wedding ring when we married, or ever bought me a pair of shoes. Of course, this was because he had no money, and it wasn't as if I didn't understand that. But this money was not money he had earned. Wouldn't the rightful thing for him to offer, then, have been to use this money, obtained by my own effort, to buy the wedding ring that I had so longed for, or buy me a pair of shoes?

But this dunce of a man could not have had such thoughts in mind. This more than anything else was what made me resentful. The shoes I'm wearing now are from a trip to Seoul a few years ago when I went to be treated for tympanitis; my husband's friend Kim Kyungho kept pressing me to take them, an old pair his wife used to wear. Think of how bad my shoes must've been for him to insist so. I cannot tell you how ashamed I was. Anyone would've felt the same way, and who would want to wear shoes that someone else had worn? But when I looked down at my old shoes, I couldn't bring myself to refuse him. I examined the proffered shoes carefully and found no holes. I did begin to want them a little then, but I was worried about what my husband would say. I sent him a letter the next day. A few days later he wrote a reply, giving me permission. I wore those shoes, but whenever I looked at them I could never quite erase my first feelings of shame.

That night, the night I held my money in my hand, the shame I felt back then welled up again in my throat. I couldn't help sobbing. I began crying with my mouth open, like a child.

My husband bolted upright and slapped my cheek so hard I could hear a ringing in my ear.

Tearfully, I screamed at him with all my might. 'How could you ... how could you hit me!'

I jumped back at him. My husband flashed his tiger-like eyes and struck a blow to my head, knocking down the lamp with a loud crash. The smell of kerosene flooded the room.

'Kill me, why don't you just kill me!' I shouted at him as loud as I could. I felt like I was ready to be done with him.

Fuming, my husband said, 'Even a hundred deaths is too good for you! You think I don't know how you feel? I see that making a little money on your own has made you forget your own husband. You disgraceful wench, get out! Take all that money and go back to your mother's house tomorrow, I can't live with a disgraceful wench like you. So, you just want to be another one of those "modern girl" tarted-up whores? Oh yes, you high-and-mighty literary types, that's what you all end up becoming! Hah! I don't fancy myself as fit to be the husband of such a high-and-mighty literary eminence. I suppose you want to fry and broil your hair like those hussies, slap some flour on your face, put on a gold watch and a diamond ring and a fur coat, and stand on some stage sighing, "Ah, the proletariat"? Get the hell out!'

He grabbed my hand and pulled me after him. He pushed me out the door.

Dearest K, I cannot tell you how cold the northern country's wind is. It's been four years since I came here, but I have never experienced winds as biting as I felt that night. The whole world seemed to be made of ice. Just looking at the moon made my eyes cold, and although I could see the moon clearly in the sky, powdery snow blew in the harsh, whistling wind. The snow was so prickly against my flesh it was as if a sharp knife was piercing my skin. I stood with my arms wrapped tightly around me.

My mind was fit to burst with all the thoughts running through it. What was I to do? I reached into my swirling mind and took up one thought at a time. The first thought I grasped was that I couldn't live with that man anymore. You couldn't pay me enough to live with him! But then what was to become of me? Should I go back home? Home ... I imagined the faces of the people and their taunting: *That wench came back, of course she would, who could stand to live with such a hussy?* I imagined the sorrow on the face of my mother. I cringed. Go to Seoul and get a job at a newspaper or a magazine? Seeing how women journalists tended to degenerate into flirts, I realized I would only fall into similar disrepute. Then where to go, what to do? Go to Tokyo and further my studies? Using what money? Considering my situation, the only study I would be engaged in would be how to be a fallen woman. When I came to this conclusion, I felt as if I were turned away by the world, that no matter where I went, no one would take me in. I felt that aside from the fuming tiger sitting in that room, no one in the world would hold my hand.

Dearest K, is this love? But what else could it be? I started to shed hot tears again. At the same time, the tiger-man's words came back to me. I thought of poor Hongsik's wife and how young and vulnerable she was, and of Eungho's face that was no more than skin and bone at this point. The mother and son who had trembled as they sent him off to prison! Moaning Eungho, who came out of prison with heart disease! The two hundred won in my hand ... Only this could save them. My own body was still healthy. And what else could all the things I wanted be but vanity?

I suddenly realized I had been dreaming a dangerous dream.

Dearest K, what's the use of a gold watch or a gold ring or a fur coat for someone like me? If I could use the money to save the life of a comrade, how right it would be if I did so. And if he is my husband's comrade, does that not make him my comrade, too? I ran back to the door.

'Husband, I was wrong!'

The door swung open. I rushed inside and hugged him. 'Husband, I was wrong. I won't be, ever again ...' Loud sobs came forth from my throat. But please know that these sobs were very different from the sobs before.

Dearest K, my husband sighed and caressed my head.

'It's not that I don't know how you feel. But while you only have a single skirt and a single jacket, you are not naked. You are clothed. You haven't the slightest care in the world. But look at Comrade Eungho, or Hongsik's wife. As long as we have money in our hands, we cannot let our comrades die of sickness or starvation! We cannot let this money turn our heads. Even I felt different from the man I was before that money appeared.'

My husband fell silent. Apparently, he had also been thinking while I was gone, and I realized that his earlier anger had been his attempt to control his own upsetting thoughts and guilt. It made me more determined than ever as I felt a hot fire take hold in my heart.

'Husband, let's buy a set of cheap clothes for both of us and a sack of rice and some wood, and give our comrades the rest! We'll soon make more money on our own.'

My husband swept me into his embrace and said, 'Good thinking!'

Dearest K, I've gone on and on at the risk of boring you. I know that with graduation approaching, you're dreaming all kinds of dreams. Even those dreams, of course, have their time and place in our lives, and I do not chide you for having them. But someday, you have to step out of those dreams and see reality for what it is.

Look at the suffering of the people outside of the city! Are there not tens of thousands of them turning away from their beloved homelands and running away here to Manchuria? And who will clothe them and feed them once they are here? They come in the hope of finding something better than what they left behind. But one woman becomes a kitchen slave, while another is kidnapped to become the concubine of a rich man, each crying an endless lament as they wander these wide flatlands. But it isn't just the people of the three provinces who suffer so. Wasn't it not long ago that the people of Ulleung Island had to make landfall en masse at Wonsan? Did you know that the poor of Korea – no, that the great masses of the poor of the whole world live in the borderlands between life and starvation?

Dearest K, here in Jiandao, the subjugating force has swept in, and the people tremble with fear at the sound of guns and swords. The farmers cannot farm or go to the mountains to get wood, so they migrate to the relatively safe zones of cities such as Longjing or Gukja, but what would they do for food when they get there? A dog's life is more valuable than a human's in a place like this.

Dearest K, you may despair because you cannot move on with your education or create a sweet home for yourself. But close your eyes for a moment and think of how meaningless such despair is. Even if by chance you managed to achieve what you wanted and more, it would only be a moment, and you would return to be where the rest of us are. What will you do when that happens? Take your own life?

Dearest K, you've gained an impressive amount of knowledge from sitting at a desk, more than enough! Now is the time to obtain real knowledge through action. You must work to increase your societal value. If you neglect this societal value for the sake of concentrating on increasing your exchange value, you will become another failure. I am not saying you are a product or a thing, quite the opposite. But these are the two ways that we as human beings create our character in this world.

Which will you choose?

February 1935

SALT

Peasants

Word came that the Chinese landowner Fang Tong had come to the village.

The woman's husband took his good overcoat down from its peg and went out the door. The woman could not help being agitated at the sight of her husband disappearing into the distance. Was it really Fang Tong this time? Or the vigilantes again, luring her husband out with a lie? She wanted to cry. Her husband put up with their terrorizing day after day without a word of complaint. It broke her heart. And there he went again, into who knew what sort of danger! She sighed. There was nothing to be done for poor people like them; the only way out of their suffering was death. What could they do except die? She found herself scratching at the wall in agitation. She looked down at her fingernails, cracked and ugly. It was so easy to be killed, yet so difficult to die. Such was life.

Years ago, they had been forcibly driven from their homeland without much more than a basket of goods to their name, and it had felt as if they faced a voyage over a vast ocean towards certain death. At least they managed to rent a patch of farming land from a Chinese landowner, but Chinese soldiers constantly threatened their lives, and the woman and her husband only survived from day to day. Every morning when they set out for the fields, they looked towards the sky and prayed they would be safe.

The soldiers, unable to survive on their pay, went around extorting the peasant farmers. This had gone from happening rarely to being a common occurrence, often in broad daylight. The peasants realized they needed to prepare bribes of money and rice if they wanted to live and had them ready even if it meant going hungry. Then the communists came, which scared the landowners and soldiers off into the city, forcing the soldiers to limit their forays into lands unoccupied by the communists. But when the communists were driven out, the militia arrived.

The woman continued to stare at her fingernails and thought about the many times she had almost died at the hands of Chinese soldiers. That she was alive today was a miracle. She looked up. Her husband was already out of sight; she gazed at a fluttering banner above a distant wall and wondered whether he had reached the next village yet. The anxiety that she had forgotten for a moment filled her heart once more. Her husband had told her he had already paid the vigilantes, so it may be true that Fang Tong had come. It was planting season; it made sense for him to visit. But if he were here, her son Bongshik, who was away, would miss Fang Tong, and Bongshik would not be able to bring back his share of the crops. She kept staring at the faraway wall. Her husband and some other peasants had built it over a period of a whole year. It looked like the fortress walls of their old home.

The wall reminded her of a night five years ago. Chaos had erupted, the sound of guns and shouting coming from all directions. They had hid in the foxhole they had secretly dug near the kitchen hearth. When they emerged days later, Fang Tong had fled, his family slaughtered. Fang Tong went on to buy a house in Yongjing, take another wife, and sire more children, ending up living almost exactly as he did before.

Since Fang Tong fled to town, the house the woman was staring at now belonged to the militia. It was their banner that flew and their guard who stood watch.

She looked elsewhere into the distance. The fields were flooded with sunlight, and birds flew high and unfettered in the blue sky. When would she and her husband get to have land like that? She sighed and stared out at the land they had managed to purchase, a plot on the red mountain. They had tamed the harsh earth of the slope, and now it was arable, but they could not plant anything other than sweet potatoes for the time being.

They could try planting millet, maybe sorghum ... She did not mean to, but she began thinking of her homeland again. Her field by the young pines that brushed her knees! Her coffin would be pelted with soil before she forgot that field! How every crop took root in it and thrived! *That bastard*, she thought as she imagined Old Man Chambong walking up to that field. Her heart throbbed, and her hands and feet trembled. She tried with all her might not to think of her homeland, to keep from flying apart in anger. She found herself standing in the yard and listening to the loud twitter of the sparrows hopping on a pile of hay in the corner.

She turned and went back into the house. Everything in the room called out for her touch. She took up the broom and swept the floor. She caressed the holes in the straw mat as she thought of how they had to have a good life and show that horrible Old Man Chambong ... She held back tears. No matter how determinedly they worked the land, their only rewards turned out to be hunger and poverty. What a fate this was, and how cruel was it that God blessed some but cursed others! She carefully swept each room. A sweet potato rolled away from her broom. She picked it up, put it in a basket of them, and started to snap off their sprouts. Most of the peasant houses had the kitchen and the main room in the same space, with a cauldron installed in the corner. She prepared her food beside it. When they first arrived, more than anything else she hated the houses, which felt like caves or cowsheds at best. There was nowhere for her to go when they had a visitor, so she had no choice but to sit while silently facing the guest. But now the presence of a male visitor did not bother her, and the house was more or less tolerable. They never forgot to keep a secret foxhole dug near the mouth of the earthen oven. Whenever they heard gunshots, the family would leap into the hole and stay inside for days on end. They kept their clothes and crops in it, taking out what they needed for their daily lives. They had to do all of this because of the soldiers and the bandits.

She finished handling the sweet potatoes and started sorting through the red beans. The sound of the beans bouncing and rolling soon echoed through the quiet house. Her eyes felt tired, and the sparrows grew louder. She began to think. If they were going to start sowing tomorrow, they needed rice for breakfast, lunch, and dinner, and if Bongshik did not meet Fang Tong then he would not be able to bring the rice, but he ought to bring home the other food for side dishes ...

Her thoughts faded as she grew sleepy. She rubbed her eyes and went outside. Her eyes came to rest on the hardened bricks of fermented bean paste hanging from ropes on the wall. That's right, she needed to hang up the rest of the bricks. She brought out a basket of the blocks and started hanging them one by one outside the door, brushing the dust off the older ones and lifting each of them from the wall for inspection. She should make some soy sauce and a jar of chilli paste ... but then, she would need some salt ...

She sighed and sat down, thinking of home once more. They used to brush their teeth with salt because it was so common ... One could flush out an upset stomach with just a handful of salt ... Compared to some of the things they had had to do without since their banishment, salt seemed like such a small thing, but she had cried many times over their lack of it. Twenty won and ten jeon for a *mal* of salt! A peasant farmer could never afford an entire *mal*, buying it instead in smaller packets. They could only afford to preserve things whenever they had some salt, and when the bean paste would rot instead of fermenting they had to make do with the sparsely-seasoned preserves, but because the preserves were so bland, any dish she made from them would be bland as well.

During meals, her habit now was to look closely at her husband's expression and feel as if she were at fault. Her husband never said a word, but there were times when he would take a bite and grimace, and resignedly put down his spoon. She would feel the rice turn to sand in her mouth, put her spoon down too, and look away. Not even able to serve up a hearty broth for her husband who came home drenched and stinking of sweat and hard work … she was worthless! Could she truly call herself a wife?

Sometimes, her husband would dump a spoonful of chilli flakes into his bowl to stimulate his appetite. His eyes would tear up, their capillaries fit to burst, and beads of sweat would form around his mouth. Why are you adding so much dried chilli, she would almost say before catching herself. And here she was, responsible for the family's meals … what was she to do?

She sighed again, looking down at the remaining bean paste blocks, wondering what she was going to serve for dinner. She heard footsteps and looked up. Her daughter Bongyeom was back from school, carrying her book bag.

'Why have you brought your book bag?'

'It's a half day. Oh, you've taken out the bean paste blocks.' Bongyeom beamed as she picked up one of the blocks and inhaled its aroma.

'Did you see your father on the way home?'

'Yes. Fang Tong is here.'

'Fang Tong? You're sure?' She let out a sigh of relief, only now realizing how nervous she had been all morning. 'Where did you see your father?'

'Fang Tong's house. He was sitting with the militia. I don't know what they were doing.'

The tension spreading to the woman from Bongyeom's sudden frown! 'Was Fang Tong with them?'

Bongyeom nodded. Then, she smiled. She took out shallots from her book bag. 'So many shallots growing behind our school!'

'Enough for a whole meal.' The woman fondled them in approval before choosing one of the bigger ones, twisting off its stem, peeling it, and eating it. Bongyeom also popped one in her mouth.

'Mother, if only I had some exercise shoes ...'

The words had escaped her by accident, and Bongyeom fearfully looked away from her mother to the shallots on her lap. She could almost see, between the shallots, the lovely exercise shoes that her classmate Yong-ae wore as she ran as light as a sparrow.

'You crazy child and your wants!' The woman rubbed her nose and glared at her sideways.

Bongyeom felt the weight of the shallots turn into that of new exercise shoes. She mumbled, 'Mother, every single want to you is crazy.'

The woman turned to her. 'What else can your wants be? When we can barely afford to educate you, and you're going on about exercise shoes! Look, child, it's only thanks to the Enlightenment that you're getting an education at all. When we were growing up, where would we have gone to learn? We had to fetch the water, weave hessian, tend the fields, and the only thing we could wish for was a pretty pair of straw sandals ... Your father and mother are breaking their backs on the fields, but you're going on about exercise shoes! Be glad you're not starving. If you want to go on about your crazy wants, don't go to school!'

'You're not the one sending me to school.' Bongyeom felt slightly scared by her own rebellion, but she persisted.

The woman's face turned red with fury. 'Fine, even if it were your father sending you to school, I would've told you to quit. What kind of a daughter are you? Talking back just because she has some learning in her head instead of being silent when she's spoken to! Yapping away with her jaw hanging loose! Fine, we have no money ... If we had the money to buy you those silly shoes, we would've given Bongshik more schooling.'

Bongyeom could barely keep down the raw shallots she had been eating without any rice or water. Her eyes filled with tears. 'Why don't we have any money? Why can't we send Big Brother to school?'

Then Bongyeom remembered something that her teacher had talked to her about, and she realized it was not her mother who was at fault for their poverty. But she could not help resenting her mother whose first instinct was always to castigate her daughter.

'How do I know why we don't have money! Why were you born to beggars instead of rich parents! You useless child, I'd be better off without you.'

Bongyeom stared at her mother. She was reminded of what happened at last autumn's threshing, how her mother and father's harvest of rice was all taken away by Fang Tong. Her mother's face then was the same as it was now. Mother and Father, who knew nothing of resisting, nothing of fighting back! Her mother, who was so wretched it was almost pathetic!

'Mother, you have to know why we don't have any money. Why can't we afford exercise shoes? Why can't we afford Big Brother's education? You must see the reason why!'

She realized as she was shouting this that there was nothing wrong with her desire for exercise shoes. She began to recall a thing or two that her teacher had said to her ...

'You stupid girl, why else would we be poor? We have no land. If only we had some land ...' The woman's heart was so full of sorrow that she closed her mouth. But she could not stop her memories of the field by the young pines, her eyes tearing up. She could almost see it through her tears, a wavering mirage.

The sound of gunshots! Mother and daughter bolted upright, their eyes wide. The dog that had been napping by the pile of hay was huddled to them in no time, barking.

Exile

They frantically went from imagining the bandits to the communists and back as they stared out at the next village. The sound of dogs barking made them feel more nervous than ever. The wind, so soothingly cool until a moment ago, turned into pure fear itself as it brushed against their skirts.

'Oh, if only your father would come ... Why are we just standing here, something seems to have happened, something has come ...'

The woman's face was contorted, and she could not keep still. More gunshots. They fled into the house. Now they were certain something had happened in the next village. People had been shot and killed, the woman reckoned, and a fire danced inside her that she could barely contain. But she dared not leave the house. She kept getting the feeling that something was coming towards them.

'What are we going to do?' the woman mumbled. 'Bong-shik hasn't come home.'

Her husband was not safe, either. And what if the gunshots had something to do with him meeting Fang Tong and the militia?

'You said you saw Father sitting with Fang Tong? With your own eyes?' Her mouth was dry, and she could barely breathe. Bongyeom could not answer with her voice, so she answered with her eyes instead.

They heard the sound of footsteps. They jumped into the foxhole in the corner of the kitchen, clinging to each other as they stood over a sack of potatoes. Someone was coming to kill them!

A while later they heard, 'Mother?'

The sound of her son's voice brought the woman back to her senses, but despite shouting back to him, she could not bring herself to leave the foxhole right away. When she finally could, she was found herself speechless again. Bongshik stood before her, covered in blood, and her husband seemed to have collapsed beside him with blood running like a stream from his neck.

'Oh!' The woman let out a shriek and fell to her knees. All she could do was stare at her husband.

Bongshik's heart went out to her. 'Mother, you must be strong! It was a communist bullet. Please help me.'

He tried to raise her to her feet, but the woman sank to the floor again. All she could do was mumble, 'Your father, your father ...'

It was only when dawn was about to break when the woman could speak again, between bouts of loud, uncontrollable crying.

'How was it you came to meet your father? Was he alive then? What did he say to you?'

Bongshik only smacked his lips as if he had tasted something bitter. 'What's the point in carrying on with this life!' he spat.

Then, he sighed. He was only venting, as his mother's expectant face made him uncomfortable. It had infuriated him that his father would act all grateful to Fang Tong and the militia, and he knew it would only come back to hurt his father someday. He had argued about this with him before, but his father was adamant. In truth, his father had little choice in the matter, as his life would have been made unbearable otherwise.

Bongshik had thought a hundred times that his father was on the wrong side, but once he heard from Yong-ae's father that his own father had been shot, his rage at the injustice of the thing made his head hurt too much to tell right from wrong.

The next day, after his father's funeral, Bongshik said he would be going for a walk. He never came back.

Mother and daughter waited fervently for him to return but come spring, they had not received so much as a letter. Unable to wait, they went off looking for Bongshik. They searched for him for a month but never found him. They came to Longjing, remembering how he would mutter about trying to work his way through school someday every time he had visited that town. But they did not find a single student who looked like Bongshik at any of the school grounds they lurked beside. After their visit to the last school there, the woman found herself going back and forth between resentment and worry over her child's disappearance. What if something happened to him? Where was he? Had he fallen in with some bad men? Where would he be sleeping tonight? Her worries only deepened.

Around sunset, they paid a visit to Fang Tong. They had thought of visiting his house since they first came to Longjing. The plan was to ask him for help if they could not find Bongshik on their own. Fang Tong came to greet them as they entered the main gate of his house.

'You're here. When did you come into town?'

He seemed glad enough to meet them. Bongyeom's mother observed his expression closely and let out an inaudible sigh of relief that at least he was not throwing them out.

Fang Tong patted Bongyeom's head. 'Where were you? I visited your house once. I was sorry to have missed you.'

'We've been looking for our Bongshik. Where might he be?' The woman's heart pounded as she waited for his answer.

'I haven't seen him. I don't know.'

She lowered her head. Fang Tong took them into the hall with a long *kang* bed-stove where a young woman who seemed to be his wife sat and eyed both mother and daughter with suspicion. Fang Tong introduced them.

His wife said, 'Come up and sit.'

They went up and sat on the heated floor. Fang Tong poured tea for them. The mother and daughter took in the scent of the light tea and glanced around. The room was wide, with the *kang* running down its length. The floor under the *kang* was paved with sparkling stone. There was a marble table by a window, and on it a goldfish swimming in a bowl and a few objects they did not know the purpose of. On the wall above the window was a framed photograph of Fang Tong and his family, along with a dizzying array of slightly faded paintings. On the wall opposite the table was a painting of Bultasan Mountain done in thick brushstrokes, and on the next wall was a mirror as large as a door. Outside the window was a flower bed, so blue it cooled the eye.

They were delirious, as if they had come into a field of stars. They became so ashamed of how their poor appearances looked in comparison that they could scarcely draw breath.

Fang Tong sat back and lit a cigarette. 'You have family in this town?'

Bongyeom's mother lifted her head. 'No.'

She felt a wave of loneliness hit her at his question. How pitiful she was to come to Fang Tong for help. She stared out the window to the flowerbed. What beautiful spring colours! The millet must have sprouted from the earth by now! She should be tending the fields, how strange not to be working. What were they to eat in the autumn ...

She looked into the patch of perfect blue sky beyond, and it was like looking into that well-watered rice paddy she used to own back home. How she loved even the waters of that field! How tall the stalks would have grown by now! And was that sky not the same one that sheltered her old field? Where her husband's solid legs, thick with black hair, had sloshed through the water as he worked ... Her heart hurt as she turned to Fang Tong again. The thought of her husband being dead while Fang Tong was so alive and well made her head heavy with her rising sorrow.

'You have no family. Where are you staying?' Fang Tong asked after a long pause.

The woman's sorrow and anger turned into tears that began to spill before Fang Tong. She lowered her head and wiped her eyes with a corner of her skirt. Bongyeom could not help but tear up too at the sight of her mother's distress.

Fang Tong was dismayed. He was quickly beginning to realize they wanted something from him, a place to stay perhaps. What a mess. If he wanted to send them away before dinner, he would have to give them some money. But what if he let them stay for a while and work? A smile crept on to Fang Tong's lips. 'You have no family here. Stay with us. Bongshik knows this place.'

Hearing Bongshik's name fall from Fang Tong's lips added resentment to the woman's sorrow and anger. When was Bongshik going to give word about his whereabouts? Had he met the same fate as his father, struck down by some bandit? She began to cry even louder. After that, mother and daughter stayed at Fang Tong's house, living from day to day doing work about the place.

Fang Tong became friendlier by the day. On some evenings, he did not leave their room until late as they talked into the night. He sometimes brought them fabric or things to eat. Whenever that happened, Bongyeom's mother was so moved that she would not be able to sleep until very late.

It was the night after Fang Tong's wife had left to go to her mother's home. The woman was mending Fang Tong's underclothes that his wife had washed and laid out to dry. There was no telling when his wife would be back, but she would want the mending work to be done by the time of her return. The woman had to work the sewing machine day and night. She had only learned how to use the machine since coming to that house, so she was still unused to it. She was anxious should the needle break or she somehow harm the machine.

She heard the sad strains of Fang Tong's reed flute coming from his room. Fang Tong usually played the flute or the zither at night. The zither sounded like a puppy scratching at the door and whining for its mother. But the flute was somewhat tolerable.

She sighed as the end of the needle energetically sprang up and down against the fabric.

'Oh Bongshik, why aren't you looking for your mother ...' she mumbled. She thought about her son all the time. Whenever someone visited the house, she listened in as much as she could in case they came bearing news of him. Her diligence was unrewarded as there was no news of him that day either. Fang Tong seemed grateful to them, but his wife made her dislike of them very clear. This made the woman resent and miss Bongshik more, and cry more times than she could count. The longer they stayed, the more she was sure that they would have to move on from this house. But she kept her anxious thoughts to herself as she could not think of a better situation. Should she get Fang Tong alone and ask him to get her a rented house? She thought of his fat face blowing the flute in his room. But how could she ask him for such a thing, and even if she did find a house, what about bowls and other household goods? How was she to run a house with nothing? She stared into the light of the candlelit lamp.

The sound of the flute stopped, and the house became silent. The only thing she could hear was Bongyeom's breathing as she slept. Sometimes, as she gazed at a cloud of mayflies tenaciously holding on to life by the light of the lamp, she thought of her husband's short life. He never once got to eat a good meal, all he had were chilli flakes that made him sweat profusely ... Why was salt so expensive here? Although this house seemed to use it liberally enough. Of course, that was because they had money. Money? Money can help you do anything. Money could buy all the expensive salt she had so longed for. Why had they not managed to save any of theirs?

She heard the sound of heavy footsteps, and the door slid fully open with a crash. Fang Tong entered, wearing black trousers and a white tunic, smiling. She quickly stood up with her sewing in her hands.

'Sit down! Have you been working?' Fang Tong's gaze moved from her face to her sewing.

The woman came and sat down by the lamp, wondering if she should ask him to find her a rented house or not. She clamped down on the words that threatened to leak from her lips as she tried to discern his mood, watching his face.

'Whose clothes are these? Mine?' Fang Tong fondled the clothes and said, 'Mine, I see ... Are you hungry? I have tea and sweets in my room.'

He pulled at the sewing. Any other time she would have followed him, but the fact of his wife's absence made her hesitate.

'I'm not hungry.'

She felt a strange shame that seemed to brush against the ends of her eyebrows. Fang Tong snatched her sewing away from her.

'Let's go. Come on, come on.'

Staring at her sewing, she felt trapped. Should she ask him about the rental now or not ...?

'Are you coming?'

Fang Tong had raised his voice. She jumped to her feet. But as she looked at the fold of flesh over the back of Fang Tong's collar, she felt a sudden distaste, and her feet refused to follow him. Fang Tong turned around at the door. His face then had a fearful anger that she could not put into words. Defeated, she came down from the *kang*.

Looking back at the sleeping Bongyeom, her heart was so heavy that she wanted to weep loudly.

Leaving

It was sunset one late summer day. The woman looked up from her sewing, rubbed her eyes. The shadow of the roof awning fell long over her red door. Was Fang Tong coming tonight? Where had he gone all day? She wanted to ask Fang Tong's wife this whenever she saw her, but his wife always seemed listless now. She dared not disturb her. But whenever it got to this time of day, she wondered whether he would visit her that night. Not that she was happy when he visited, but somehow, she missed him when he did not come. How nice it would be if he came... *I must say something to him this time, but what?* Her ears turned red. Did he even know how she felt about him? Of course not, men were like that; they were not interested in her feelings. She imagined Fang Tong's face, and in her mind, she gazed at it with resentment.

Ever since that night, Fang Tong's attitude, no matter how she considered it, had gone cold. At first, she thought it was because he was a stately older man and his finicky wife was by his side, but as the days passed, jealousy began to rear its ugly head. On the other hand, she felt an affection towards him that was careening down a path into the unknown. She sighed and wiped the sweat from her forehead. When would she be able to talk to Fang Tong comfortably and receive his love? The more she thought about him, the worse she found herself wanting him. The thought brought tears to her eyes. She envied his wife no end.

Her thoughts then fell to the fact she was with child. Her

head dropped in silent despair. That night seemed to conjure itself up from the point of her needle. Did not Fang Tong jump on her like an angry tiger? And was she not so afraid that she had accidentally ripped the tarp over the windows of that dark room, and was that not why she was with child now? She had committed no sin. But why was it so difficult to talk to him? She could not even ask for the noodles in icy broth that she so wanted. Everything felt like it was her fault. Why could she not talk to him, why was she hesitating? She would talk to him this time for sure. She would! She was going to ask for a bowl of noodles, too. Her mouth watered at the thought. This was all just a fantasy, she thought as she gave out an empty laugh. It was almost funny that despite the mountains of difficulties that lay ahead, all she could think of were cold noodles. But she wanted them badly. Her throat itched at the thought of them, and she could barely sit still.

When she had first realized she was with child, she tried to do everything in her power to miscarry. She punched her belly, tripped over her own feet, and beat herself against a wall. When that did not work, she thought of drinking the caustic soda used for laundry, and almost did so several times, sitting up in her bed in the middle of the night. Even in those moments, she wanted cold noodles. She kept feeling as though people were hiding them from her nearby. In the end, it would just be too sad to die without having had the noodles she wanted so much. That and the thought of Bongyeom made her throw the bowl of water mixed with caustic soda away from her lips.

The rounder she got, the more she was unable to think of what to do. She wrapped her stomach as tightly as she could and ate only one or two meals a day. She tried to avoid others as much as possible and worked alone when she could.

Suddenly, she heard the sound of a carriage. Then she heard Fang Tong's children run out of his room, all shouting, 'Baba, baba!' He was here! Her heart beat so quickly that the baby in her belly kicked her. She pressed down on the folds of her skirt that were skipping to the baby's kicks. She heard footsteps, and quickly stood up, thinking it was him.

Bongyeom popped her head through the door. 'Mother, Fang Tong is here. He wants to see you.'

Relieved yet disappointed at the same time that it was not Fang Tong himself, the woman suddenly felt a wave of shame hearing that he wanted to see her. She could not speak, and her hands and feet shook.

'Mother, are you sick?'

Bongyeom had cut a neat fringe into her hair like a Chinese girl. She blinked at her mother through the fringe, staring.

The woman turned her head away. 'I'm fine.'

Bongyeom seemed to think for a while. 'Mother, I think Fang Tong is angry about something.'

'About what?'

'I wish I knew.'

Bongyeom thought of Fang Tong's face a moment before as she stared at her fingernails that were in a bad state from tending the stove.

Fang Tong's wife shouted, 'What's keeping you! Come this instant!'

They went into Fang Tong's room together. The tone of Fang Tong's wife's voice was not a good sign. Fang Tong was surrounded by his children. He frowned at the Korean mother and daughter.

Fang Tong's wife pouted her lips. 'Hmph, so it seems that you've raised your son a communist. Ten deaths aren't enough for such scum. We don't associate ourselves with communists. They are our sworn enemies. You can't live in our house anymore. Get out.'

Her eyes were like daggers. The woman and Bongyeom were completely taken aback. Their minds turned blank.

'My husband and Zhang were in town today. They saw Bongshik being publicly executed.'

The woman and her daughter heard a ringing as if they had been struck with a steel bat. The woman slowly turned her head to Fang Tong. Fang Tong avoided her gaze and looked down at his children, but he seemed to agree with what his wife was saying. A shock ran through her body. *It can't be true,* she screamed inwardly.

'Get out! In Manchuria, communists are put to death!' Fang Tong's wife's earrings jiggled as she pushed the woman and her daughter out of the house. The two still could not believe what they had heard, and the woman still wanted to hear it from Fang Tong himself, but Fang Tong only felt distaste when he looked at her. From the moment he had satisfied himself with her, he had felt a strange compulsion to kick her behind. He avoided her as much as he could. They needed help around the house because his wife was not good at housekeeping, but that would have meant providing board and wages, so the woman and her daughter had presented a temporary solution that he had delayed replacing until now. Simply put, there had not been a good excuse to kick them out.

Then he saw Bongshik's public execution. The police would be after all the family members of a convicted communist, which would mean danger for him. The other thing was, the mere mention of communists made him shudder with absolute disgust.

As he watched his wife push mother and daughter out of the house, he thought of the scene of Bongshik's death.

He had been in town with a friend when he heard there was to be a public execution of communists. By the time they got there, ten or so had already been killed, and only one was left. Regretting he had come so late, he pushed his way through the crowd for a better view. Just then, a man was being led before them by a policeman – it was Bongshik! He rubbed his eyes several times, not believing what he saw. He cursed Bongshik loudly enough for him to hear. Fang Tong despaired at the loss of his hope that Bongshik would repay his pitiful act of charity when he made some money and returned for his mother and sister.

The yellow-uniformed executioner poured water over the blue steel of his blade. The sword shone as the clear water dripped off it like pearls. Examining his blade, the executioner grinned. He turned to Bongshik. Bongshik's face was white, but he stood tall and calm. There was a hint of a sneer on his lips. Fang Tong found it more than a little disturbing. He thought of the time his life had been threatened by communists, and he was suddenly sure beyond all doubt that Bongshik was one of them. Bongshik shouted as the blade swung towards him. His head fell to the ground and the crowd, feeling a chill as if they had been splashed with cold water, took a step back as his blood spurted out into the air.

The memory made Fang Tong shudder as he drew his children closer to him and wished the mother and daughter were gone.

The woman had thought Fang Tong would come to her defence, even as she was now over the threshold and out the door. But even as they stepped out with their bundles hugged to their chests, Fang Tong did not appear. Enraged, the woman turned around and glared at the back of Fang Tong's head through the window. Just as she was about to shout at him, Fang Tong's wife and a strange man turned her around and pushed her out of the main gate.

They wandered the streets before leaving the town and came upon the banks of the Hailan River. The river seemed to block their path. Where could they go? The question refocused their thoughts, scattered by anger. The sun was about to set over the mountains, and the willow grove by the nearby village resembled the one by their own old hamlet. The woman felt if she went back there, Bongshik and her husband would be waiting for them. But she only rubbed her eyes and collapsed to her knees where she stood. She stared at the river flowing noisily before her and thought of throwing herself down into it. The news of Bongshik's death was sinking in; her heart was cracking in two. She did not want to believe it. Bongshik was a clever child. He would never join the communists, whom his father had hated so much when he was alive.

It was all a lie to drive them out of the house!

The woman whipped around and glared at the town behind them, gritting her teeth. 'That bitch, saying my son is a communist. Huh, they'll get struck by lightning someday ... Who are you calling a communist? The day will come when you'll die for your words. Who are they calling a communist!'

All those houses in that town, and not a single one they could go to. No doubt, they were each filled with terrible people like Fang Tong. The woman despaired. Despite her hatred, every time she saw a faraway figure approaching, her heart ached with the hope that it was Fang Tong coming to take them back.

When twilight descended, they were more dismayed than ever. Bongyeom sobbed and said, 'Where are we going to sleep tonight, Mother?'

The woman wanted to run into Fang Tong's house and stab everyone and then kill herself. She jumped to her feet. But when she looked down at the wide road they had walked down, she thought of Bongshik coming to find her, his plodding footsteps echoing on this very pavement ... But what if he was dead like Fang Tong said? She had to fight down tears again. Should she go into town and ask around if it was true? If it was, she would kill everyone and then herself! Determined, she started on her way.

They spent that night in a shed owned by a Chinese family living on the banks of the Hailan. They were allowed a night there only after mother and daughter begged them and did some work preparing spinach and leeks for the family to sell in the market. The woman's belly felt worse as the night wore on. She realized the baby was about to come and hoped Bongyeom would go to sleep soon. But Bongyeom was too busy cursing Fang Tong and his wife to go to sleep. She and her mother should never have worked so hard for them, she grumbled.

Finally, Bongyeom muttered, 'I wonder what Yong-ae is doing. I wonder what's going on in school.' She fell asleep.

Her mother sighed once more and decided that if she had the baby while Bongyeom slept, she would kill it and throw the body into the Hailan. She pressed down on her belly.

Drops of rain fell at the sound of the wind.

Good, she thought. There would be fewer people about when she went out to throw the body away. She caressed her daughter and covered her up with more of their old clothes. She moved her to a part of the shed that was not leaking and lay down underneath a leak herself. The rain began coming down in torrents. Her pain intensified.

She bit down on her lip, trying hard not to make a sound and wake Bongyeom. But her cries threatened to leak through her nose, jumping up from inside her like flames. Rainwater fell on her hair and into her collar and lips.

'Mother!' Bongyeom sat up and touched her mother. 'You're drenched.'

The mother only realized it was still raining when she felt the touch of her daughter.

'The roof is leaking, Mother, what are we to do?'

The woman could barely hear what her daughter was saying. She kicked and groaned, 'Unh! Unh!' She banged her head against the wall, but when even this would not allay the pain, she ripped at her hair.

Bongyeom could only shake her mother in wonder and collapse into tears.

The woman pushed her daughter away and pushed with all her might – and a long time later, they heard the cry of a baby. Bongyeom crept up to her mother and shouted, 'A baby?'

The woman groped in the dark, finding the baby's neck.

In that moment, the mother's eyes lit up like a pair of blue flames.

The maternal instinct that ran through her like electricity! It stifled her, and her grip on the baby loosened.

Her sweat flowed like a waterfall, and she turned to her side.

'*Aigo!*' she cried. She sobbed aloud.

Wet Nurse

She had overcome the horror of childbirth and failed to kill her baby. Now she felt a profound hunger. How much lighter her body would feel if she could have a bowl of seaweed stew! Her husband had made seaweed stew himself with some white rice, ladling it into a bowl for her ... She closed her eyes. She was drenched, and the wet floor stank of earth and blood.

What was she to do? She had to eat before she could work for her children's food, but she had to have a bowl of boiled water at least to get herself on her feet. But unless she picked up a handful of earth, there was nothing to put in her mouth. Should she wake Bongyeom and get her to ask the household for a meal? She could not bear it in her shame, having birthed an illegitimate child. Then what? It was going to be light soon, she was going to have to beg them herself ...

She opened her eyes and looked around the shed again. It was still dark. When would the sun rise? Did this house not have a rooster? She listened. All was completely silent, save for the sound of insects, chirping in the vegetable patch outside, like starlight against the black of night. She held her baby against her beating heart and felt determined to live whatever the cost. She was not going to die, she would live! She was going to live for the sake of her children. She kept muttering this over and over. Talk of death had constantly passed her lips before she experienced this childbirth, this pang, and she had often wished that she would die. Now that she had stood before the threshold of death, she found herself no longer wanting it. If anything, she felt a strange joy towards life. She had experienced difficulty many times before, but until her husband was taken from her, she had never truly realized what death was like. She was no longer so mindless about death.

That morning, the mother shook Bongyeom awake. Bongyeom immediately sat up.

'Go wash these. You only have to rinse them.' The woman handed over her bloodied underwear and rags to her daughter. She felt ashamed before Bongyeom and detected a feeling of disgust in her gaze.

Bongyeom's heart was still trembling, everything seemed like a dream, and her mind was full of questions and fears that felt like cobwebs in the dark. She quickly left the shed.

She must be so cold, thought the mother as she watched her leave, and she felt filthy sitting in the gloom.

Bongyeom's footsteps faded away, and the woman looked down at the baby's face. Her love grew the more she looked, and she could not bear to not put her nose against the baby's. She heard sounds coming from the house. Were they making breakfast? Surely, they would spare them some. She thought of seaweed stew again, and a bowl of it seemed to waver before her like a mirage. She grew hungrier by the minute. She had to eat; she could not live on determination alone. The thought made her fearful. She looked around the shed again. It was still dark in there, but she spotted something in the corner. A pile of leeks! The woman of the house had stacked them in the shed to take to the market. She would feel more like herself once she had some. She quickly went over and picked out a leek. She brought it several times to her mouth but put it down, in fear that the owners would come bursting in. Finally, she took a bite of the green stalk. She felt an electric shock go through her teeth. She grimaced and kept her mouth open for a long time, in pain.

If she wanted to live, she should at least swallow the saliva coming down her chin. She put the leek into her mouth and did not chew, instead poking around with the tip of her tongue as she moved bits of it down her throat. How stiff the stalks were, and her throat was in such pain she was about to cry. Could one survive on leeks? She grimaced again, staring out at the blue sky through the crack in the shed door.

The door flew open.

'Mother! I met Yong-ae's mother at the washing place on the river, she's coming!'

Yong-ae's mother immediately followed Bongyeom into the shed. Bongyeom's mother got up, clasped the other woman's hands and started to cry. The two families had lived in the same village and were close. Yong-ae's mother had been glad at first to see Bongyeom, but now that she saw how pitifully Bongyeom's family had fallen, she wished she had not come. She could not think of anything to say to comfort them.

'Oh my, what happened to you!' Yong-ae's mother said after a long pause.

Bongyeom's mother reined in her sobs and replied, 'It's only my terrible fate. My fate to live instead of die ... But why are you in town?'

'We moved here last year. The village is abandoned. The fighting was too much, so everyone left in the night. No one could make a living growing crops. But things are no easier here.'

Bongyeom's mother was glad to see her and realized in a flash that she must not lose this opportunity. She decided to tell her everything that happened and beg for help.

'I gave birth to a baby last night. This thing ... what am I going to do? Please save my life. Let us stay with you for a few days. I am sorry to ask. How terrible for you to have met a woman like me …'

She collapsed into tears again. Meeting Yong-ae's mother made her think of both her husband and Bongshik at the same time. Others had their husbands and children and lived normal lives, why did she end up with such a terrible fate?

Yong-ae's mother hesitated for a long time, but in the end, she sighed. 'All right. Stay with us.'

She was so reluctant the words had to be forced out of her mouth. Standing behind her, Bongyeom felt she had been saved and let out a sigh of relief.

'Thank you! How can we ever repay this kindness …?'

The woman tied the baby to Bongyeom's back. Yong-ae's mother led the way, anxious about what her husband would say. *Are we going to have to take them in forever?* Her footsteps were heavy with worry.

Four days passed without incident at Yong-ae's house. Yong-ae's mother worked as a laundress and would leave before sunrise for the washing place, and her husband likewise was out all day on account of his working to build the new railway. Their hard-up lives made Bongyeom's mother ashamed of having to impose on them. She tried to spend as little time recovering as possible.

That day, she met Yong-ae's mother when she came back from the washing place.

'I can take in laundry, too. Find me some work.'

Yong-ae's mother's eyes grew wide. 'You should be lying down! Heavens … don't worry about us.'

Then she seemed to remember something and turned to Bongyeom's mother again, blinking. They were in the kitchen and could hear Bongyeom playing with the baby in the other room.

'You know, one of the houses I do laundry for, they're looking for a wet nurse … They said it's all right if the nurse has a child, as long as she can give enough breast milk. The money will be less because of it, but ... What do you think?'

Bongyeom's mother's ears perked up. 'Really? It's all right if I bring my child?'

Yong-ae's mother hesitated. 'Well ... if they give you about twelve or thirteen won a month, you can get a room for Bongyeom and the baby. You'd only be able to visit them occasionally to feed the baby, and maybe use some cow's milk, too. You'll be paid less if they learn your own baby is still so young. So lie to them and tell them your child is past feeding. Then you ought to have enough money.'

Bongyeom's mother was overjoyed at the thought of possible work. 'Then please let them know about me.'

She was determined to make money and pay back Yong-ae's mother's kindness, but at the same time, she looked at her own baby and wondered if she could really leave it to feed another.

Bongyeom's mother regained her strength after a few days. She was hired as a wet nurse and had to live away from Bongyeom and the baby, who were put into a small room. Bongyeom took care of the baby from then on. The baby cried every night as if set on fire and refused to sleep. Bongyeom would carry the baby on her back and pace around the room, pinching herself to keep from falling asleep. Sometimes, she would cry right along with the baby, and look out into the darkness for her mother.

A year passed this way, and the baby cried less but still had not learned to use the toilet. The baby was given half of Bongyeom's name and was called Bonghee. Bongyeom did her best to care for the child, but she would hit the baby if Bonghee scattered her toys or cried too much when Bongyeom's friends had come over. Bongyeom hit the baby especially hard when Bonghee went to the bathroom on the floor. This was not because she hated the baby, but because she was too tired and miserable to do anything else. Bonghee did not drink cow's milk anymore, and only occasionally drank from her mother's breast. She could just about crawl. Sometimes, she stood on her legs and took a few steps. She was oddly bright. Sometimes she would go to the bathroom on the floor and cry loudly before her sister could even hit her. Other times, when Bongyeom had friends over, she would pretend to sleep so that Bongyeom would not beat her for making a sound, and she would lie sweating with her eyes closed. She did not gain much in flesh and bone, but did in such tricks and the size of her head, which was as big as a small gourd and hard as a rock. The hair on top of her big head was as light-coloured as the day she was born. The only thing alive about her was this head, and sometimes it seemed that it was too big for the rest of her body and that she could die early from being crushed by the weight of it.

Bonghee recognized her mother. She cried every time she left. Whenever this happened, the three would hold each other and cry for a long time before parting.

In summer, Bongyeom caught a fever and spent her days lying in bed, unable to even eat. Her body was so hot she could hardly tell where she was sick. Bonghee kept crying beside her. Wishing her mother would come, Bongyeom gave Bonghee her leftover rice. The baby stopped crying and began to eat. Bongyeom closed her eyes and brought her arm to her forehead. She thought she heard footsteps and quickly opened her eyes, but it was only Bonghee dragging the rice bowl.

Bongyeom was furious. 'You stupid girl! Why can't you eat in one place!'

Bonghee's mouth twitched with the effort it took to hold back her cries. She turned to the door. Bongyeom thought Bonghee was also waiting for their mother, and she wanted to shout out, 'Mother!' with all her heart. She gritted her teeth and fought back tears as she looked back at Bonghee.

'You want to see Mother, too, right? Shall we go see her?'

She had spoken without thinking. Bonghee stared at her,

pushed the bowl aside and ran to hug her. She should not have spoken so soon! Bongyeom hugged her sister tight. She realized that two hot trails of tears were coming down her face.

'Why won't Mother come! It's time for her to come. Isn't it, Bonghee?'

Bonghee, not really understanding her, answered, 'Yes ...'

'Come on, Bonghee. Be a good girl. Finish your supper.'

Bongyeom gave Bonghee's head a pat and put her down. Bonghee picked up her spoon again and began to eat. Bongyeom stared at the ceiling. Her mother used to come often and sweep the room, but now there were cobwebs on the rafters. How could she not come, even when enough time had passed for new cobwebs? She could barely remember when she had last come to see them. Bongyeom turned on her side and wondered if her mother would come out of that house after breakfast with her charge, the baby boy Myoungsu, on her back ... Surely she must be past the Chinaman's store by now. She could be right outside the door. Bongyeom stared at the door again, but there was no sound of footsteps, only the sound of Bonghee's spoon scraping the bowl.

Bongyeom sprang up and flung open the door. Bonghee, not understanding what was going on, stared at her sister for a while and crawled towards her.

Bongyeom felt out of breath and collapsed on to the floor.

The sound she had heard was of the woman next door flinging her white laundry on to the fence to dry in the sun. The tips of the neighbour's fingers that Bongyeom could see over the fence reminded her of her mother's kind hands, and it made her think her mother, with her breast-milk stink, was standing on the other side. Sitting in that stink made her feel more at peace than anything else in the world.

She yearned to throw herself at her mother and be held. She was thirsty, so she drank the water that she had mixed with Bonghee's rice, but she was then somehow thirstier than ever. She fell into an uneasy sleep.

Bongyeom awoke with a start.

Bonghee was gone. Had her mother come and taken her out somewhere?

She quickly got up and ran outside. But her mother and Bonghee were nowhere to be seen. The sun was so hot it looked as if it would bake the lawn red. Where was Bonghee? And her mother? She ran outside the fenced area and bumped into the woman next door.

'Have you seen my mother?'

'I haven't seen her ... Are you ill? Hey!'

Bongyeom ran off, only caring about what had happened to her mother. She ran around until her eyes were bloodshot red, and she returned to the room. Then, she heard a sound from the backyard. She jumped up and ran to it.

There in the corner, where the water used to wash the rice was stored in a bucket, Bonghee had dropped her large head and was sucking at the surface as if it were a breast. In the sunlight, her hair was as red as flame.

The Heart of a Mother

Bongyeom died four days later. Her mother had to quit her position and left Myoungsu's house. Bonghee also became sick and died not long after. The landlord, furious that she had brought disease into his house, ordered her to move out. The woman was so angry that she fought loudly with the landlord's wife. She declared they would have to drag her out of that room and spent her days lying in it doing nothing. There was a time when she was too shy to even give excuses to the landlord when her rent was late, but now she surprised herself at her new daring.

She had fought with the landlord's wife long and hard the day before. If the wife had carried the argument on any longer, Bongyeom's mother had been ready to stab her. Thankfully, as if detecting a line was about to be crossed, the landlord's wife had stood down.

'Huh! How dare she try to make me leave. I'm not going anywhere.' The woman glared at the door as she said this to herself. It was unsatisfying that the landlord's wife had retreated so soon. She felt enough fury to till a hundred fields.

Once her anger subsided, she again thought of Bongyeom and Bonghee, and of little Myoungsu. The more she thought about them, the more she thought she had killed her own children. If only she had been with them, they would not have become sick, and even if they had, they would have survived. She beat her chest.

'I killed my own children while looking after someone else's ... You stupid girls, how could you leave without your mother. Take me with you.'

She cried so loudly that soon her throat closed up and she could not make a sound. Her throat felt torn. She coughed, stared out the door, and thought about the events of the past few days.

It had been raining hard. The woman, having seen Bongyeom so sick, had scarcely been able to sleep. She sneaked out of her employer's house in the middle of the night. When she first moved in there, she had gone to sleep in her clothes and crept out to feed Bonghee as soon as everyone in the house had fallen asleep. But once Myoungsu's mother realized what was happening, she watched the woman like a hawk. The woman had dared not sleep in her clothes again and ended up running back and forth in her bedclothes. That night, knowing that Myoungsu's mother would never let her go having already allowed her to visit her daughters during the day, the woman had crept out as soon as the family was asleep and ran home. It was so dark she could barely see in front of her, and the rain had beat down on her bare shoulders. The thunder and lightning made her hair stand on end with booms, crashes, and flashes of light that seemed to split the very sky in two.

None of it had mattered. All she cared about was her daughters, and the storm only seemed to be an expression of her own fears.

When she reached the room, the sight of a white lump by the door had surprised her. Her daughter, Bongyeom! She hurriedly embraced her.

'You stupid child! Why are you lying out here, you'll kill yourself!'

Bongyeom's wet body had been as hot as fire. She had trembled so fiercely that it frightened the woman. What use was her wet nurse position now? She must quit. Once she laid the girl down in the room, her head had filled again with troubles. Myoungsu must be crying so loud as to raise the roof, his parents awake and grimacing, determined to ask her to leave, nay, already having thrown out her things. The thoughts had flitted through her mind as she stroked her sick daughter.

She had stood up. Bonghee, whom she thought was asleep, had ran to her and grabbed her breast. 'Mommy!' she had cried. Bongyeom did not have the strength to ask her mother to stay. She had cried instead, gripping the edge of the woman's skirt. 'Just a little longer ...'

That trembling voice ... the woman felt she could still hear it. She would remember it forever.

She stood up. She paced the room, trying to clear her thoughts, but the memories leapt at her like sparks. She remembered Myoungsu's face. That beautiful, smiling baby ...

'I wonder if he's crying right now.'

The words had slipped out of her before she knew it. Then she forced herself to say what she did not really feel.

'It's because of that bastard child that Bongyeom and Bonghee are dead! Be off with you!'

But Myoungsu's face persisted in her memory. She could just about touch his hair ... She bit her hand. The pain from the bite hurt as much as her longing for the child. She restrained her own steps from going towards the house again by forcing herself to recall how Myoungsu's mother had turned her away at the door. 'Huh! You foolish woman, you killed your own children, but you want to take care of mine? Why are you even alive, still? If you die now, you won't suffer so much!'

It reminded her of the time she had wanted to kill herself after her husband was murdered. This terrible misfortune was all because she had not followed through on that urge. And the communists who had killed her husband, they were the worst of them all. Fang Tong would never have done what he did to her if her husband was still alive. Yes, this was all because of the communists! She thought of Bongshik, who supposedly had been executed for being a communist. Fang Tong's face sprang up in her memory.

'You bastard, my son is no communist ... If you wanted to kick us out, you should have just kicked us out! Dirty bastard ... But is my son alive or dead?'

Saying her son's name out loud gave her a sliver of hope. She was going to go into town to look for Bongshik, but first, she thought she should go to see Myoungsu.

'Oh, Myoungsu!' she called out and squeezed her nipple. He must be calling for her at this very moment ... She ran out of the room. But then, the face of Myoungsu's mother suddenly loomed large in her mind, and she stood up tall.

'You bitch! How dare you stop me from seeing Myoungsu; you only gave birth to him, but it was me who raised him! Of course that baby loves me more. Myoungsu is mine.'

Her eyes bulged in determination. But she realized in the next moment that she would never get to touch even a single hair on Myongsu's head again, and the sad thought made her hunch over.

It was a silent night. The silence weighed heavily on her

heart, threatening to crush it. But she could smell roasting sweet potatoes! It was the season after all. She looked about, trying to find the source of the smell. If only she could have a warm sweet potato ... *Hmph!* How ridiculous of her to want to eat something, to go on living! She leaned on a wall and stared up at the sky. The moon floated high above, and the stars twinkled. Some twinkled like Bongyeom's eyes, others twinkled like Bonghee's eyes. And there were ones like the clear eyes of little Myoungsu. The eyes she would gaze into as she massaged her breast.

'No, get away from me!'

She banished the memory again. She thought of Bonghee and Bongyeom's eyes, swollen from crying and missing their mother. She would never see those eyes again!

She visited the cemetery. There were countless graves spread out before her. She did not like this. She shivered with cold fear as if she were drowning in a roaring torrent. She was afraid of remembering Myoungsu's moon-like face again. She thought of death, thought about how frightening it really was, and gazed into the distance. Suddenly, she broke into a run as if she had been startled by something.

The moonlight shining like snowfall between the awnings of two distant houses had reminded her of the white blanket Myoungsu would be lying on right now as he called for her. But it was only the moonlight after all, which struck her face like a slap. She held her cheeks as she stepped into the light, and restrained herself from crying out, 'Oh, Myoungsu!' by staring up at the utterly unperturbed moon. Love was such a shameful thing!

She stared down at her shadow and pondered whether she should live or die. She felt that dying and forgetting everything that had happened to her was the last happiness she had left in this world. Her body felt so heavy that death seemed the only way to rid her of its weight. How should she die? Caustic soda ... No, that melted the organs, it would be too painful ... Jumping into the river... She imagined the swirling blue currents and it scared her. She shivered and leaned against a wall. No, she would live as long as she was able. Then she would be reunited with Bongshik and watch those bastard communists die by their own swords. They would never prosper, not when God watched over all. *Let's see how well they do.* She gritted her teeth. She heard the sound of footsteps and thought it must be the landlord's wife, coming for round two. She turned her head towards the room, but heard a voice coming from the opposite direction.

'Why are you standing here?'

She turned around and was glad to see Yong-ae's mother. She must be bringing news from Myoungsu's family. 'Have you seen Myoungsu?'

'Myoungsu? In the morning, for a moment.'

'Does he cry? He must be crying all the time!'

Young-ae's mother gave her a sympathetic look and thought of how Myoungsu had indeed thrown a tantrum that morning. She could tell immediately how much Bongyeom's mother wanted to see Myoungsu.

'I heard you went to their house yesterday.'

'Yes, that woman, that horrible woman wouldn't let me see him! Huh! That useless bitch.'

Yong-ae's mother hesitated before saying, 'Don't go there anymore. I don't know how she found out, but she was livid that your daughters died of typhoid. You shouldn't go.'

Bongyeom's mother felt a wave of resentment at her friend. 'Typhoid! What typhoid? My children are dead, anyway. What is the use of crying over someone else's child? So what if I never see Myoungsu again! It's not like I would die!'

She was shouting as if Myoungsu's mother was standing before her. Yong-ae's mother tried to calm her down. 'Enough talk about this. Have you had your supper?'

Young-ae's mother, crouched down with her skirt wrapped around her legs, smelled faintly of herring. It suddenly occurred to Bongyeom's mother that her hunger was making everything feel even worse. She asked Yong-ae's mother for some leftovers, if she had any.

'You've starved all day,' said Yong-ae's mother, 'and I knew you would. I was just about to bring you something. Wait inside, I'll be right back.'

Yong-ae's mother stood up and left. Bongyeom's mother, so hungry that the lower half of her body felt like it was about to break off, crept back into the house.

Yong-ae's mother returned. 'Come, try this. Get yourself together. You've got to figure out how you're going to live from now on ... Do you know what you might do?'

Bongyeom's mother stopped her hasty eating and stared at her.

'I might have something for you,' Yong-ae's mother went on. 'It's good work, lots of profit. My husband just left to do it himself.'

'What kind of work?'

Yong-ae's mother lowered her voice. 'Selling salt.'

Bongyeom's mother's eyes grew wide. 'But what if you get caught?'

'You have to be ever so clever. Making money isn't easy, after all.' Despite her resigned words, Yong-ae's mother became worried again about her husband. They sat in silence for a while.

'Anyway, you should try it too, when you've got your strength back. In Korea, salt is thirty jeon for one *mal*, but here, it's two won and thirty jeon! Think of the profit.'

The prospect of work breathed new life into Bongyeom's mother, but her spirits deflated once she remembered her dead daughters. Others were smuggling salt for the sake of feeding their sons and daughters but for whom was she struggling? When she realized it was for herself alone, she was awash with melancholy. Still, if she did not try with all her might to live, who would so much as lift a spoonful of rice-wash water to her lips? Starving scared her more than dying. It was harder to bear. Was she not despondent before she ate, and so different now that she had something in her stomach? Was not the air that seemed to press down on her chest much lighter for it? In this life, one absolutely had to eat ... She remembered the leek she tried to chew when she gave birth to Bonghee in the Chinese family's shed. The memory made her shudder. She had to acknowledge that despite her suffering during her time with Myoungsu's family, at least she had never gone hungry. She thought of Myoungsu's face again and wondered whether his constant crying would convince Myoungsu's mother to take her back. She put down her spoon.

'What, finished already? Have some more. You've got to get your strength up.'

'My strength ... such is a person's greed ... my husband is dead, my son, daughters ...' Her voice trembled as she stared towards the door. Her face looked so gaunt in the moonlight that Yong-ae's mother sighed.

'If you can't die, then you should at least keep your strength up. Don't even think about the past.' Yong-ae's mother approached her and began tidying up her hair. This reminded Bongyeom's mother of Myoungsu's fat little baby hand grabbing at her, and her calmed heart suddenly beat wildly again. She unconsciously grabbed Yong-ae's mother's hand.

'Do you think Myoungsu is asleep right now?'

Then, she buried her face in Yong-ae's mother's lap and cried loudly. Yong-ae's mother also shed a tear or two at her friend's distress.

'Don't cry. Don't think about other people's babies! There's no use.'

'If I could see him just once ... Could you take me there? Please, my friend.' She was convinced she would be allowed to see Myoungsu if her friend accompanied her.

Yong-ae's mother felt uncomfortable, thinking of the curses Bongyeom's mother had shouted about her former employer only a moment ago. She did not answer. Bongyeom's mother leapt to her feet and grabbed Yong-ae's mother's hand, urging her up.

'Look here, you must calm yourself! We'll go to see them tomorrow.' Yong-ae's mother sat her back down.

The moonlight continued to illuminate their faces.

Smuggler

The autumn of the northern country was bleak. On a night when the wind blew as loudly as thunder, Bongyeom's mother put four *mal* of salt into her sack and followed the others. They were a group of six, and Bongyeom's mother was the only woman. The ageing tracker who headed the group had smuggled salt for the past ten years and was able to find the route with his eyes closed. The rest of the group had to be completely obedient to him. They had to maintain absolute silence during the time they carried the salt, even if that meant days with only gestures to communicate with each other.

They walked in a line through the unrelenting wind, paying close attention to the person in front of them. Sometimes, the wind sounded like footsteps or the shouting of a policeman, which made them hold their breath. They would remember rumours about a smuggler being shot on this very route the day before. The dread blackened their hearts to the very shade of the darkness that surrounded them.

The others wore padded clothes, but Bongyeom's mother wore layers and rubber shoes her toes protruded out of. The weight of the salt carried on her head banished all thoughts of the cold. It was like being hit on the top of her skull by a steel pipe, and sometimes as painful as carrying a ball of flame. She had taken on six *mal* of salt at first like the others, but the men had managed to convince her that it would be too much. Now, not even ten *li* into their journey, her head already hurt.

She grimaced and tried to lift the load slightly with her hands, but it was no use, and now her arms felt like they would fall off from fatigue. She was seized with a compulsion to throw down her load and just die there in the middle of the route. But that was just a feeling. Her feet continued to follow the men. If only she could carry as much as the men ... Perhaps she would be able to if she used her back instead of her head ... But she would need rope, and there was none ... How about resting for a while? She almost said the last part out loud but bit down on her words. Her hands continued to try to lift the sacks and sooth her pain.

Her forehead and back sweated so much that she could feel wetness on the soles of her feet. Her shoes were so soaked in sweat she was afraid she might slip and fall. She had to concentrate on not stumbling, which made her fall further behind the others. Running after them made her lose her breath, and her side would hurt. She should have taken on just two *mal* ... Should she spill it? Should she? Gripping the sacks in her hands, she knew she could not do it.

Soon, she heard the sound of the river. It soothed her heart. They could put down their salt and rest for a moment and drink all the water they wanted. But what if something lurked on the other side of the river? Her anxiety grew with the increasing sound of the water. Even this happy sound had turned into needles prickling her eardrum. She felt she would die of exhaustion soon. Then, the man walking in front of her stood still, and she stopped, too. The sound of insects mixed with the sound of the water. The man in front of her seemed to have sat down. She also dropped her salt sack and collapsed. Then, she forced her eyes closed; they had been opened wide from her exertions. At the same time, she kept an ear out on the men lest she be left behind.

Now that the immediate pain had subsided, her whole body trembled from exhaustion. Just as she leaned forward, hugging her stomach, the man in front of her gave her a poke.

She quickly got up. The sound of the men taking off their clothes made her more nervous than ever. She hesitated for a moment before taking off her own clothes and making them into a bundle to tie around her neck. Rubbing her neck, she wondered if her head would still be attached to her body by the time they reached Longjing. She hoisted the salt on her head again and began to walk.

The splashing sound made her think the men in the front had entered the water. She felt her feet touch sand and soon she was in the river. The water was a cold, rushing black void, its sound so loud it filled her ears. The water lapped about her, and she felt her hair stand on end from the icy cold. She took a deep breath, close to a sob.

The deeper the water became, the rougher the ground got beneath her feet, from sand to pebbles to large stones. Their slick surface made her mind go white with fear every time she almost slipped. The water came up to her breasts now.

Just then, her foot slipped, and her body fired up as she tried with all her might not to let the salt drop from her head. Her foot kept slipping, and her legs were getting wider and wider apart. She wanted to shout to the men in front of her for help, but she was too out of breath, and something in her chest blocked her voice. The tiny yelp that slipped out was drowned by the wind and the gushing of the water. She used her last remaining strength to keep her left foot steady. All thoughts of death or fear were distant from her mind; the thought of the salt dropping into the water and melting kept her ramrod straight from the tips of her toes to the ends of her hair.

The men had almost reached the other side of the river when they realized Bongyeom's mother was not behind them. The tracker had to retrace their steps, and luckily, he found her. The tracker knew that if he had arrived even a moment later, the woman would have perished. He steadied her with his hand and shouldered her burden of salt. Prodding the riverbed, he found the rock that she had almost slipped on and wondered why she had gone that way when he had taken care to go around it. He gripped her hand as they made their way to the others.

Bongyeom's mother regained her wits bit by bit as they continued to walk. She was still dizzy and wanted to vomit, but the salt was still on her head, so she gritted her teeth to keep it in.

When the two finally reached the riverbank, the others waiting all stood up and embraced them both. A few of them even shed quiet tears. As pitiful as their own lives were, somehow the life of this poor woman was even more unfortunate. They also sighed as they thought of their wives, children, and parents who were waiting for them, sleepless, hungry, and worrying.

The night was too fearful for them to rest long, and soon they were off. This time, they put Bongyeom's mother in the middle of the line. They seemed to be walking in an irrigation ditch as dried stalks cut her feet through the torn soles of her shoes. Several times she had wanted to take off her shoes, but she could not bear to throw them away. She always had trouble making decisions. Even now, she hesitated. Her shoes were so ripped that the soles kept getting caught in the millet and sorghum roots, but she still could not throw them away.

Then, when they reached the summit of the hill, they heard a loud voice shout, 'Who is that? Freeze, with your hands up! Or we'll shoot!'

A blue light flashed in their faces. The group shielded their eyes with their hands as if the light was a sharp blade or a bullet flying towards them. *We're going to lose our salt!* They despaired at this shared thought. They hoped the people with the light were communists or bandits; these were the two groups who were not interested in salt and would let them go if they begged them.

Their bodies were searched. The light went off and there was some low-voiced talking. The darkness made the woman shiver all over again, and she wondered if they were being threatened with swords or guns in the dark.

Then, a voice spoke from the shadows.

'Comrades! Do you know why you are forced to smuggle salt under cover of darkness?'

The steely voice boomed as it spoke on through the surging of the wind. They were communists! Their salt was safe. The woman thought of ways she might beg them to let them be on their way. The voice continued to speak. She wished they would stop speaking and just let them go. She was worried there were patrols that would hear the communists' speech in the hills ahead. The voice reminded her of a speech that she had heard when she visited Bongyeom's school; it had been delivered by her daughter's teacher. She raised her head and tried to see who was speaking, but all she could see was pitch blackness. She wondered if her Bongshik was among them. No, her clever boy would never be stupid enough to join such a gang. Now that she had been reassured about her son, she began to wonder if their talk was a ploy to steal their salt.

The voice in the dark finished talking and even bade them good luck on their way. The smugglers began walking again. The woman hurried, afraid they would be followed by guns and swords regardless of the words they had just heard. Only when they came down the hill and into a field did she manage to give out a sigh of relief.

They really had been communists! She thought of herself as the most pitiful person in the world, to quake in her shoes before them like that. They killed her husband and ruined her life, but she could not say a word as she faced her greatest enemy! She could barely muster the courage to even think of her hatred before them! Even she, the most pathetic creature, was carrying salt to save her own life. She realized then, the more stupid and pitiful a creature, the more it strove to save itself. Her only question was: why had not the communists

taken the salt from them? When they kill people like flies ...
Now she had no trouble cursing them in her mind.

During the following days, they hid in the mountains or
among reeds and reached Longjing only on the fourth night.
Bongyeom's mother did not know where to hide her salt, but
after a long hesitation, she put it in a box and shoved the box
into a corner. She collapsed on the floor. The room had a
draught and the floor was like ice. She rubbed her head and
feet and broke into loud sobs. Having returned home, she was
confronted again with the memories of Bongyeom, Bonghee,
and Myoungsu. She cried for a long time and twisted in agony
thinking of everything she had gone through in the past four
days. She realized that even the tears she was shedding now
were a luxury. She calmed herself and lay down, thinking of
how she was going to sell the salt. The others would have sold
theirs by now, but who would come to buy from her? No one
knew she had salt yet, should she go around the houses and
tell them? What if she met a policeman on the way? She tried
to stand again but cried out as her legs gave way beneath her.
She stayed still for a long time before making her way to the
box.

She listened to be sure that no one was approaching and
put her hand in the box and stroked the salt. How much
would this make her ...? Eight won and eighty jeon! She could
clear off her unpaid rent ... and what remained would last only
another month. She ought to use it to fund a new business.
But what could she sell? She absentmindedly put a little salt in
her mouth and her appetite came back in a rush of saliva. She
craved a bowl of rice. No food tastes good without a bit of salt.

That was it! She remembered her family and how she had
dreamt of making preserved side dishes if she had just a little
salt. That she would think of this only after having lost her
husband and children! She simply had to continue living, only
because she could not die. She sighed. The life she had lived
was like meals without salt. A terrible life. So terrible ... She

touched the top of her head. It was so sore that the slightest graze of her fingertips pained her. She leaned her face against the box of salt.

'Oh Bongshik, whether you're alive or dead, please come find your mother ... I cannot bear this life!'

A while later, she woke up to bright morning light and was shocked to see two men in uniform and her salt box at her feet. The sack of salt had been removed and the men's eyes were boring into her. Policemen! She trembled like a leaf.

'Where is your salt licence!'

She did not have one. She could not breathe, and her eyes went dark. She felt a sudden sharpening of all her senses, just like that time in the river when she strained against the currents, trying not to drop the salt into the water. The tracker had saved her that time, but who would save her now against these men with guns and swords?

The policemen knew very well she had no licence. 'You despicable woman! Selling private salt! Get up!'

One of them grabbed her arm. She felt a jolt of electricity run through her as she remembered the words spoken by the voice on the hill, the voice she had listened to with contempt.

'You are our comrades! Only when we work as one can we fight against the rich bastards who are our real enemies!'

Those words thrown at her from the dark! Her heart was fit to burst. The communists had not taken her salt. She felt that if they were by her side right now, they might even help her. Surely, they would help her! And the real enemies were the rich bastards who were stealing her salt! She was shouting this aloud before she even realized. All the resentment she had harboured until now was blasting from her like flames.

She sprang to her feet.

May–October 1934

THE AUTHORESS

The woman suddenly raised her head and opened her eyes wide. She looked about her. Only when she realized she was alone did she let go of some of the tension in her body. She had woken up to the sound of birds – *chi-rrup, chi-rrup* – and wondered if she were still dreaming. She must look a fright.

She sat up in bed, staring at the door.

The chirruping of the birds, as if it were a serenade to her youth, infused her with a sense of new energy. All the beauty and glory of the world seemed to exist just for her in that moment.

She caressed her breast and thought of how wonderful it would be if her hands were a man's. She blushed at the thought, and though she quickly removed her hands, a glow of pleasure remained. As she pulled on her clothes and looked in the mirror on the wall, she caught a glimpse of her lovely shoulder and the curls of her hair, black as ink, tumbling behind it. She stood still for a long time, possessed by her own reflection.

Light began seeping into the dreamy, dim room. The street lamps blinked off. She came out of her reverie and finished dressing.

She opened the back door. The fresh wind that swept over her whole body made her feel as if she had wings. The dewy poplar forest emanated a green fragrance of spring. She leaned on the door and looked up at the crown of leaves, like stars on a crescent-moon night. The blue sky showed through, as did red rays of sunlight. She was flying among them.

She thought of that pretty shoulder of hers in the mirror and of the faces of the countless men who were in pursuit of her. She thought of her photo in the magazine and her poem that had been published with it.

She smiled at herself and mumbled, 'Those idiots. They'll never pin me down.' The smile shaded slightly to a sneer.

The more letters she received from men and the more her writings were published in magazines, the greater her pride grew. She felt herself standing tall atop a pedestal.

The woman was as sensitive as she looked. Everyone has a period of time in which they might write a line of poetry or be swept up by a novel or two. She had been going through such a phase, and so she would turn first to the literary section of whatever newspaper or magazine she happened to be reading. She playfully wrote a few verses, and a poem she had written in response to a man's love letter had ended up being published, making her an 'authoress' overnight.

She did not try to think seriously about how easily she had become an authoress. All she knew was that she had an uncommon talent. It got so that she assumed every person she met knew her name – Maria – even the ones who did not utter it in her presence. When she walked the streets, she was sure that everyone was looking at her because of the immense talent that shone through her. She admitted to herself that this must be, as writing talent in a woman was so rare and herself so singular.

Pride filled her heart at the thought of this. She eagerly observed the scene before her, looking for a possible writing prompt. There was some potential here and there, but once she picked up her pen to write, the idea vanished from her mind.

'Miss, breakfast is served.'

Surprised, she glanced up at where the student stood and then looked back down at her wrist. Her wristwatch was not there, just the pale skin where the watch face would have been. She felt a touch disconcerted until she turned her head to the mirror and her watch lay on a shelf next to it, cheerily ticking away.

She smiled, her mood lightening. 'What sort of breakfast is served this early?'

'Miss, you're supposed to go out of town today.'

'Oh, yes ... I forgot. I'll be right there.'

In that moment, she recalled how she had stayed up late the night before trying to remember a certain Bible verse. She then remembered the place she was to go, the name of which translated to 'Two-Headed Village'.

The student turned and left. Her braided ponytail fell in a neat line down her back, making the woman nostalgic for her own time as a student in this school.

As the student's footsteps faded away, she washed her face and approached the mirror in her room again. She could see her voluptuous shoulder once more. She applied some cream to her hands and massaged it gently into her flushed face. The room filled with the scent of the cream.

A lone ray of sunlight flickered in the middle of the room as the leaves outside her window shook lightly in the breeze. The room brightened. As did her face.

Once she was done with her makeup, she picked up her Bible and gave herself another look in the mirror. *I, too, would fall in love with you if I were a man*, she thought and nodded her approval. Even when she was alone, she always took a quick glance behind her during these moments in case anyone was looking.

She flicked through the Bible until she came to the verse

she had searched for the night before and was lost in thought. A vision of the peasantry going about their lives. The faces of the familiar peasants from back home. *Would they understand what I mean?* She frowned.

The peasants she had known seemed to know only about eating, having children, and work. The ones that knew a bit more had a scattering of old proverbs and stories, but otherwise, they were not aware of what was happening in their own country or to their people. All was peace and quiet for them.

They had wrapped up a few gourds for possessions and led their children out of their beloved homelands without even thinking about why they were being banished or what was to become of them. All they could do was cry and trust that there may be a better fate for them soon.

She was having second thoughts about going to the Two-Headed Village. Peasants were peasants everywhere you went, after all. They were the most pathetic people on earth, and also the most pitiful. They could not be saved no matter what you did.

Maria ate her breakfast, and her students escorted her to the carriage. An older missionary lady carrying a black book bag followed her inside. A whiff of horse manure made Maria hold a handkerchief to her nose, and the light scent of cream on the handkerchief made its way even to the missionary lady sitting next to her. The harsh-looking carriage driver shouted something and cracked his whip. The horse broke into a trot.

She had already said yes to this trip, and it had been ordered by the principal no less, so she was more or less forced to go. It irritated her, but presently she decided that every literary personage needed to travel once in a while and that mingling with the peasants and the natural beauty of the countryside might inspire her to write a masterpiece. Her spirits lifted.

This was the first time she had left Longjing since coming to the city. A Christian wives' society had asked the principal of Jeonghwa Girls' School to send a lecturer, and this was why the woman was setting off so early.

She looked back. There were still students waving at her. As she waved back and smiled, the carriage turned around the corner of a house. The smell of vegetable oil assaulted her nose and the crackling sound of frying food filled the air. Through an open gate, the woman glimpsed the red mouth of a kitchen furnace.

Maria was struck by a sad mood. She turned to look once more over the rooftops at the green canopy of the line of poplar trees that served to fence in the school, before facing forwards again.

What if I were to be sent home, never to work at the school again?

The thought made her look back yet again.

Longjing in the morning was awash with the smell of vegetable oil and pork. They heard the creaking of the water sellers' racks and the Chinese peddlers calling out in broken Korean their wares of meat and vegetables.

Beside every little store stood a sign on a stick with the name of the proprietor painted in clear letters. A door, decorated with colourful paper crumpled into balls on either side of it, had a black plank lain in front with fresh dumplings letting off wisps of steam.

Once the carriage rolled on to the main road, she could see the deep green of the trees along the avenue and Chinese and Korean children holding hands as they ran and played together on the street. Every crossroad had a policeman, their backs slightly bent and apparently still cold in this weather as they continued to wear their padded uniform jackets, rifles slung over their shoulders. They glanced at every person who passed by. Their foreheads were oily, and their talon-like fingernails occasionally flicked at their nostrils.

Surprised by the loud clanging of a bell, Maria darted her eyes around her, only to realize the source of the noise was the very carriage she was riding. She grinned at the back of the carriage driver's head. *He's good at ringing that bell, at least!*

At the sound of the bell, a vegetable seller ran up to them with his wares. Their cabbages, carried in a wide basket, were slightly dewy and soiled with earth.

'Look at those cabbages! So large!' exclaimed the missionary lady. The carriage driver turned to look and smiled at them as if he understood, showing his yellowed teeth. Maria was so surprised that she had to avert her eyes. She tried not to throw up her breakfast.

The missionary lady saw her distress and smiled. 'I don't think they've ever brushed their teeth in their lives.'

'Good heavens ...'

Maria had to wonder, could such people ever be considered civilized?

Soon they were out of the city. Maria gazed at the green pastures and looked back at the city once more. The dazzling disc of the sun was shining over the red and blue bricks of Longjing's buildings. The faraway mountains were still shrouded in milk-coloured fog, but the blue of the sky was shredded to a thousand pieces by the rays of the sun, and somehow made all the bluer for it. The earthen walls surrounding the houses along the way were white with bird droppings, sad as an old woman's expression as she waits for the grandchild that never visits. Tiny blossoms, white and yellow, were scattered by the road. Somewhere in the green grass, ants would be digging their tunnels and dung beetles would be rolling their balls of cowpat. All of this, wrapped in the single embrace of nature.

By 2 p.m., Maria was standing tall at the altar of the church in the Two-Headed Village, giving a lecture on John 3:16.

The church was a small one but packed. Of course, Maria knew all too well that not everyone was a congregant. Every person who came through the door was dark-skinned from working in the fields. Just looking at them made her shudder.

Her mouth went on and on while her mind kept thinking of

other things. She felt like a phoenix among chickens, a white person among black. How pretty she must seem to them, how touching her words, she thought, and the ardour of her words increased without her having intended it.

She had the Bible out before her and was ostensibly talking about faith, but her talk veered on to the subject of labourers and peasants and criticism of the state of Korean society.

Her audience felt as if they had just come out of a storm as they watched Maria blabber on, her eyes darting this way and that. She seemed like a different species from them, one with no heat or blood, more like a pretty doll that could speak – all this talk coming out of her mouth about labourers and peasants made them feel uncomfortable and pity her. They also could not help doubting that she really knew much about labourers or peasants.

Her face was like that of an early consumptive, and the only thing alive about her were the eyes beneath her painted eyebrows. Those rapidly speaking lips were completely unnatural to them. Was this what an 'educated New Woman' really was like?

'If you die, you must die on your own land, but above all, you must live on your own land! Why did you have to come all this distance! Am I right, or am I wrong? I have never forgotten that it was our old land that knit my very bones! It is the only destiny that I have! Do you know this, or do you not? We must live and die for the land!'

Maria pounded the podium with her ivory-like hand. Her audience, who had been silently mocking her, sighed at her words. They were remembering the days when they were kicked out of their own homes, dragging their children behind them.

'If you had your own land, you wouldn't have to endure this pain, this humiliation. What have you accomplished by wandering out here? What? Only our own blood will look out for us. Who else will be happy when we're happy, cry when we're sad? Is it not our own people? This is why we must stand our ground and live on our own land, even if it means cutting off our heads, even it means the destruction of our bodies!'

Maria was tearful at this point. The audience raged silently and could barely keep still. They were imagining their hated landowners. Oh, the earth that they had broken in with their bare hands! The land they loved so much and knew so well – every blade of grass that grew on it, every little stone, every inch! The senseless loss of it, being ripped from it; their hearts had broken then!

If they had any pleasure or joy in their days, or any reason for courage to get on with life, that land had been it. But they had been cruelly banished from it at the utterance of a few words from fearsome lips. Were Maria's words any kinder or more sympathetic to their plight? When did people like her ever stop, even for a moment, to consider what they were going through!

The eyes of the landowners seemed to materialize before the audience, those hated faces large and clear, as they were taken back to the moment they were banished from their lands.

From a dark corner, a cry cut through the church like a bolt of lightning. 'What use is nation! What use is country!'

Maria was startled.

She suddenly remembered something about the peasants of Jiandao: they were a fierce, fearsome people.

But she shrugged off her fear. *I studied at the best college in Korea, I am a rare authoress, and what's more, I'm beautiful.* She stared down the audience with what was clearly a sneer on her lips.

And you're just peasants.

The audience realized from her expression that the woman they had regarded as no more than a silly doll was a completely different person from what they had assumed. They suddenly abhorred the sight of her. She was the kind of rich little girl that they detested above all else, and the memories of their poor wives, sisters, and daughters who starved to death without so much as a bowl of rice gruel to save them came back with a vengeance, their ghostly figures populating the stage on either side of Maria. Had their wives and sisters died to feed this woman sweet food? To pay for this woman's education and for the whitening of her skin? They had sacrificed their own food, clothes, and any hope of an education, and bit their daughters' thumbs until they bled, giving away their own flesh and blood so disease would mercifully take them.

Their thoughts turned Maria and the pastor and the church leaders standing behind her into vampires.

No! They had always been vampires.

They jumped to their feet. But before they knew it, the church started to cave in around them and the belfry collapsed.

Maria was standing next to the bell that wailed its last ring. Her clothes torn to shreds, she was holding her face in her hands as she shivered, afraid her beauty would be damaged.

September 1932

DARKNESS

His eyes, sunk into dark circles over his high cheekbones, scanned the outpatient room before he realized it was empty. The man lowered his head and leaned heavily on his cane as he dragged his bandaged leg through the door.

His hair had not been cut in a long time. It covered his forehead like a fur-lined hood and roughly tumbled down to below his ears. His clothes were yellow with dried sweat and stuck to his body, outlining his emaciated frame. A stick-like arm protruding from a sleeve stopped abruptly at his knobby hand, which gripped tight to the cane. It looked as if his skeleton would show through his skin at any moment.

Sitting on a swivel chair, the doctor glanced up from his medical journal but quickly pretended the man was not there. Irritation knitted his brow as he pretended to read. The whispering nurses stopped chattering and stood silent.

The oldest nurse among them almost shouted out, '*Oppa!*' but upon closer inspection, he was not her older brother. Young-sil forced herself to lower her gaze. The floor was dark. Her ears rang, and her heart beat fast. She was sure he had been her brother, but in the blink of an eye, he had turned into another charity case, the kind she hated dealing with. Was she going mad? What a disaster it would have been if she had not stopped herself from calling out! She looked up at him again. Did her brother truly sacrifice himself to save people like him? A flame of deep frustration burned in her as she picked up some clean cotton and alcohol and approached the man to tend to his bandages. How could her brother care so much about people like this? The dizziness in her head made her hands tremble. A putrid smell coiled up from the man's unravelling bandages.

Had her brother really been executed? Or was that a lie? Her mind kept busily asking these questions as she pressed down on the man's leg to make the pus leak out before cleaning the wound. Red blood mixed with the pus as it flowed. She pressed her fingers harder, and could feel the bone beneath. Spots of blood and pus came off on her fingertips. She thought of her brother's face. She thought of how her brother had sacrificed his life while she complained about dealing with patients. Darkness descended over her eyes and an inexplicable feeling welled up into tears.

The pus stopped and only blood flowed. She scrubbed the wound with alcohol and gauze using a pair of pincers, covered the wound with more gauze, and bandaged it. The patient wiped the sweat from his forehead and leaned on his cane as he stood up. The stink of his old sweat jumped at her from his dishevelled hair as he turned and left the room. The unkempt hair that came down to his tunic, his trousers crusty with dried pus and blood – clearly a man with no parents or wife. The nurse washed her hands by the basin near the radiator. *I only have a mother, too*, she thought as the cresol solution splashed her hands. Tiny beads of sweat studded the skin behind her ears.

She surreptitiously glanced at the doctor. He frowned as he continued to read his medical journal. Bad mood today. She could not tell if it was because a repulsive patient had come by or because there was a difficult sentence on the page. She could not help but snort at an old, unwelcome memory.

Ten years ago, when the doctor was first appointed to the hospital, he was full of enthusiasm for his work. He would charge poor patients only half, and sometimes if they begged him enough, he charged them nothing at all. He constantly fought with the head of the hospital over this and had been rumoured to be leaving soon.

Time passed. Perhaps his passion passed as well, as he had turned into the doctor before her today. He was hardly the only thing that had changed; since her brother left, Nurse Young-sil's body and mind had also altered considerably.

'Listen, sister. We are have-nots, and we have to look out for other have-nots. And more than that, we have to keep fighting to get out of this living hell.'

She had begged her brother that night not to go, feeling that something terrible would happen. Indeed, since that day he had never returned.

'*Oppa*, it's not right what you did, if you could only see Mother now. The whole world thinks the worst of us and wants us dead ...'

Her gaze moved towards the curtains. They were infused with orange light, and through her tears they looked dim and yet beautiful at the same time.

The noon bell rang. A siren followed. It sounded through the halls of the hospital. She thought it was saying, '*Waaaaaaa – your brother has been executed!*'

The siren made the floor ring before ascending into the sky and fading out.

The doctor closed the medical journal, took out a clean white handkerchief, wiped his face, and left the room. The sound of his leather slippers dragging on the floor made Young-sil realize she had had her ears open for the sound of his footsteps. But the doctor had long forgotten about her and was engaged to another woman. Why could she not forget him, too? Now that he was gone, she let out the sigh she had been keeping to herself all day.

Lovers change. The older brother you waited for day and night is gone forever. She had yearned to tell her brother the secret she had hidden from even her mother, but now that hope was taken from her. She could feel her eyes getting bloodshot, so she blinked and sat down on the edge of a bed. The smell of cresol crept up from her hands.

'Oh *Unni*, are you thinking of your brother again? Don't do that. You've got to accept it, there's nothing you can do.'

It was Nurse Hyosook, looking at her with sympathy. Her cheeks had a healthy plumpness and the white teeth showing between her thin lips were as round as marbles. 'Come on, let's finish the cleaning.'

Nurse Nakagawa also gave her a gentle look over Hyosook's shoulder. 'Don't be too sad, Lee-*san*.'

Young-sil managed a nod. She took a deep breath. Her co-workers at least had some words of kindness for her, but the doctor was going out of his way to ignore her. This angered her and made her refuse to show any of her sadness or vulnerability before him.

Hyosook discreetly looked away from the trembling of Young-sil's eyes and grabbed a bucket to gather hot water. Her dainty nurse's cap sat slightly askew on her head and her hair came down in a neat ponytail from underneath it. Nakagawa collected syringes, pincers, and other equipment to put in the sanitizing vat. She twisted a knob and the water began to boil and give off steam. She tossed in the equipment. Beads of sweat appeared under her nose.

Young-sil dragged herself to the doctor's desk. Her hands automatically reached out to rearrange the objects on top of it. The yellow cover of the journal gave off a scent of tobacco. It was like the doctor's breath grazing her cheek. She frowned and turned her gaze to Hyosook to distract herself, but she was reminded of the doctor's lab coat in the white of the nurse's uniform. She turned her eyes to the ceiling, but even there it seemed to be written, *Your brother was executed.*

Hyosook chattered away as she mopped the floor and wiped the desk, chairs, and cabinets. Her bird-like movements gave the young woman a buoyancy that Nakagawa lacked. Nakagawa stood by the vat, steam landing on her dry hair while she took out the medical tools one by one and wiped them down, and interjected an occasional, 'Oh, yes' or 'You don't say?' Neither of them looked as if they had a care in the world.

Once the clean-up was over, the two gave a quick bow to Young-sil and skipped out the door. The lunch bell rang soon after. Young-sil had not eaten since the evening before, but she did not feel hungry. She had begun to skip a meal or two on occasion since the doctor announced his engagement three weeks ago. She had lost her appetite the moment she heard the news.

She closed the door to the corridor and put her hands in her pockets. Her fingertips brushed the newspaper cutting she had folded in there. She trembled, and gooseflesh travelled up her body. She touched her cheek. If only she had misread it. Who knows? Maybe she had. Her hand entered her pocket again. She began to sweat, and her arm shook. She gripped the newspaper. She slowly drew it from her pocket. Looking at it felt like knives slicing her eyes. The photograph of her brother standing among the other condemned prisoners. It could just be someone who looked like him; she would need to check the name again. Before her eyes could reach it, she threw the newspaper aside. She felt bound with steel wire, she would never be able to escape ...

'*Oppa!* What am I to tell Mother? I've managed to lie to her so far, but what am I going to tell her now ...?'

It was the doctor who had handed her that newspaper! The unbelievable news! She had fainted on the spot. She should have died right then and there. If she had, she would not have to endure this pain. She found herself biting the back of her own hand. Blood bloomed.

'*Oppa*, you're a bad person. You let yourself die young, before Mother. How could you? How could you! What am I going to tell Mother?'

She paced the room. If it were not for her mother, she would have swallowed some pills and followed her brother into oblivion. But her mother was seventy and needed her care. Her mother, who still waited day and night for her son's return.

My dear Young-sil, you must've seen in the newspaper that we have been executed. But we are not dead. One day, I'll see you and Mother again, so wait for me. Please hide Mother for now. My dear sister ...

She received this letter after her brother's sentencing. She wanted to believe in his words and in his goodness. But what good were his words and beliefs if he ended up dead? She snatched up the newspaper, tore it to shreds, and threw the remains out the window.

The garden outside hurt her eyes with its vibrant colours. The slats of the surrounding fence stood side-by-side in an orderly manner, curving with the shape of the grounds. Spring had come after all.

The news had to be a lie. A letter was sure to come from her brother today. She looked at the clock.

The door opened. Thinking it was an orderly delivering a letter, she held back a cry and turned her head. The doctor, startled by her presence, paused for a moment before wordlessly going to his desk. He held nothing in his hands, much less a letter. He lit a cigarette.

Her mouth twisted from the effort to hold back her tears. She averted her eyes and bit her tongue to keep him from seeing the poison in her heart. She tasted salt and felt the beginning of a headache. The doctor had gone to the sink and was wiping his hands with alcohol-treated cotton.

'Did you have lunch?'

Young-sil's eyes opened wide at the doctor's question.

'No answer?' The doctor smirked. He was mocking her! She glared at him to prevent her tears from spilling out.

She was repulsed by the stray, wafting strands of his pomaded hair, and his eyes exuded distasteful arrogance as he avoided her gaze and concentrated on scrubbing his hands. Where had the conscientious doctor of the past disappeared to? There was not a trace of him in the coward that stood before her. She could not believe she had given him her precious virginity and, more importantly, her soul; her innocent soul that had once been the exclusive purview of her good brother. It was her own foolishness she was disgusted with. She wanted to run up to that man and stab him to death.

Perhaps detecting her feelings, the doctor shuffled out of the room. She stared daggers after him until he was out of view and went up to the reception room herself.

The windows opened wide on to a sky that looked down on a world without her brother, and two lilies in a vase on the table had their heads tilted towards that sky. She sat down and stared at the sky herself until she heard footsteps coming up the stairs. Suspecting it was the doctor, she whipped around in her seat. But it was only Mr Kim, an orderly. She turned away, unwilling to show anyone her eyes swollen from crying.

Mr Kim silently walked up to her.

A sudden hope welled in her heart. 'Is there a letter?'

He scratched his white hair with his knobby knuckles and looked away. 'No letters.'

'There simply has to be a letter today!'

She stared at him, and Mr Kim hesitantly returned her gaze. His eyes, usually full of smiles, were only sad today. He must know about her, too. This time, Young-sil did not bother wiping away her welling tears. She stared at him harder, as if to defy him, and the scraggly white beard of the orderly blurred in her vision.

'There, there. You must be brave,' consoled Mr Kim, bowing over her.

She wanted to call out, '*Mr Kim!*' But her throat had closed.

She and Mr Kim were the people who had worked at the hospital the longest, and they were also its poorest employees. They understood each other, and of course he would know about her affair with the doctor and her brother's execution as well. He understood her better than anyone else.

*

It was nine at night.

Hyosook and Nakagawa had gone to the baths and only Young-sil remained at her post. She checked patients' temperatures and pulses, writing them down with blue and red pencils. Her hands kept nervously fumbling over the charts. She was worried her mother would have heard the news by now and was perhaps running towards her this very minute or had fainted in the streets. She tossed aside the charts, and the pencils fell to the floor. If she asked the doctor on the night shift to let her go home, he would only force her to tell him the whole story. He would not be understanding, anyway. Why were those girls taking so long with their baths? The rowdiness of the pool table downstairs carried up to the ward. She felt like she was in a different world from all of them.

Burying her face in her hands, she sighed as she thought again about her brother's execution. It simply had to be a lie, he had to still be in prison. If no letter came tomorrow, she was going to ask for leave and go to Seoul. She had to get to the bottom of it herself; the newspaper was printing falsehoods! She felt she was spinning round and round where she stood.

But if it was real? She went to the window and opened it. Unconsciously, she asked out loud, 'Can it be true?'

There was no one outside. Her head was ringing, and cold air whipped her hair and snaked down her body. The scattered lights outside blurred with her tears. She could see the hospital chief's house, the nurses' quarters, and the house of her former lover, the doctor who was second-highest ranking at the hospital. The light at the door of that last house was especially bright against the night. His fiancée must be visiting. She shook off her useless feelings of jealousy and turned her back to the window.

Young-sil, I can't live a moment without you. Your beautiful, white hands clean the dirty wounds before I examine the patients, which allows me to see how I can cure them. Your hands! Your pretty hands are forever mine.

Such were the lines in a letter he had sent her.

'The devil!' she muttered, and slammed the window shut. The myriad machines of the city seemed to whisper, *The doctor's hands! Young-sil's hands!*

She bowed her head. Together their hands could accomplish any complex surgery. The pale, nimble hands of the doctor! They seemed to know exactly what was needed, what apparatus and what medicine, to accomplish miracles. Young-sil brought her own hand to her lips. She wanted to bite down on it.

Was she crazy? She thought she had just heard her mother cry out for her brother! '*Young-sik! Oh, Young-sik!*'

'*Unni*, do go take a bath,' Hyosook said as she came up the stairs with Nakagawa. Their faces were flushed red from their ablutions, their hands giving off the scent of lotion.

'Actually, I have to go home for a moment. If there's an emergency, try to take care of it yourselves and don't tell the doctor I'm gone. I've already prepared everything you might need here, all right?' Young-sil gestured towards the surgical tray. She quickly changed out of her uniform and bounded down the steps, passed a long corridor, and left the hospital.

It was pitch black outside. The sky was spread with stars and there was only an occasional streetlamp throwing light down to the ground. She felt as if her feet were sinking into the pavement, and her legs threatened to give way beneath her. She kept hearing the sound of her mother's footsteps, and the street was unfamiliar despite her having walked it countless times. She kept looking behind her. Her breath turned into puffs of white steam and swept back the way she came.

The front gate of her home was locked. Through the gap between the doors she could see a faint light. Her mother was inside ...

She turned around and took a deep breath. So, her mother did not know what had happened. But if she found out the following day, what would Young-sil say to her?

Please hide Mother for now.

She sank down before the gate. At least when her brother was alive he had told her what to do, but who could she listen to now? What on earth was she supposed to tell her mother? She writhed in frustration.

She had run all this way the night before, too, but had turned back at the gate. Young-sil knew she would burst into tears at the sight of her poor mother, but she could not hold off telling her indefinitely.

Slowly, she got to her feet. She was going to do it. She was going to cry out, 'Mother!' But her throat closed again.

She rubbed her eyes, and her elbow knocked loudly against the gate.

'Who's there?' It was her mother's voice.

Young-sil tried to run away but she tripped on her own feet. She sobbed. Footsteps. She bit her lip and stood up. It was now or never.

The gate creaked open and she could see the white of her mother's skirt.

Young-sil's mind went dark but she gripped the fence and cried out, 'Me! It's me!'

'Is there news from Seoul?'

Young-sil turned her face away from the sweet scent of her mother's tobacco and thrust her cheek against a slat of the fence next to the gate. She could feel a splinter make its way into her cheek, but it could not distract her from the tears that were about to fall.

'Your brother was in my dreams last night, so I thought there might be news today. I went to see you at the nurses' housing, but they said you had the night shift.'

Her mother patted Young-sil's arm. Young-sil fought hard against the urge to throw herself at her mother and burst into tears. She held on to the fence for dear life.

'Were you berated by some doctor today? What's wrong?'

Young-sil wanted to reassure her, but she could barely open her mouth. Her hand gripped her own throat. She stepped away from her mother and removed her hand but still could not open her mouth.

'Child, say something!' Her mother's voice was laden with sympathy.

Young-sil took a step away from her. 'Go back inside, Mother.'

Her words did not reach her mother. Young-sil took a deep breath and tried to say it again, louder, but she erupted into tears. She flung her hands over her mouth. Angrily wiping her face, she looked up to see her mother in white, standing before the gate, just out of reach.

'Mother! What are we to do!' she shouted.

Abruptly, Young-sil forced herself to walk away. When she had gone a distance, she turned around to see her mother still standing there. What would become of her mother? Would she come after her to the hospital again? Would she go back to the old village where she grew up?

Young-sil changed her mind. She determinedly walked back to her mother's house. But her mother no longer stood at the gate. This comforted her somehow, and she walked away again.

Then, when she turned to look once more, she saw something white standing by the gate. She rubbed her eyes and ran back to the gate. Her shoes were giving her trouble, so she took them off and held them in her hands as she ran.

Looking through the gate again, she saw the lights were on in the house. Her mother must be inside... But she could not face her! Young-sil could offer no comfort in this state. Her tears threatened again, so she turned around and walked away for the third time.

She passed by the local school and a wave of nostalgia hit her. The darkness of the central building that rose into the night seeped into her soul. She remembered the countless mornings she had climbed the hill to this school, holding her brother's hand.

They wore patched-up clothes and had no backpacks. Her brother carried their books in a book bag full of holes that their mother had obtained from the Japanese house she worked for.

Their mother disappeared for work early every morning, so it was her brother who raised her. He changed her diapers and taught her to count. When she began school, he held her hand all the way to her classroom. She sought him when she was sick and when she fought with her classmates. If she hurt her hand during a game, he was the one who blew on it to make it better. Her brother! Her dear brother! She stomped her feet like a little girl.

There was a day when it snowed so much they had to almost swim through it when leaving school. Her brother had carried her on his back and told her to close her eyes.

He had made a path through the glittering particles of ice piled up as high as their heads. The packed snow grazed Young-sil's face and slipped into her scarf, prickling her neck. She had begun to cry. When they finally arrived home, their mother was not there. Seen through the torn paper screen of the door, the inside of their house looked colder than the outside. Her brother had brushed the snow off her and wiped her face with his sleeve.

'Mother is coming with sweets. Don't cry.' But he was crying as well. Inside, they stared at the door, and every time it
rattled in the wind, they called out, 'Mother!' and rushed
to open it, but it was not her. Young-sil would cry in disap-
pointment, and her brother would carry her on his back again,
both of them in tears as they waited for their mother to come
home ...

Young-sil walked, frantic. The memories tore at her heart.
She fell on the pavement and thought her brother's footsteps
might still linger on that very street.

Someone approached; a woman who looked like her
mother!

'Mother!' She ran towards the woman, crying, but it was
only a perplexed stranger who quickly moved away from her.
Young-sil stared at her as she disappeared into the night. Was
her mother sleeping? She wanted to go back to her again but
felt she would never leave the house if she did. She put her
shoes back on. She could see the hospital in the distance, and
she needed to be ready to work again.

Her father died in the March First Movement of 1919, and
now her brother might have met his fate in a terrible way as
well. Was their family cursed?

The hospital was busy with activity. Oh no, was there an
emergency patient on the operating table? She glanced at the
operating theatre and saw the light was on, and through the
windows saw the doctor and various assistants bent over the
table. She hesitated but went up the stairs to the office.

Hyosook jumped up from her seat. '*Unni!* You must go
down. There's an appendicitis patient. The doctor keeps calling for you. He shouted at us. We had to tell him the truth,
and he was furious. Hurry!'

The young nurse helped her change, the scent of her lotion
seeming to hit her in the face. Young-sil had no strength left
in her at this point, and allowed Hyosook to dress her as if she
were a lifeless doll.

Hyosook dragged her down to the operating theatre and pushed her through the door. It was hot and humid inside, and she had to grip the wall to keep from fainting.

The patient was already on the operating table, the doctor standing over him. Nakagawa stood by with a tray full of tools. Three other nurses wiped the doctor's forehead, chased the moths that occasionally flew in, or poured cold water on the cement floor to cool their feet. In the corner sat a woman in her forties, presumably the wife of the patient, her eyes and mouth wide open in shock.

The doctor sneered as soon as he saw Young-sil, and his expression replaced her feelings of guilt with that of violent hate. She went to the basin and scrubbed her hands.

The rhythm of her scrubbing prepared her mind to work, encasing it in cool ice.

'Ah! Ah!'

The patient kept shouting and kicking his legs. The nurses held him down, making him scream even louder. Young-sil saw that the doctor had just cut him open. The white layer of fat became visible underneath the epidermis, and the clamps on his aorta seemed to be clamping her own eyes. Nakagawa handed the doctor a snowy puff of gauze, which was handed back to her as a clotted mess of blood.

Young-sil finished scrubbing and came up to Nakagawa. 'I'm sorry. Thank you for filling in.'

'Lee-*san*!' Nakagawa sounded relieved to see her and nodded a greeting, sweat dripping from her head as she did so. She stepped back and let Young-sil take her place.

Young-sil took up the pincers. The feeling of this tool in her hand! Strength rushed back into her body through the solid sureness of the pincers. She felt ready to flip over a large machine with them if necessary.

'Suture!' The doctor held out his hand and looked up. He was taken aback by Young-sil and gave Nakagawa a hostile look. 'Who told you to switch?'

He pushed Young-sil's hand aside and picked up the tool himself from the tray. Nakagawa made a face and grabbed Young-sil's pincers from her and pushed her out of the way.

Young-sil felt as if the pincers had been taken from her forever. The shock was so great she could not move from where she stood.

Everyone in the operating theatre gave her hateful looks, the nurses who had once been so respectful of her and her position.

She bit her lip and stared at the doctor as he concentrated on the operation, holding a scalpel in one hand and pincers in the other. Had he once not trusted her more than anyone else in both work and life? Had he once not wanted to entrust the rest of his life to her?

'*Aigo! Aigo!*' The patient's screams seemed to scratch at her very bones.

Her brother! She suddenly thought the man's screaming sounded like her brother's voice. She quickly realized the patient was not her brother, but her heart beat fast and she started to tremble again. She tried to run but felt like she was about to vomit. In the next moment, as she bit down on her bottom lip, it felt as though her throat was being ripped from her body and it was as if someone had punched her right in the nose. The room went dim around her.

She saw the glint of the scalpel in the doctor's hand. It looked like a knife headed for her brother's neck.

'Mother, Mother! That man is trying to kill *Oppa*!'

Young-sil ran at the doctor, who stumbled backwards before he righted himself and kicked her. Young-sil fell on the cement floor but got up and ran at him again. Her nose and mouth were bleeding, her face smeared with crimson.

'That bastard! That bastard is killing *Oppa*! *Oppa*, wake up, that bastard, that …'

The others finally realized Young-sil had gone insane. The other nurses rushed to restrain her.

'Mr Kim! Take that crazy bitch out of my operating theatre!'

Mr Kim, who had been readying a gurney outside and had run into the room when he heard the shouting, froze as he saw the nurses dragging Young-sil out by her arms.

One of the nurses yelled at him, 'She's crazy, she's gone crazy!'

They handed her over to Mr Kim and pushed the two of them out of the operating theatre, slamming the door. The walls rang from the impact.

Not knowing how to restrain her, Mr Kim slung her over his shoulder.

Young-sil struggled in his grasp and beat against him. 'You bastard! Oh *Oppa*, oh Mother, stop darning socks and come out now. Ha ha ha! That bastard!'

Mr Kim ran down towards the quarantine ward, but in the chaos of the screams he forgot what the room number was. He ran up a floor but none of the room numbers jogged his memory. He carried her back to the door of the operating theatre, but then in a strange fit of frustration, ran with her out of the hospital.

The night was dark.

January–February 1937

THE MAN ON THE MOUNTAIN

I wonder if that man is still throwing rocks at us, with that rope tied around his waist?

It's become a habit of mine to think this whenever I worry about my mother back home, or read one of her letters. It all comes back to me, the rope soaked in blood, the crimson of it almost piercing my eyes. I shake my head to get rid of the image, but oddly enough, two years after the events of that day, the memory is clearer than ever.

His eyes were like dark spheres and his nose, which bulged at the tip, was shaped like a tadpole. It dampened the effect of his brow, making him seem solid and steadfast rather than intimidating and fearful. I always thought I might run into him again as he hurled his stones, the rope still tied around his waist and draped about his torso. The thought makes me shudder. Perhaps I've become oversensitive these past few years.

Rumour has it that he was the illegitimate son of a certain local official named Kim, who was the richest and most powerful man in our village. The man with the rope belt was the result of an affair Kim had with a married woman. Kim hid them away in a mountain hut and never had anything to do with them again, until the son appeared before him one day, brandishing a knife.

I was once extremely curious about this man and tried to find out as much as I could about him, but everything had happened so long ago that details were thin on the ground. From time to time I thought back to that desperate moment where he almost lost his life. Doing my needlework, on nights the rains came down, or when I'd look up at the cliffs of my home village and see the sky above moving like a turbulent blue ocean ... If it hadn't been for him that day, what would've become of us ...?

It all happened two years ago, around 20 July. I received a telegram saying that my mother was ill, urging me to come home immediately.

I was already worried about her, as she was over seventy and often sick, and I felt my world go dark in that moment. I just about pulled myself together and looked at the clock: 3 p.m. There was an express train at 3.05 p.m., so I grabbed a bag and rushed out in my house clothes with my husband.

The station platform was almost empty as most of the passengers had already boarded. I ran through the turnstiles, stumbled several times, and jumped on to the train as my husband hurriedly bought a ticket. He thrust it at me through the train window and said, 'Your slip, your slip!' Only then did I realize that I'd been stumbling because I had stepped on my slip, which had come down below my hem. I was too out of breath to even hike it up. My head pounded as if it had taken a serious blow.

I looked back to catch my husband's face when the train began to move, but it was too shadowed to make out anyone on the platform. Even the cool July breeze blowing through the window felt sad to me, and the plains, spread like swathes of indigo light, made me dizzy. The telegraph poles which once whipped past the train windows seemed to crawl now, and I was annoyed by the persistent sight of the low mountains that indicated we were still far from our destination. I kept telling myself that I might as well have taken the all-stop train.

I finally caught my breath, but for some reason I thought then of my mother's fragile, wriggling chin, and gradually the rest of her face. How could I have not seen her for five years? What had I been doing all that time that was so important? I admonished myself as I buried my face in my hands. I wanted to cry like a baby. What if I went but it was too late, and I was never to hear my mother's voice again? My anxiety ran ahead of the clanking rhythm of the train.

My mother, who had no sons, whose daughters had scattered east and west as they married. My mother, who had no one to lay a cool rag on her head or make her a bowl of rice gruel if she fell sick. I couldn't stand the fact of my circumstances, or to be exact, the very social system that prevented me from having my mother live with me. I closed my eyes and leaned against the window frame. The wind blew through my hair and my memories, reviving scenes that I thought I had long forgotten. The time when we lost Father and had to climb a twisted mountain path to go live with my aunt. The time when we were gathering pine straw and I cried because I was hungry, and my mother stripped a pine sapling and gave it to me to suck on. The murmur of the people on the train and the cigarette smoke seemed further away from me than these memories. I wiped my tears and looked around me. The car was filled with the yellow faces of the other passengers, which so repulsed me that I stuck my head out of the window instead and felt the misty rain wrap itself around my neck.

The sky was bereft of the sun, and the birds seemed to be refusing to sing. I thought I saw the face of my mother on a faraway hill crying out, 'Child! My child!' I saw her running towards me, jumping over mountain after mountain. The smell of the leather seating in the carriage was almost enough to choke me.

Only when it started to rain in earnest did I finally close the train window. The sound of the rain pounding against the glass helped maintain an ominous mood in my heart. We arrived at Jangseong Station at 2 p.m. the next day, whereupon I transferred to the Gyeongeui Line in the midst of a horrendous downpour. I could barely sit still for the anxiousness I kept feeling about my mother.

The windows of the next train were all shut, trapping all manner of little sounds that set my teeth on edge: a woman constantly whispering, a man droning on and on about something inconsequential, a child buzzing his lips on a willow leaf for an instrument, the clomping of footsteps, the slam of the door. I was also sat next to the lavatory, and the acidic stink turned my stomach.

The winds and rain seeped through the edges of the shut window, and raindrops trailed down the pane like tears. The rising and falling of the telegraph wires alongside the train was like the flight of a baby bird searching for its mother. The low mountains were huddled in the wet, red light as I pressed my face to the window until my nose almost froze. I begged the rain to stop.

Finally, I was let off at Sariwon Station and I rushed through the rain and boarded the light railway. I gathered my wet skirt around myself and looked outside, and what I saw was not reassuring.

The scene near Sariwon Station looked as if everything was covered in red. The sky, chaotic with falling raindrops, was empty of birds, and only the faraway hint of the mountains could be seen. One of them barely seemed to keep its peak out of the water, and it was almost as if the thatched-roofed farmer's houses were cowering in fear of the deluge.

There was no toilet on this train, so at least the stink was gone. The interior of the carriage was thick with worry. The passengers seemed to have forgotten about smoking as they smacked their lips from time to time, staring silently out the window.

The closer we got to a familiar elevation of mountains, the more my heart raced and limbs trembled. What if I was rushing all this way only to be too late? I was so nervous that I kept opening my window, much to the annoyance of everyone else in the carriage. The train was practically ploughing through a flood. I kept thinking it was going to sink, which made my body scrunch up to a fraction of its size. Finally, we arrived at my station. The few of us who disembarked were met by some of the station staff in a waiting area that was otherwise empty, save the sound of the pounding rain and a sour smell. The concrete walls were gaudy with posters, and there were only a couple of chairs in the corner for resting.

'The bus may not come today, so please find a room at the inn,' shouted a staff member over the din of the rain.

I couldn't believe it. To be trapped here, only a few *li* away from home! I stared down the road, wondering if I should walk the remaining distance. The new road, sprinkled with white sand, stretched into the grey of the rain. There were no pedestrians. I looked back at the other passengers to see if any were about to brave it, but they were all looking at the red body of water approaching the road. A staff member said that once the water flooded the road, the station and the town it served would be swept away.

Suddenly, one of the station staff announced, 'We've called the next station, and they say the bus has left. Buy your tickets!'

We passengers rushed to comply, buoyed by a sudden surge of energy and chatter. I stared up the road as I shivered and willed the bus to pull in.

The bus really did arrive, a big one at that. We boarded, and soon the vehicle was running along the road at a great speed. The driver said the road before the hot springs was about to be flooded so we had to rush. He concentrated hard on the road ahead, moving only to turn the steering wheel. We were as nervous as he was and could barely stay calm in our seats.

The millet fields we passed were submerged but the patches of grass growing by the side of the new road were bright green. Sometimes, to our consternation, the road looked washed out, but the bus would mightily drive through the deluge to the other side. The air was fragrant with gasoline, and the engine rumbled courageously as we sliced through the torrent.

The sky, the mountains, the fields, they were all speeding past now. The bus felt faster than our train was. Soon, it came upon a pine forest and climbed a sharp incline. The road was much more familiar now, wider than I last remembered it, and the colour of the earth was the exact shade of red that I remembered from my childhood. The pine trees, sitting demurely by the road, looked beautiful in the rain, their tufts of needles looking soft like the hair on the head of a baby. We climbed and climbed, and the dark mountain on either side of us was like black smoke. The rain hitting the pine needles sounded like the roar of the ocean. The rumbling of the engine kicked up a notch.

Once we turned a corner, the bus abruptly came to a halt. The driver tried to restart the engine but failed. He hopped off the bus with his assistant. Anxious, I looked out of the window and was scared out of my wits to see that the front wheels of the bus were perched precariously on the edge of a cliff!

The passengers were in such a rush to get off the bus that my face got mashed against the chest of one of the male passengers. Too afraid to sit by the bus, I went to the side of the road and crouched down by the face of the mountain. I was too relieved to have escaped with my life to think about anything else at that moment. My eyes were met with the deep blue of the bellflowers growing on the mountain. The inside of the bus had been cold, but the outside was even colder, and my teeth loudly chattered as I tried to get warm. The passengers gathered around the driver and his assistant as the two assessed the situation. The people on the bus seemed to be mostly students returning for the holidays. There was also a fat man with a woman who was his sister or wife, and a man with a large head who wore a traditional white robe.

The driver tried to dig the wheel of the bus out and occasionally threw a worried glance down the cliff. His speeding had brought the bus to this. He discussed something with his assistant for a long time before the assistant, under orders of some sort, ran down the winding mountain road.

If it were a matter of pushing the bus we would've pitched in, but the bus needed to be pulled from the edge. The back wheels were sunk in mud so the bus couldn't be driven backwards, either. The road we had come up was obscured by the turns we had taken, and half the sky was simply mountains flanked by more mountains. Because of the weather, I could only see the little section of road we stood on. I felt as if we were floating in the clouds.

I noticed a faded path through the pine trees in the mountain, neglected now because of the new road. At the other end of it, I could make out through the mist a field of millet that was hugged by two ridges of the mountain range, slender as horses' backs.

I was pinning my hopes on the assistant as I sat there, shivering in my inadequate clothes. The rain soon thinned, and the green carpet of the pine disappeared into the white fog as the forest ran up towards the sky.

Everything that was happening felt like punishment for having neglected my mother these past five years. I swallowed my sighs when I spotted the assistant in the distance. He was passing some millet fields, approaching a thatched-roof house on the mountain. As I puzzled over the fact that someone should be living here in the mountains all alone, I saw the assistant quite deliberately enter it, as if it were the house of a close acquaintance. What on earth was he doing there? Was he getting help or borrowing some tool? I rubbed the mist from my eyes and looked again. The fence made from millet stalks looked as if it were made of matches and the roof looked low and old. The tiny yard shone from puddles, and the mountain itself seemed to fence in that small house. The assistant emerged with a man who seemed twice his size. I was glad for the help, but the sight of the bus teetering on edge was more than making my blood run cold; I was afraid a terrible disaster was about to happen. One couldn't help having terrible visions of the vehicle plunging into the valley below.

I couldn't quite make out how far off the assistant and the man were now. I waited for them, staring down that path through the pine trees I had noticed before. The blue mountain seemed to appear and disappear behind the mist. The other passengers saw the two men come up the steep path before I did, as they were closer to them than where I was sitting, loathe to move as it was so cold. The students cheered as the man appeared, helping the assistant up the path. He carried a thick rope in his hand. The assistant, exhausted, promptly collapsed on the road as soon as the man pulled him up to it.

The driver quickly took the rope from the man and bent over the back of the bus. The passengers crowded around him. I wondered if I should go up to the bus myself but crouched down again after a few steps. I was too hungry or sick by then to make the effort.

The assistant seemed to have caught his breath as he pushed the passengers aside to help the driver. I looked away for a moment and saw the man who had brought the rope, who was now standing a little way off, staring down at his house.

He was very tall and broad-shouldered, with a slightly bent back and thick hair that grew outwards in all directions rather than lying flat. It hadn't been cut for a long time and was tangled rather unattractively. It was streaked with white, which made him look as if he was in his forties or fifties, but his demeanour was somehow younger. He looked worried as he stood there, staring off down the mountain.

The driver stood up. 'All right, then! Pull the rope.' He held out the other end of the rope to the man.

The man calmly took hold of it and glanced among us to see if anyone would help him, but no one stepped forward. Understanding he was alone in this, he tied the rope to his waist. The passengers gathered behind the wheels and wherever they could get a hold, intending to help push the bus back. I decided I should pitch in as well and joined the others, gritting my teeth as I got ready to push.

'And – push! *Push!*'

We all shouted it together. The man stood a few steps away from the bus, pulling at the rope, with a generous amount of slack between his grip and the end that was tied to his waist. His calloused heels in his peasant's straw sandals went up and down with our shouts. His toes were so long they were practically fingers, and they were heavily calloused as well.

'Push! Push!'

The length of rope between the man and the bus was taut, and I could hear the fibres in it snapping. My heart was chilled at how the effort looked like a tug-of-war between the man's very life and death. One false move, and the bus would go careening down the cliff, the man with it. But strangely enough, there wasn't a single person who suggested he not tie the rope to his waist. The backs of his feet were soon caked with mud, and the thick veins of his hairy legs coming out of his short trousers were popping out from his exertions. The pushing had helped with the cold, but now I felt as if I was going to vomit from the effort. I stepped away and went back to my old spot on the other side of the road. The world was spinning around me. I had to close my eyes to calm myself. When I opened them again, the passengers looked as yellow as the bus itself. My gaze stopped on the man. His head was bowed and he was panting, his white-streaked hair wild about his face, his deep-black eyes half-closed, blue veins standing out above his thick eyebrows. His clothes were wet, and I could make out the outline of almost every bone and muscle in his body. The rope was wrapped tightly around his waist.

I heard a sound. The man had fallen on one of his legs. The rope around his waist looked more dangerous than ever. He got up as if nothing had happened and still pulled with all his might. His large, furious eyes and the mud splattered on his face made him seem otherworldly. He must have torn his trousers when he fell, and his muddy knee showed through the tear.

Only when he had righted himself again did the passengers continue to heave and shout in unison. Seeing how they had barely managed to keep the bus from slipping when he was down, it must've been a very dangerous moment for them indeed.

A woman who had been worriedly standing by the bus ran up to me and said that bits of the cliff supporting the front wheels were breaking off. I quickly got up, and the woman and I searched for rocks to wedge underneath the wheels for traction. We searched as widely as possible but there weren't many that would suffice, frustrating us no end.

Darkness was falling quickly on the pine forest. It made all of us afraid. The woman and I dug around until our fingernails were practically falling off. But soon, we had a good enough rock to wedge against the wheel, and some of the students helped us with the search for other rocks.

The man fell again. While we stood holding our rocks, staring at him in worry, he fell yet another time.

He was, by then, more covered in mud than not. His trousers had torn at the crotch, but he immediately got up and pulled again. He threw the rope over his shoulder and wrapped it around his body once more under his arms, his chest straining towards the sky as he pulled. His straw sandals had come off and were rolling around in the mud, his toes gripping the earth.

We got the hang of what we were doing and got more rocks to spread near where the man was standing. When I approached the man with a rock, I saw that his knee was bleeding, and I quickly turned my head away and fled. Whenever I came back with a rock, I carefully looked at the cliff as much as possible and not at him. A student said he'd found an abandoned gold mine, and we were carrying rocks from it to the bus when we heard shouting coming from the passengers who had stayed.

We stood frozen in place, not knowing what was happening. One of the students who had stayed waved at us to come join them. By the time we came down to the bus, we saw the vehicle was beginning to budge!

We quickly laid out our rocks and pushed again with all our might.

'Push! Push!'

The bus was moving back bit by bit. I was standing so close to the woman in front of me that I could smell the camellia oil in her hair. I couldn't stop worrying about the cliff behind us and the man in front of us, so I kept glancing up to see if he was there.

'Oh!' cried the woman in front of me.

My heart jumped at the sound. The man had fallen on his leg again. As he righted himself, he was pulled a few steps back, the bus also edging back to the cliff. He pulled again, flailing his arms in the air.

We shouted as we leaped back from the bus.

The man ignored all else as he sustained his effort on his one good leg, dragging his injured one behind him.

His hair stood on end, and every muscle in his leg bulged. The black hairs on it seemed to writhe like living creatures.

We shouted our mantra as we took hold of the bus again and pushed as hard as we could. The man, perhaps tired now, kept teetering, but he always righted himself. Our throats were sore from the shouting.

And, in a flash, the bus was in the middle of the road again.

The man collapsed, his head on the ground, unable to get up. We ran to him as he lay there in his torn trousers. His red legs were shaking like leaves in a storm.

But when the driver and his assistant came to help him up, he quickly got to his feet on his own.

His tunic had been torn to rags, and his chest and under-arms bled where the rope had grazed his skin.

'Shall I carry my mother here now?' he asked the driver in an urgent voice.

His words stopped my heart.

The driver hesitated as his assistant untied the rope from the bus and carried the coil over to them.

'I'm awfully sorry,' said the assistant, 'but there is so much rain today and it's almost dark, and we don't know if the bridge by the hot springs is passable, so what about tomorrow instead?'

He then turned and urged us to get on the bus.

The man stared at the assistant and the driver. From his eyes, I finally realized the man was really a young man, only about twenty years of age.

The driver tossed him a perfunctory farewell and turned away. The man collapsed.

The rain began to fall harder.

As the bus started again, we felt sorry for the man and opened the windows to at least apologize to him once more, leaning out into the rain. The man, who had been silently still, got up with a rock in his hand and flung it in our direction. We quickly leaned back and shut the windows, our guilt turn-ing to terror.

The bus sped along as it had previously. *Clang!* I flinched at the sound of a rock hitting the bus.

'What was that all about?' asked a passenger to the driver's assistant. Shivering and wondering the same thing, I turned towards the assistant myself.

'He wanted us to take his dying mother to the hospital, but she was in such a state that it looked like the bus might as well be a hearse by the time we got her there. If we had known the bridge by the hot springs was all right, then maybe ...'

I finally understood why my heart had stopped when the man had mentioned his mother. I burst into tears.

I leaned out of my window to catch a last glimpse of him. He still stood there, the rope tied about his waist, throwing rocks.

August 1938

ANGUISH

'You poor damn bachelor!'

My husband's spoon clanged against the floor as he grabbed R's wrist. R was drunk, almost as drunk as my husband, and he had been getting up to leave.

'Oh, please let me go. I'm drunk. I must go and sleep. I'm very sorry, ma'am. I keep coming here and disturbing your peace ...'

'Don't be ridiculous, please sit,' I urged him. 'Why don't I go buy more drink ...?'

'Yes!' my husband said. 'That's a good wife. Go get some more drink.'

R snatched away the empty bottle my husband was putting in my hand. 'I really can't drink any more!'

'Oh, you old bachelor!' My husband grabbed the bottle back and gave it to me. I took it and practically fled the house.

The night was dark, and I felt a cold breeze against my face as if I were entering a gloomy forest. By the time I returned from the Chinaman's store with the bottle refilled, R, who must've heard my footsteps, burst out of the gate and took the bottle from me.

'Thank you, ma'am, thank you so much ... I am so sorry to trouble you,' he said, his breath in the cold air like alcohol-tinged rice steam. I silently followed him back into the house. There was the rictus of a smile on my husband's face at the sight of the bottle!

'It's very dark outside, no?' R said as he poured the drink. I thought again what a nice man he was.

'So,' my husband interjected, 'are you really not going to get married?'

I sensed they were carrying on a conversation they were having while I was gone. I glanced at R. He smiled, took a long swig, and said, 'Well ...'

My husband sang '*Sakewa namidaka* (Is Wine Tears?)' so hard that the tendons on his neck stood out.

R nonchalantly chewed on the side dishes and said, 'Prison is a terrible place. It makes one so useless.' He sighed. 'Ma'am, I was trashed when I was in prison. I have a story to tell about what happened afterwards. Would you like to hear it?'

Sadness filled his narrow eyes. I blinked, taken aback by his sudden intensity, and turned to my husband. All he did was beam at the bottle of wine.

'Let's drink that a bit later and listen to his story first,' I suggested.

My husband regarded me with affection. 'My dear wife knows nothing about man and his nature. Don't you know there's nothing like listening to a good story over a long drink? All right, young Rhee, speak!' He gave a hearty laugh.

R laughed along, but there was something sharp and focused on the sound as if he were gathering his thoughts together.

'I'm telling you this story only because I'm drunk ... You must forgive me.'

'All right, I will. We will.' My husband was beginning to slur while R sounded clearer than ever.

R smiled wanly.

*

As I've told you before, I've never been married. I was never interested in marriage, and later on, I couldn't afford it, anyway. My friends who had married were full of regret. Think of how difficult and frightful it is for people in our situation to get married.

I was born in Hamheung, but I grew up in Vladivostok. I call Vladivostok home. The people of Russia at the time were fraught with civil struggle between the Reds and the Whites. Then one day, I was forcibly taken in by the Reds and emerged from brief captivity as a Bolshevik. I was a young man and my re-education period was short, so what new consciousness I would have achieved then was meagre. It was just the mood of the times. From then on, I took up arms and joined the Red Army. A few years later, Russia entered its constructive phase, and I came out to Manchuria.

In Manchuria, I was too busy running about to sit and give my behind a rest. We had many successes and failures and were chased by government troops one week and bandits the next. I had long decided to live and die by the Red cause, living day to day as I walked the line between life and death. Who could think of marriage in such a thrall? It wasn't as if I didn't feel aroused by women, but to us, sex was such a small problem. Oh, the invincibility we had back then!

I felt like I could race across the Manchurian plains with just a few Chinaman's dumplings in my pocket. Fanning the flame was the consciousness of the people rising as the winds of the era began to blow. The people of Jiandao! Koreans made to flee from their unbearable country, ready to live or die in a foreign land! No one has suffered more under blade and bullet than the people of Jiandao have. How many massacres, even just the ones we know about, have they lived through?

The world they found themselves in was what created their fearful rage and determination.

*

R paused in his telling.

I took a deep breath and glanced at my husband. He was snoring, his face down on the table. I brought out a pillow, slipped it under his head, and pleaded for R to continue.

*

I suppose that's enough background ...

I left prison around this time two years ago. I'd been incarcerated for seven years, across eight calendar years. I had never imagined the world would've changed so much during that time. A little change is inevitable but ... What was truly foolish was that I thought, once I stepped off the train at Longjing Station, that the platform would be crowded with my comrades. Stupid of me. I had known that I was a little obsessed with honour, but ...

So, I stepped off the train at Longjing with great hope in my heart. And who was there to greet me? Not a single face I knew. The platform crawled with troops in uniforms I'd never seen before. I felt my body become as heavy as iron. The entire platform seemed to empty out in a few seconds. That was when I burst into tears like a child. The sorrow welled up in me and I could not keep it down anymore.

I left the station with no comrades, no parents, nothing to contradict the notion that I'd fallen out of the sky. I stood around and didn't know where to go. The people who were on the train with me were marching on far ahead. I felt so empty ...

I decided to drop in on an old comrade. The city was very different from seven years before. It took me two hours of wandering and asking around to find out his whereabouts.

I learned that he had gone somewhere to earn money and had left his wife to look after their children. She didn't know when he would be back. I learned only later on from another comrade that he had moved to Yanji. I had wasted my whole evening looking for him. I was so exhausted that I didn't have the courage to keep on looking. I spent that night in an inn and went out looking for him again the following morning.

Finally, in the afternoon, I bumped into someone I knew on the street. He was wearing a consulate guard uniform! Ma'am, I should not talk more about him. I understand, now, that changes in one's circumstances force changes in one's mind. But back then, I was enraged. My anger was as if my flesh and blood had sloughed off my bones and my skeleton had caught fire. I began to abhor the sight of Longjing. After spending the rest of the day loitering in one of its parks, I left the city for good.

I tried to go back to Russia, but the borders were so heavily policed that there was no way to enter the country. I wandered into a place three *li* away from Longjing called Myeongdong instead. I realized this was where the house of a jailed comrade stood. I went to it, and his mother greeted me warmly. She eventually collapsed in tears thinking of her own son in jail. I'd been looking for a chance to cry as well, and cry I did, hugging the old woman as we both wailed. Such is life!

My story is getting too long. My comrade's mother had lost her husband in a failed rebellion and had nothing to look forward to in life except the safe return from jail of her only child. As for the wife of my comrade ...

(R coughed.)

She'd been married to my comrade for ten years, but she had never been with him for more than four days. There she was, dutiful and diligent, taking care of her mother-in-law while suffering through all sorts of hardships. What a pitiful sight they made, living in such gloomy conditions, such unspeakable sorrow ...

In any case, the two women were very happy to see me. I hadn't planned on going there in the first place, and I knew how difficult things were for them, so I tried to leave the next day, but the mother cried and refused to let me go. She declared that if we starved, we'd starve together, and bade me to stay until her son came back. I did feel sorry for them. While I stayed there, I visited the school in Myeongdong, where I found that they had a teaching position open. I got the job and ended up moving into that house permanently.

Working at the school, I was able to give all of my salary to my comrade's mother, small as it was. I helped her by sweeping the yard every day, cleaning the outhouses, watering the plants, examining the pumpkin vines, and occasionally tending their vegetable patch. I cannot describe how wonderful it was to handle the earth freely and breathe in as much of the clean morning air as I wanted.

How I had longed for such freedom during those long years in tedious solitary confinement ... In that house, I realized that no torture was more terrible than to live in isolation. One can't stand up or lie down straight. Long summer days are spent sitting down. And to have no one to talk to! The sound of people talking in the next room drove me crazy. My words were like fireballs stinging my mouth and I wanted to hurl them at anyone and anything. The words burned in me, unused.

*

'Dear God!' I said before I could stop myself.

R blushed, his face as red as fire. 'How could I not appreciate, then, the breeze cooling my hair, when I could touch anything I wanted with my own hands? Sometimes I found myself mumbling, "You're not in prison anymore!"'

He laughed. 'Oh, but ma'am ...'

*

My comrade's wife, Gyesoon, had a reputation for being very plain. She had no pretty features, and one might say her face resembled a fist! There was no charm to her forehead, and her eyes and nose were spaced so far apart, you couldn't but take pity on her. But the teeth concealed in her demure mouth shone like pearls. Her heart was as strong and pure as those teeth. Her demure posture, her handling of food, and the fall and tuck of her clothing were just as straight and orderly.

For one thing, her washing shone white. You may say, ma'am, that everyone washes clothes white, but Gyesoon's washing was as white as gourd flowers, and the garments were rinsed so thoroughly that there was not a hint of soap or scum, only the scent of spring water ...

*

'You know laundry so well!' I couldn't help but exclaim.

He smiled. 'That's because I had to wash my own clothes since I was seventeen. I also washed my comrades' clothes before I went to prison.'

'Really? A thing like that.' I was thinking how his sparkling eyes and pointed nose made him look like an artist.

'I don't know much about food, but during the year I was in that house, I never bit down on gravel while chewing or found a single hair in the rice. Each rice grain shone as if polished, and that taste lingered deliciously in the mouth. I can still taste it now ... She never made any extraordinary side dishes, but they were wonderfully savoury. Not like the meals at inns where the food flatters the tongue using *Ajinomoto* or sugar. Her cooking had a much more expensive, high-quality taste. I'm very particular about food and clothing. My word, your husband sleeps well.'

R's face, which had seemed to shine until a moment ago,

suddenly went dark. I glanced at the lamp, thinking it had gone out, and looked back at him.

'Ma'am, since the day I ran out of that house, I haven't had a single delicious meal. This is going to be very rude of me.' He grinned. 'But I could immediately tell if something was made by Gyesoon or someone else. I could even tell whether a handkerchief had been washed by her or not! I felt almost like a child with his mother. I trusted her in everything. My heart grew dark and my body lost its vigour when she was out of sight even for a moment. Do you think this is what people call love?'

*

And how could this be, that a man would fall in love with his comrade's wife?

How could this happen to a man who all but flew across Manchuria in the name of class struggle? Was it not the time to truly immerse myself in the work of fighting the enemy?

But I would feel despondent whenever I thought of this. How far I had fallen. How weak I had become in prison.

These foolish thoughts cost me the health that I had recovered since leaving prison. I lost sleep in the endless clash between reason and my ever-growing passion. But whenever I saw Gyesoon, my face would break into a smile. How I wanted to touch her lovely, plump hand ...

*

A vein in R's forehead popped as he closed his mouth. I felt so embarrassed that I could not meet his eye. He poured himself another glass and knocked it down his throat.

'Are you sleepy, ma'am?'

'I'm fine. Do go on.'

He thought for a while.

*

Please forgive me for boring you so...

This was last summer. My comrade's mother had to go to Longjing for a family wedding. I saw her off, and on my way back to the house, my mind was seized by an overwhelming feeling of ... All through my teaching that day, I kept dropping my chalk and correcting my letters and numbers on the blackboard to the giggling of my students. After the school day ended, I felt too afraid to go home. I remained in the classroom by myself. I tried to think straight, knowing that if I went home without having thought things through, I might end up doing a terrible deed. But I only felt an urgent need as if to urinate and could not for the life of me hold a coherent thought in my head. All I ended up doing was pacing around the school. I went in and out of every other classroom before finally leaving the building.

The school grounds were so lonely. The sports field looked wider than I had ever seen it before. I walked around it until my feet hurt, and when I looked up, I saw that the little stream in front of the school was blood-coloured. I ran to the stream, feeling the sunlight on my hair, and the clear smell of the stream hit my nose. It was the scent that came from Gyesoon's clothes.

I longed to go home then but instead walked for a long time, not knowing where I was going. I eventually came back to the stream and sat down on the bank. Birds chattered above me, and the stream babbled, but my mind was empty of all thoughts. Then, I suddenly stood to attention. *I need to be a man and stop getting so distracted. I should do what I want to do and get on with it!* The idea had struck me like lightning, and I took a few steps forward. Then I thought, *But I'm only human after all*, and sat down again where I was. The pebbles in the stream gleamed white and the blue shadows of the willow trees carpeted the ground like moss. Little fish swam in pairs. They were mating. And how the tips of the branches of the willow trees would almost touch the water, and how oblivious the water seemed!

I couldn't bear it. I left the willow trees and kept walking.

It was soon sunset, and every tree and blade of grass before me started throwing shadows. Far away, the sun over the horizon seemed to tease me with a refrain: *Won't you cry, won't you cry?* I bowed my head and kept walking. It became twilight, and the insects began to sing louder. I reached home and, after some hesitation, quietly opened the gate. Gyesoon sat on the porch waiting for me as if she were my wife. She gracefully stood up. I felt heat darken my vision. I quickly went into my room.

After a while, I heard her say, 'Why don't you wash?'

I jumped up and came out of the room. Gyesoon was moving away, having placed a basin of water on the porch in front of my room. I wanted to run to her and grab her waist. My heart pounded, and my whole body trembled. But I stood firm where I was. It took every ounce of my past experiences, where I walked the line between life and death, to stand firm. But for a moment, I could've crumbled. Thank God Gyesoon went into the kitchen, else ...

I pretended to take in a few spoonfuls of dinner before deciding to spend the night at a friend's house. Once I had this idea, my body relaxed, and I felt a few jolts down to the ends of my bones. I wanted to lie down a bit before leaving, so I did. I heard the sound of dishes being washed, then silence. I was wondering where Gyesoon went when I heard the scratch of a match being struck.

It sounded as lovely as a voice saying, *Here I am.*

I closed my eyes and imagined Gyesoon's face. Oddly enough, I had trouble imagining it; when I thought of her eyes, her nose disappeared, and when I thought of her lips, her eyes disappeared, which was saddening. More than anything else, a voice kept tormenting me by whispering, *Just go to the master bedroom, just go to the master bedroom.* On what pretence could I go to the master bedroom? To borrow a needle to mend my worn-out suit? But I already borrowed a needle from her yesterday. Then what?

Oh! What about water? But she had already given me water. No, that was rice gruel, so this time I could ask for water... I jumped to my feet. Then a voice in my ear seemed to shout, *Stop it, you bastard!* I slunk down again and looked at the door. The room was dark, and the door was a pale rectangle of white. The ribs of the door's lattice crisscrossed the white of the papering, startling me. They reminded me of prison. I thought of all my comrades trapped there. Especially Gyesoon's husband, whose face refused to vacate my mind. I thought of all the times in our past when we worked side by side. I felt as if I'd swallowed a rock and it had caught somewhere down my throat. I struck at my chest. Tears flowed from my eyes.

I thought that this couldn't go on, so I prodded the surface of my desk until I found the textbook I'd brought with me and got up. Why was it so hard to get up? I came up to my door and stood still. Then, after a long hesitation, I opened the door. How the light from the master bedroom door shone like sunlight through the papered lattice screen! I wanted to call out, 'Gyesoon!' I wanted to push aside the thoughts of my imprisoned comrade and leap into the master bedroom. I put one bold step forward. Then another. And another! My heart was heavy, my face felt as if it were on fire ...

Had the mother suddenly returned? The thought gave me pause. I realized it was only the light of the door that made me think so, but worries started pouring forth regardless. I looked back, examined the yard, and took a glimpse into the kitchen. Then, thinking the gate wasn't locked, I crossed the courtyard to check it. Once I reached the gate, I became worried about who might be outside it, so I stood for a long while listening before quietly locking it. My body felt so light that I thought I would walk right into the sky. Once I returned to my room, I put my book down on the desk and breathed deeply. How smooth and soft the surface of my own desk felt, like a woman's hand!

Oh, ma'am, you must forgive my language.

*

R wiped the sweat from his forehead and looked up at me. I blushed and glanced at my husband who was still sound asleep as if he didn't have a care in this world.

'What happened next?' I asked, curious.

He swallowed and, after a moment's pause, continued his story.

*

I thought about how I was going to talk to Gyesoon, how I was going to act towards her, and worried that she would refuse me ... I thought about it for a long time. I was overjoyed just to be thinking these thoughts. And excuse me for saying this, but why did I keep salivating ...? I kept swallowing like a man eating cold noodles.

I jumped to my feet again. *Not now, wait just a bit longer ... and if someone burst in, wouldn't that be a terrible thing?* I sat down again. Whenever I sat down, I felt a fire on my behind, and my anxiety that I was letting a good opportunity pass by was as relentless as the blows from a torturing policeman.

I got up again. I paced in my room. I listened for sounds from the master bedroom, my hand gripping the lock on my door. My hands sweated profusely. The lock became slippery in my grasp. It made my hand smell of iron as if I made a living selling fish. Thinking of my sweaty hand grabbing Gyesoon's, I wiped my hand on the wall and my suit trousers, but that wasn't enough, so I went around my room looking for a towel before hitting my head on the side of my desk and realizing that the room was as dark as a cave. Oh no, my lamp was not on; that was why Gyesoon was not coming to me! I struck a match to light the lamp. Why couldn't I see the lamp that was supposed to be right next to me? I had wasted a match looking for it. Then, I had a thought. The lamp should be there. Did Gyesoon take it? I struck another match and saw that the lamp was still there, right where it should be. My room was a mess. The children's composition assignments were scattered everywhere.

That's when I came down to earth in a rush. I picked up one of the compositions. I got bored after about three pages and gathered up the compositions and placed them on the desk. I got up again. I was determined to make a decision now. When I opened the door, I saw the light was still on in the master bedroom. Gyesoon was finding it as sleepless a night as I was. I came out into the yard.

After a brief hesitation, I called out towards her room, 'Please bring me a bowl of water!'

The master bedroom door slid open and Gyesoon stepped out. How ridiculous, because the moment I received the water that she brought from the kitchen, I became braver.

'Did you sleep?' I asked her.

'No.'

'Would you like to talk a little before you sleep?'

Gyesoon did not reply. I took a step towards her and she took a step back.

'Did Mother-in-law say she'll return tomorrow?' she asked with a trembling voice.

I felt as if cold water had been splashed down my back.

'P-Perhaps,' I said, my throat closing. Only then did I notice the bowl of water in my hands. I quickly gulped it down. She took the bowl from me and moved away. The light flowed down the left side of her skirt, softly like skin.

Unconsciously I followed her. 'Look here!'

Gyesoon quickly moved into her room and popped her head out the door.

'Would you ...' I had to say something through my stuttering. 'Would y-you like to write a letter to prison?'

I felt another chill down my back. Why did I keep saying things I didn't mean?

Gyesoon hesitated before answering, 'Wait until Mother-in-law gets back.'

Her voice sounded like pleading. I felt as if a steel wall had come down between Gyesoon and me. I wanted to shout at her, *Why did you have to be the wife of my comrade!*

Gyesoon's cheeks turned red, and she shut the door. I heard the clink of the lock as I ran towards it.

This third splashing of cold water threw me into an unspeakable rage. *You locked the door. What have I done for you to lock the door!* The words filled my mouth. But the fire of my passion, nay, the wildness inside me was making the hairs on my head stand on end.

'Gyesoon!' I pulled at the door and pounded it.

I could see Gyesoon's shadow stand and sit and stand again, agitated by my crazy behaviour.

Presently, she came to the door and said, 'Mother-in-law ... Wait until Mother-in-law gets back ...' She started to sob.

I shuddered as I also burst into tears. I collapsed at her door. Gyesoon had been suffering as I had all this time! How pitiful we both were! Gyesoon could not bring herself to open the door as she continued to cry. A woman's tears ... Oh ...

I jumped to my feet. 'Gyesoon, please forgive me for what I've done today ... I'm going to a friend's ... I'll be spending the night there.'

My voice shuttered. I ran out of the house without saying goodbye.

The night was dark as ink. I walked for a long time. A lively breeze coming from a vegetable patch seemed to caress my chest. I thought of Gyesoon's solid figure as I trudged along my way. The reeds growing on either side of the road swayed in the cool wind. I came up to my friend's house, but I couldn't quite make myself enter. So I went to the school. I circled the playground a few times before looking up and realizing that I had lost track of myself and I wasn't at the school anymore, I was before the gate of our house. It was such a surprise I laughed out loud. I walked away, uncertain on my feet, like a bird with a broken wing. Then, I thought I ought to tell her to lock the gate before going to sleep, so I walked back to the house. But once there, I looked up to the heavens and took two deep breaths before determinedly walking back to school. To rid myself of foolish thoughts, I dashed back and forth as the children like to do. Dust rose high and my breathing became so fast that I collapsed where I was. Sweat flowed from my forehead, and I teared up at the incomprehensible, tortured feeling within me. I lay there, exhausted. I imagined that the glowing master bedroom door was shining in the corner of my eye, persistent as an errant eyelash. I was seized by sleep then woken up abruptly, surprised by something. The light was returning. A cold wind seemed to seep into my heart. I thought of the events of the day before and shouted, *You crazy bastard!* to myself over and over again.

I leaned against a willow tree before me and thought about my past while at the same time looking down the road of my future. The chattering of the birds above me sounded like my young students reciting their lessons.

Oh my, you must be sleepy now, ma'am.

*

He stood up.

I stood up as well. 'But what happened next?'

He smiled and said, 'That's for next time. Good night, ma'am.' He ran outside.

I followed him out the gate, but by the time I looked out of it, he was long gone.

June–July 1935

OPIUM

'But I'm registered!' Bodeuk's father protests as he leaps to his feet.

The police officer rushes towards him and grabs him by the lapels. 'What are you going on about, you woman-killer? Bastards like you will be dealt with by the law!'

'What? What woman? A-a woman?'

Bodeuk's father stares at the policeman before attempting to duck when the latter goes to strike his face. Bodeuk's father grasps his cheek, bewildered, as his eyes dart from the policeman's lips to the sight of Bodeuk crying as if he has caught fire.

'Mommy! Mommy!'

The father is convinced his wife will come running any minute, her dark face wearing that deep frown she always has on her wide forehead. He is about to say, *Dear, don't let Bodeuk cry*, when he turns around and sees that his wife is not there and only the child stands crying, almost stepping on the unravelled tunic ribbon that dangles from his heaving chest. That black hair his wife had stroked until it lay flat has slowly raised itself up again during the night.

'Move!' The policeman kicks Bodeuk's father, who tumbles into the courtyard.

*

The dark is so dense it is like water around them. Grass, wet with dew, brushes against their feet. The forest is thick with tangled vegetation, the stars peek out from the heavens, and the moment she looks back at the change in her husband's footsteps, she is seized with an inexplicable fear.

Why are we on this unfamiliar mountain? Why was he so intent on Bodeuk falling asleep before we left? If I'd known we would come so far, I would've carried him on my back. I must try one more time to talk to him.

Her throat burns with questions but the more she needs to speak, the less she can form the words. She is well aware that she cannot talk to her husband when he is in this mood. She bites down on the words at the tip of her tongue. Her husband had told her they were only going to take a short walk; in hindsight, his lie is so cruel that she could almost cry.

She feels pine needles brushing against her shoulders. The stars blinking through the scent of pine sap shine like Bodeuk's eyes. The sight slows her feet. She had only followed her husband into the dark because she was afraid he would shout at her again. She tucked her child in not knowing the distance they would come. She hates herself for trusting her husband and being so afraid of contradicting him. The soft sound of insects in the wake of her walk reminds her of Bodeuk's breathing.

Is he bringing me here to murder me and kill himself, too?

The thought comes to her from the starlight, fine as a spider's thread, as she remembers that time two years ago when she saw her husband hanging from the apricot tree by his neck. She shivers.

Is he going to kill me because I stopped him then, and then kill himself to finish the deed? What will become of Bodeuk?

They carry on making their way up the mountain road. She wants to sink to her knees but manages to keep walking. All she can think of as the wind encircles her body is the tip of Bodeuk's tongue on her nipple as he suckles and refuses to let go. She turns around and a spray of pine needles slaps her face.

'I-I must go back to Bodeuk, he must be awake now.'

Her husband wordlessly pushes her from behind, urging her forward. She wants to scream, to call for help. Once they are over this peak, her knees will surely give way, and her husband will no doubt drag her deeper into the woods ...

She is shaking violently once they reach the summit. The lights below look like torchlights approaching them from the town ahead. She wants to burst into tears.

'This is a rough part. I'll lead.'

Her husband goes in front of her. The impulse to scream brushes past her mind along with her fear, and now she begins to tremble at the prospect of the town.

Maybe he's taking me to them to exchange me for a sack of rice.

She recalls how she has begun to fear her husband since he started partaking in opium. Since he lost his job and attempted to kill himself, he has started to associate with an unsavoury crowd and become an opium addict. How he screams and cries at her! The other women of her neighbourhood mocked her about how he was caught trying to steal from a store and beaten.

Crazy bitches! He would never do such a thing.

But the bruises on his face made her throat constrict.

Once they are through the mountain trail, the path to town becomes flat enough to make her want to put Bodeuk on her back and run, if he were with her now instead of at the home they left behind. The sound of the wind overhead makes her think that the cries of her baby are following her footsteps. She cannot help but mumble, 'Bodeuk will be crying now ...'

When they make it into town, they stop in front of a dry

goods store. There's an occasional pedestrian, but the streets are quiet.

Her husband goes into the store, and a Chinese man who seems to be the owner greets him with a glad expression. 'You're here! We waited for you.'

The man smiles as his bloodshot eyes take a quick glance outside the store. A scar shines dully on his forehead. Her husband stands wearily with his fedora pressed down on his head, his paleness in stark contrast to the plump Chinaman. There was a time when he would refuse to give the Chinese the time of day ...

The beautiful blues and reds of the silks on sale fill the room like a dreamy fog. When her husband turns his head towards her and nods, she jumps out of her skin, thinking he is gesturing to a mob of opium sellers behind her, but she quickly realizes he is telling her to follow him inside. She almost stumbles in, her face turning red. The scent of silk makes her wish for a length of it to make a jacket for Bodeuk. Her eyes remain low, fixed on her husband's shabby trousers as they make their way out the back of the store, where there is a courtyard with a stale smell. Her husband sweats profusely, whether from exhaustion or the prospect of the opium sellers who are always in pursuit. Scared of the Chinese man noticing his weakness, she almost grabs her husband's arm several times but relents.

Her husband quietly discusses something with the Chinese man in front of a red door before he tells her, 'Stay in this room. I'll be back soon.' He pushes her in.

Thinking the opium sellers are about to barge in, she does not say a word as she enters the dark room but opens the door to catch the sound of her husband's footsteps disappearing. The back door of the shop has opened and shut.

I should've told him to hurry back.

She leans against the doorframe, and the memory of Bodeuk's face resurfaces. The time when he tripped over a threshold and fell to the floor. She feels her own heart fall and smash at her feet. 'What am I to do? What am I to do?' She paces the room.

A long time later, she hears approaching footsteps and runs out to the courtyard. 'Has Bodeuk woken up?'

But it is only the Chinese man, whose name is Jin. In fear, she stands up on tip-toes to look over his shoulder and calls out, 'Husband!'

There is no one behind Jin, only a dense darkness. The hairs on the back of her neck stand on end.

Jin suddenly grabs her hand. 'Byeon, you know, he's gone home.'

She whips her hand out of his grasp and presses down on the tears that threaten to burst, trying to get past Jin. He grabs at her skirt.

'Bodeuk's Father!' She pounds away at Jin's chest.

Jin grins as he lifts her off her feet and pushes her back into the room, locking the door behind him.

'Husband, help me! Husband!'

She feels as if she is trapped in a palanquin, panicking and helpless. All she can think of is that she must escape this room. She screams for help, but her voice becomes hoarse and she tastes ash in her throat. Jin's gaze becomes more menacing as he punches her and grabs her and tries to push her down to the floor.

'Help me! Save me!'

She pounds the walls as she screams, but her voice is too hoarse to be heard from the outside. All it does is make her feel like a fire is burning up from her stomach to her lips. Jin blocks her mouth, a sweaty, smelly hand that prevents her from breathing. She bites down hard and shakes her head. Fast as lightning, he makes a fist and punches her face. There's a cracking sound, and blood flows down her neck. Jin's eyes grow as wide as lamp-oil containers, and he grumbles in Chinese before stuffing her mouth with a dirty rag. The pain is like biting down on a mouthful of thorns, and the rag feels like it is creeping down her throat. She coughs and strikes the base of her own neck. Jin takes off his belt and ties up her flailing arms and legs, wipes the sweat from his forehead, and grins again. His bloodshot eyes flash with an animal energy, and his panting is mixed with the sour smell of dog fur. He is drooling yellow saliva, and his blue trousers are halfway down, revealing his repulsive belly. She closes her eyes because she does not want to see, and she imagines her husband's prominent nose and his limping walk as he comes back from having had opium somewhere.

'Husband! Husband!' she screams at the door, but her words only turn into moans.

Jin does not leave her alone the next day. She has a fever, and Jin lays wet towels on her burning forehead. Now that her body has been defiled, she tries to calm herself and concentrate on gathering her strength, but the fever and pain in her broken teeth have only worsened. From time to time, she thinks she could even make a life of it, if only she had Bodeuk with her. That dawn, she had begun to think that her husband had sold her to this man. But the thought had been fleeting, and her head is now filled with worry about whether her husband had made it home the other night or is lying dead somewhere instead. Or if he has gone home, how distressed he will be at having to take care of Bodeuk.

She raises her head at the sound of a towel being squeezed over a basin.

That sounds like Bodeuk peeing!

She closes her eyes to hold back her brimming tears.

Jin smiles. 'Think carefully. I can give you a gold ring, I can give you silk clothes.'

She tosses aside the towel and turns over. Her breasts fall to the side as she does so, and her hands grip them, shaking. She can almost feel Bodeuk's breast-milk breath on her cheek, making it blush, and the sound of his calling for her as he runs around the village, his little feet and knees cut and bleeding from the reeds that grow around their home. She sees this as clearly as if it were happening before her.

She suddenly asks, 'Did Bodeuk's father go home last night?'

Jin is glad that she is talking. 'He went. With the money.'

She bursts into tears at the mention of money.

Bodeuk's mother lives through that day pinning her hopes on that night. She tries to distract Jin, attempting to make him let his guard down. Jin is happy, going back and forth from his store to the room, bringing her food, and medicine for her teeth. But he never leaves her alone for more than ten minutes, always returning to keep watch over her. She abhors the very whites of his eyes. Why had he made such a large fire under the house? The room is as hot as a boiling pot. His yellow hands peel fruit, and sweat flows like grease down his forehead. He makes an effort to ingratiate himself. He offers her a slice of fruit so many times that she decides to accept, just to make him more complacent. But the second she bites the fruit, her teeth hurt and it feels as if she is biting into Bodeuk's flesh.

What can my baby be eating now?

She spits out the fruit. Blood drips from her mouth.

Some hours after midnight, she carefully lifts her head. Thankfully, Jin is asleep. She holds her breath and quietly raises herself, trying not to disturb Jin. Her nervousness swirls around the room. The sound of every breath, every insect, the ticking of the clock, the light coming from the door, even the very smell of fruit makes her jump. She slips out from under the blanket, and the smell of sweat that puffs up makes her think of diapers. Her heart pounds with the thought of running to Bodeuk and taking him in her arms. She gathers her courage, picks up her coat, and slowly walks to the back door. When she opens it and comes outside, her legs and arms shake loud enough to be heard, and her heart is almost beating outside of her chest.

She can almost hear Jin shout, *'Where do you think you're going!'* She quickly goes towards the outhouse and looks about. She cannot leave through the store, so the only way out is over the fence. There's barbed wire around the top of the fence, but climbing over the outhouse is the easiest way. She keeps her ears open as she gets to the top of the outhouse and gives the room and store another look.

If I hesitate and Jin wakes up again ...

She throws her coat over the wall and perches on the top. She is terrified that someone will grab her ankle at any moment and is driven mad by her heart urging her to hurry. She dips a little and the barbed wire scratches her face. She grabs the wire to steady herself. She thinks that if she fails now, she'll never see her husband again, never see her baby. The wire makes a loud creaking sound. The thought that Jin might have heard it spikes her panic. She slips, and in the next moment, she finds herself hanging upside down on the wall on the other side, the barbed wire wrapped around her ankle and tangled in her underwear. She pulls at her foot and falls to the ground. Something hits her head and she thinks it is Jin, but just as she strikes at it with her hand, she finds that it is a rock fallen from the wall. She jumps up and runs as fast as she can.

The joy that wracks her body! She pierces through the darkness and runs as if she has been turned into a storm, flying out of the town and up the mountain path. The mountain wind wraps around her as she imagines she can hear her baby crying his adorable, pitiful cry ... She almost stumbles at the thought of it. The fire burning on the soles of her feet makes her glide across the mountain path. She thinks of her husband lying next to Bodeuk, unconscious from opium without a doubt, and all she wants to do is to get there and let her tears spill. She feels no resentment, only gladness and sadness taking turns in her heart. Her husband will surely ask for forgiveness, maybe even give up opium. The scene in her mind moves her so much that she stumbles and falls. 'Husband!' she shouts as she gets up again to run. Whenever she stops to catch her breath, she falls down and feels faint. Sweat or something else keeps pouring from her head, bothering her eyes and seeping into her collar. It is about to rain but she cannot afford to pay attention to that; she has to keep looking back to see if Jin is following her. She thinks she hears the barbed wire creaking. She thinks she is still holding on to the wire as she grasps the air and falls again.

I must make it, yes, I must make it and raise Bodeuk!

She cries as she gets up again. The disappearing lights of the town below are like lights strung up along steel wire. Let them follow her. The thought that she feels desperate enough to kill anyone who gets in her way flashes in her head like the lights that she is leaving behind.

She runs through the starlit forest, the hope of meeting her husband and Bodeuk almost driving her mad. She stumbles again and again, but she gets up and continues to run. Her body smells of blood and breast milk, the stink dripping from her hair. Whenever the wind shakes the forest, she whispers, 'I must make it, I must make it.'

Still whispering, she falls to the ground. She writhes as she tries to get up again but cannot move her body at all. She touches her forehead and realizes she is bleeding. She tries to tear off a strip of her underwear for a bandage, but her hands are too exhausted. She feels for her coat but realizes that she left it behind at the wall in her haste to run away. She tries to tear her underwear again. She is so tired that all she gets from her effort is her own grunts.

I must make it! I must make it!

Her mind is fading. She tries to get up, but her body is as heavy as iron. When she raises her arms, her legs will not listen, and when she tries to raise her head, all she produces is dry heaves.

I can't die now. What will become of my Bodeuk?

She gets to her feet but falls again.

'Baby! My baby!' She chokes on the dust as she cries. She rubs her ear against the ground, yearning to hear an answer from it. She opens her mouth and calls, 'Baby ...'

There is no answer. Her eyes look up. She thinks she might see her husband carrying Bodeuk on his back, coming to find her through the dark. She gets up again but falls just the same. Why does she keep falling? She bites down on her hand, willing herself awake.

She cries into the air, 'Baby, I have breast milk for you, drink ...'

That patch of empty sky, is that her husband's jacket? She blinks; it is not. A tear escapes her. She thinks she might try to crawl home, but her arms and legs shudder as they give up their strength.

Baby ... baby ... come on, get up ... my husband, what about him ... maybe he'll become a registered opium seller ...

Her life leaves her body, peacefully.

November 1937

SYMPATHY

'Have a cup of cool water every morning and go for a walk.'

Ever since the doctor gave me this advice, I had been going to the banks of the Hailan River each morning to drink a cup of water from the well there.

At first I only carried a towel, my soapbox, and a cup, but I was so struck by the sight of the women bringing water from the well that I soon brought a water bucket of my own to carry on my head. The well was almost always surrounded by women, and I would have to wait for a long time for my turn. I suppose this was because it had the best-tasting water in Longjing.

There was a woman whom I happened to meet every time I carried my bucket on my head and passed the eggplant field studded with baby eggplants or the dewy millet field next to it, and we would not say a word as we walked more or less together to the well. She happened to be the only other person passing by those shoulder-high millet stalks, and she was also the only woman by the well who never spoke.

Here she is again! And she's still ignoring me!

I couldn't help thinking this whenever I ran into her.

Soon, the autumn elongated the pearls of the eggplants and coloured them a deep purple, and the millet stalks made a whooshing sound as they swayed in the cool wind. I heard footsteps plodding behind me; lo and behold, it was her.

Her face was swollen, and there was a large bruise on her right cheek. I wondered if she had fought with her husband or stumbled somewhere the day before. Perhaps it was my curiosity that made me want, more than ever, to hear her speak.

I finally got up the courage to ask, 'Are you all right? What happened to your cheek?'

Her downcast eyes looked up at me and she smiled. Then, she sighed.

'It's nothing, just my bad luck ... Where do you live? You're always coming from that direction.'

I was glad to find she was happy to talk to me as well. 'I live behind Yongshin School. What about you?'

She was silent for a moment as we walked. Then, she sighed and said, 'What kind of home would a wench like me have?'

It was obvious that all was not well with her. 'Why say such a thing? Even a bird has a nest to return to, and you are a person, no less ...'

'Ha! I'm no better than a common bird. In fact, I wish I were a bird! I could fly through the sky to my heart's content.'

She looked up at the sky, and I could tell she was near tears. It broke my heart. I wanted to know what made her so sad.

We reached the well. We were a bit early today and there was only birdsong to greet us. I filled my bucket and took up my cup to drink underneath the willow trees that let down their long branches by the well.

The woman made splashing noises as she filled her bucket to the brim. 'You always have a cup of the water. You must like this water a lot.'

I didn't want to tell her about my illness, so I simply agreed with her. I gulped down the water, wiped my chin, and said, 'Would you like to go for a walk?'

She hesitated for a moment before saying, 'Why not.'

We pushed through the thicket of grass and came out to a long path. The drops of dew dangling on the tips of the grass were like the stars at night, and the dark green of the grass made the jewel-like dewdrops sparkle all the prettier. The breeze, scented with a hint of freshness from the mountains, lightly encircled our skirts and made them flutter.

'Wonderful!' The word escaped my lips before I knew it.

I looked back at her. She was only sighing, her swollen eyes still filled with sadness. Then she smiled for a moment as if in answer to my sentiment, but the smile faded quickly. I wondered again what made her so melancholy. Flocks of birds twittered above us, and the poplar trees were so thick that I could hardly see the sky. The white trunks of the poplar trees stood out in the shade as they stretched straight and tall into the canopy.

I always think of idealistic young people whenever I see poplar trees. At the same time, there's also a feeling of nervousness; their roots seem so weak. The pine trees of the hills of my home are just as grand, but they are rooted firmly into the ground. The lovely fragrance of their sap! The red-black bark of the pine that has weathered years and years of harsh mountain winds! The sound of the river almost lulled me into my memories.

I bade the woman to sit down with me beneath a willow tree.

'So, why do you sigh?'

Some men smoking their cigarettes gave us a quick look as they passed. From the corner of my eye, I noticed that the woman's nostrils flared slightly when their cigarette smoke reached us, which made me wonder if she knew how to smoke.

'It's just a habit. I try not to, but I can't help it now. Silly of me, isn't it?'

'Not at all ... Oh, but your face must be hurting. What happened?'

'Well ...' She smiled sadly and brought her slender fingers to her face, rubbing the bruise. She sighed again and looked at me. 'Look at me. Tell me what you think I look like. A wife? A mother? Or a wench working at a bar?'

I did give her a look. 'Well ... you must be a wife ...?'

I quickly realized there was a whiff of the demimonde about her. Only then did I notice how neatly her eyebrows were drawn, like two slender willow leaves. I felt something like disgust, but at the same time, pity.

'What are you, then?'

'Ha! You know of prostitutes? Whores?' Her grin had twisted into a sneer. I was suddenly at a loss as to what to say.

'I'm a dirty wench, I am. Do be careful of me from now on.'

After a long pause, I said, 'No one does that work because they want to. I'm sure your circumstances made you so.'

When I turned my head, I saw milk-coloured clouds floating by Majae Mountain across the river. Sunlight began to spread in the blue sky.

The woman stood up. 'I should go back. I can't be late again ...'

I followed her back to the well.

*

A few days later, we met at our usual juncture.

'Why would I waste your time with that?' she said whenever I urged her to tell me her story. But this time, she relented.

'I was born in Pungcheon in Hwanghae Province. My father was a peasant. He sold me when I was twelve. Looking back, I think it was because he had debts. I didn't know anything back then. I wonder what would've happened if I had tried harder to stay. It wouldn't have made a difference ... Mother and Father said if I followed this man, he would feed me white rice and provide me with nice clothes. They took the rod to me when I refused. How could I not do as they said? I left home with the strange man, crying. I fell on the road

SYMPATHY

with every second step. I looked back and saw the jujube tree in our yard was heavy with ripe, red jujubes. I bawled, sitting in the middle of the road. My father had to beat me with the rod again to make me get up. Those red jujubes are what I remember the most.'

Her eyes had a faraway look as she thought back to her past.

'We walked to Shincheon. The next day, my new father took me to a troupe of *sori* singers and told me to learn *sori* from that day forward. I cried a river then, too.

'One night, I woke up in bed with my new mother sleeping beside me, and in my confusion squeezed my new mother's breast. I was only half-awake and had mistaken her for my old mother. My new mother beat me senseless, shouting, '*Twelve years old is too old to be touching Mother's breasts!*' I missed my mother so much. After the beating, I couldn't stop myself from calling out to her, so I muffled my cries by throwing my blanket over my head.

'When my new mother fell asleep, I pushed back the blanket and got up. The window was full of moonlight. Just like the window at my old house. I thought of my little toys that I had stacked in front of that window. The thought made me open the door and walk out. The yard shone with moonlight as well. The night was just like the ones where we would light a little fire against mosquitoes while we shelled beans. I thought my mother might be hiding somewhere in the yard, so I kept calling to her in my heart as I looked in every corner. Then I looked up at the moon. I thought, just as any child would, that if I kept running to the moon, I would meet my mother someday ... Oh, it still breaks my heart to remember such thoughts.

'I ran as far as I could, asking other children along the way, sometimes an adult, looking for the way to Pungcheon. I ran with all my might, but my new father caught me in the end and beat me, hard. I didn't dare run away after that. But when the sun went down over the western mountains or the window glowed with moonlight, it made me miss my mother so much. How can I describe it? It was like thirst. No, it was worse than thirst. I just wanted to see my mother. Whenever I saw a long road, I wondered if it would lead to my mother and wanted to run to the end of it. It got better as I grew up. I was singing "Arirang" by then and my survival came to depend on dealing with men. Oh dear, let's stop talking about this.'

She sighed and tried to smile through the terrible resentment that darkened her face.

I gripped her hand. 'You've been through so much. How large is your debt now?'

'Five hundred won, they say. When my new father handed me over to a restaurant the first time, it was three hundred. Now it's five. I make my own clothes and do everything I can to save, but that's the way it is. I fetch the water and do the washing on top of the other thing, but it's never enough. I'm doomed to my rotten luck for the rest of my life. I didn't even do anything wrong yesterday, but the proprietor did this to my face.' Her eyes flashed with rage. 'Oh, when will this terrible world end? When will the war blast it to bits?'

After a while, I cautiously asked her, 'What about a lover? I hear one can buy you out.'

'Ha, lovers. What kind of a lover would a woman with my luck have? Men are like dogs to me. They only know one thing, these men. Hah.'

This irked me at first, as I thought of my husband, but I realized she had good reason to curse men as she did, considering her circumstances. I was always sorry for her. She had a certain dignity about her that was rare in one so young, and I was drawn to how determinedly she held her ground against any man in her life.

'When I was eighteen, I fell in love with a man. I poured everything I had into him. I'm ashamed of it now but look at this hand. I even cut my finger off for his sake.'

She spread the hand she always held in a fist.

She sighed. 'I saved up the money I made from my customers, and when the proprietor wasn't looking, I would slip the money into my lover's pocket. He promised me ... promised ... a future together. What a foolish girl I was. He must've married some lady student by now ... Come on, let's go.'

She jumped to her feet. It was clear how wrenching these memories were for her. I held her hand and begged her to visit me at our house sometime. And from that day on, we would often take a walk together. I sympathized with her no end.

*

It was a windy night, the dead leaves sweeping down the street. I was about to turn the lights off when I heard a voice from outside.

'Sister, are you sleeping? Please, open the door.'

I immediately realized it was Sanwol and rushed to open the door. As she walked in, all I could see was her bloodied cheek and messy hair.

'What is it? So late... Oh no! Were you beaten again?'

She bowed to my husband and slowly sat down on the sofa. My husband only stared, taken aback. She was clutching a wrapped bundle of clothes close to her chest.

Her eyes flashed as she looked up. 'Sister ... I want to leave this city!'

I suddenly remembered an offer I'd once made her, that if she ever wanted to run, I would give her some money. *She's here for the money!*

I felt a sliver of irritation. My next words left my mouth before I could stop them. 'But you have nowhere to go!'

We donated three won to the flood relief musical benefit last night, must we spend more money now? We'll have to give up saving any money this month.

She only sat there, silent. But I could see the shifts in emotion on her face.

With my broken promise lingering in the air, my words

tumbled out of my mouth with defensive uncertainty. 'If you have to go, you must have a destination in mind. You might want to discuss it with me, I can help you think it through. And you've got to tie up your loose ends here. What if they come after you? You must see that I'm right ...'

She gave me an unreadable look. Then, she stood up, and ran out of the house without another word.

I felt guilty and relieved at the same time.

*

In the morning as I carried the bucket on my head to the well, I thought of Sanwol and wondered if she really did run away in the night. I reassured myself that she didn't have the money to do so. I looked forward to seeing her at the well again.

A woman ran up to me, out of breath and pale as a sheet.

'Don't get your water from there ... Someone fell in... that pretty one... you know... the one, the one who's your friend. She's dead!'

Shock seized my body, spreading like liquid, numbing my mind. Without a word, I turned around and walked home in a daze.

As soon as I opened the door, I said, 'The girl ... Sanwol is dead!'

'What?' My husband got to his feet. 'Sanwol? Where!'

'She fell into the well ...' Frightened out of my wits, I ran to my husband and held on to him as I cried, 'Sanwol is dead! The poor girl!' I couldn't stop sobbing.

Was her untimely death because my sympathy had stopped only at words? Or was it because, secretly, I wasn't sympathetic to her at all?

Somehow, I know that only one of these thoughts is the truth.

October 1934

FATHER AND SON

'When you meet your uncle, thank him for the rice. Don't forget!'

Bawee's mother said this to the back of his head as he left after finishing his dinner. Bawee did not answer her.

He walked to Hongcheol's house, wondering if there was any news that day. After some hesitation by the gate, he entered the courtyard and coughed. The door to the main room opened, and Hongcheol's wife stuck her head out.

Before Bawee could say anything, she said, 'I'm afraid there's no news today, either.' She came out of the room with a child in her arms. 'I think something is up. That's why there's no news. I think I'll go out there.'

Bawee was always shy before Hongcheol's wife. He never looked directly at her face and kept his hands clasped before him in silence.

She said, 'Isn't the town a hundred *li* from here?'

'Yes.'

Bawee had said the single word with some effort. He kept his head bowed. Hongcheol's wife knew he was being courteous, but she felt sorry for him all the same.

'Would you like to come in?' She had made the offer but was at a loss herself as to what they could make conversation about.

'I must be off.'

Like the other times, he left after saying this. Once outside, he let out a relieved sigh.

Hongcheol was an important figure in the seaside village. He had graduated from middle school and was a dedicated teacher at a night school for ambitious, disadvantaged youths. The authorities, however, had suddenly ordered his night school closed, searched his house for secret documents, and taken him to the station in town. There had been no word from him since.

Bawee plodded along. He knew what would happen to Hongcheol from the beginning. Now that it had actually happened, he was not exactly dismayed, but he was worried that they had nothing to eat and he would need to find some work tomorrow.

He had been walking with these thoughts running aimlessly in his head when he looked up and lo! In the distance, the farm with the acacia forest! How grand that farm was, day or night! This farm was the only thing in the world that seemed glad to see Bawee.

Six years ago, Jeonjung, the current director of the farm, came out to their village and used the authority of the district administrative office to gather the local farmers and propose a new project. They were going to make the marshland behind their homes arable, and once that was done, the farmers who helped would be allowed to farm on it for three years free of rent, and what's more, they would each receive a new house in the bargain.

Word spread of the proposal, and farmers came from miles around. The village was thrown into chaos for a while as countless farmers were turned away, some resorting to fist fights in the struggle to be part of the deal.

The selected farmers gathered at five every morning with their hoes.

The marshland resisted their every effort. There were rocks the size of houses embedded here and there, not to mention the numerous tangles of arrowroot and thorny vines. But their hopes were as large as mountains, and no one said a word of complaint about their difficult work.

Sweat rained from them as they dislodged the giant rocks. Jeonjung would smile and say, 'Hard work, isn't it? But once you've tamed the fields through your hardship, they're yours.'

They felt strength and comfort at these words.

But what were these sweet promises now, six years later? Bawee broke into a cold sweat at the thought.

He had lost the farm he was now gazing at. Lost it, because he had fallen out of favour with Jeonjung, who hated the night school. More than that, he hated Hongcheol. Jeonjung forbade the farmers from attending it, but Bawee had ignored him and was diligent in his studies. Soon, he was kicked out of the farm under a ridiculous pretence.

He had known this would happen since the day he first met Hongcheol, but now that it had, he realized what a terrible thing it was that had been done to him.

Since his banishment, Bawee despised the sight of the farm that he had worked on every day. But somehow, his footsteps kept taking him towards it.

The moon was now rising over the pines. How beautiful the farm looked, bathed in moonlight! Soil would hit his coffin before he forgot the farm. The fields he created by hacking away the thorny vines! The injustice of how the loam he had caressed and coaxed for six years now belonged to a landowner who had never touched the soil in his life!

Bawee wanted to stamp his feet and beseech the sky. This land! To whom did its loam belong?

He was so enraged that he felt the blood rush to his head. He turned his bloodshot eyes towards Jeonjung's house. A silo stood next to it, its shine in the moonlight like a shout toward him.

A moment later, he heard a creaking noise and was surprised to see himself twisting the lock of the silo with his own hand! Dazed, he opened his eyes wider to rid the illusion of Hongcheol's face floating before him.

He retracted his hands and listened hard, afraid that someone had seen him. He heard the sound of a drunken voice speaking Japanese from the direction of Jeonjung's house, followed by applause.

He sighed and quietly made his way to the acacia forest. Still nervous, he looked back towards the farmers' housing this time. The houses that stood in a circle, a distance from the silo, were dark. Then he heard the creak of a door opening, which made him take a step back while keeping an eye out.

Someone was coming towards the silo. Bawee stiffened, but when he rubbed his eyes and took a closer look, he realized it was Elder Suh, his father's friend who was in the group of farmers with him as they reworked this land. Bawee clasped his hand to his mouth before he could call out Elder Suh's name.

He felt he might suffocate, and tears flowed down his cheeks without a sound.

He ran out of the acacia forest. Once he had made it over the fields and could stand tall, he shouted, 'That's right! I am a member of the XX Committee!'

The sorrowful memories of his father, whom he resented heavily to this day, came rushing towards him.

*

Champion Kim, as his nickname implied, was a man of great physical strength. The people would jokingly call him 'the champion', and the moniker stuck.

Champion's parents died early, and once he was orphaned, he became a live-in worker at a shipowner's house. Over the decades that followed, he became a fine fisherman and earned the shipowner's trust, and this trust along with his strength meant he became a well-respected man. He was, however, distressed to find himself still unmarried at thirty. When he heard of a young widow living in a village nearby, he kidnapped the woman who became Bawee's mother, forcing her to live with him. Bawee's mother hated Champion for making her break her widow's vows and tried to run away at every opportunity, but Champion always caught her again and beat her senseless. She never managed to escape.

Bawee was conceived. Bawee's mother gave up trying to run away and concentrated on building a good life for the baby, who was eventually born on time and in good health. Having once thought he would die an old bachelor, Champion was overjoyed with having a wife and a fine little son. He quit his drinking – he had once drunk wine by the jarful – and put all his effort into making money.

Months after Bawee came into the world, he opened his petal-like mouth and said, *'Abba! Abba! Umma! Umma!'* Champion thought he had never heard a more enchanting sound in all the world. His son's affection melted away his fatigue at the end of the day, and his hope for the future became greater with each year.

Bawee turned five. Every afternoon, he would run out on his little legs to greet his father, and Champion would arrive home with his son in his arms.

One very windy day, Champion had not come home despite the late hour. Bawee tried to run out to greet him as usual, but his mother held him back.

'Your father will come soon. You can't go out in that wind.'

'No, no, Daddy is coming!'

Bawee tried to twist out of his mother's grasp but ended up sitting on the ground and crying. His mother gathered him in her arms and could not help feeling anxious about her husband being so late. On days of strong wind and rain, she was in the habit of laying down her sewing and going out to the yard, where she would stand on the flagstones for the large preserve jars and look out towards the blue ocean in the distance. Little Bawee's frustrated huffing made the house feel strangely quieter. She carefully laid her exhausted son on the warm part of the floor and stood still in the middle of the room.

The wind continued to rage outside. Raindrops pattered on the mulberry paper screens of their doors. She did not know why she felt so nervous. Pacing back and forth, she listened hard for approaching footsteps, sometimes mistaking the sound of the wind for the plodding of feet. She was never before so aware of how significant her husband was in her life.

She decided to go to the shipowner's house but then looked back at her sleeping son. How peaceful he looked! His long eyelashes curled over his chubby cheeks. What if he were to wake and she was not there? She sat down with a thud.

After a long while, she determinedly locked the house behind her, wrapped her skirt tightly around herself, and made for the shipowner's house. The wind was so strong she felt like she was suffocating in its grasp. Even when she briefly stopped to gather her wits, she kept an ear open for her child's cries.

Her dress had hopelessly unfurled in the wind and her hair was flung from its bun by the time she arrived at the shipowner's house. She could see the light coming through the tiny crack between the double doors of their gate. Her fear subsided somewhat as she shook the door.

After she gave a few shouts, she heard the sound of footsteps coming up to the door. 'Who's there?' a man called. 'Is it Champion?'

The question made her feel as if she were plunged into underground darkness. Her husband was not there in the house!

The gate opened. 'Who is this?'

'It's me. Is Bawee's father here?'

The man was glad to hear a woman's voice. He came closer. 'Ah, it's Champion's wife! No, he hasn't come in yet. The head-winds are probably forcing him to spend a night on one of the islands. You came all this way in the dark?'

The man's chatty attitude gave the woman some relief. 'Are you sure he's spending the night on an island?'

'Yes!' He even laughed. 'Don't worry about him. He is an excellent sailor, is he not? Go home and rest.'

His words made her anxieties and fear melt like spring snow. 'Thank you so much. I'm sorry to have bothered you.'

She could almost picture her son getting up and crying, so she made haste to go back home.

The next day, Champion did return, but on the back of a stranger. His surprised wife ran out to meet them, shouting, 'What has happened?'

Champion opened his eyes with effort and called out, 'Bawee! Bawee!'

He fainted. Bawee, standing next to him, called out, 'Daddy!' His small hands tried to make his father's eyes reopen.

The fisherman who carried Champion caught his breath and said, 'Thank the heavens this man held on to a rock! The others were not so lucky ... Don't know if they're dead or alive ...'

Champion opened his eyes. 'Where's Bawee?'

'Daddy! Daddy, did you bring me fish?'

All the innocent boy cared about was that his father would bring home fish for dinner.

'Oh! I'll bring you some fish now,' said Champion as he hugged his son tight. Bawee's mother gazed upon father and son with tears in her eyes.

A few days later, she asked Champion what had happened at sea.

'What is there to talk about? I survived, what else is there to say ... It was the headwinds.'

He did not elaborate on the ship's sinking. His pride was

hurt. His wife, having heard what happened through the other villagers, did not press him further.

A little over a week later, Champion rose from his sickbed despite not being fully recovered from his ordeal. More than anything, he wanted to be back at sea and casting his nets. He missed the sea as if none of his hardships had ever happened. He shook off his imploring wife and trudged on towards the docks.

First, he dropped by the shipowner's house.

The shipowner, surprised, forgot to stand up to greet him. 'Ahoy, but isn't this our Champion? Have you regained your strength?' He stared at Champion as the man listlessly sat down before him. 'You look like you should be in bed.'

'I am feeling well, thank you.' Champion bowed his head, grateful for the shipowner's words.

The shipowner stood up and lit a cigarette. 'But your ship, it's destroyed ... You can be a bit brash sometimes ...'

He forcefully stubbed out his cigarette on an ashtray. Champion was tense.

The shipowner frowned. 'You're going to have to rest for a while before I buy a new boat. There's nothing for you to do.'

'Oh, but ...'

'I know, I know. A new man is taking the other boat.'

Champion was dismayed. The shipowner had never given him time off before, but he was choosing that day to break with precedent. What was he going to do now? More than anything else, the thought of poor Bawee brought tears to his eyes.

The shipowner observed him closely. 'Don't feel too bad,' he said. 'I am only saying you should get stronger and relax for a while. If we ever get a new boat we shall hire you again.'

Though he had no such intention and planned to be rid of Champion for sinking his ship.

Champion thought he heard reason in the shipowner's words. 'All right, then. I shall wait until you have a new boat.'

He ran out of the house. Far away on the western sea, he could see his fellow fishermen's boats floating sleepily over the silky waters. He could not help exclaiming, 'What good weather for sailing!'

How he missed the sea to the point of distraction, and how sensuous the calm waters were and how stirring the bravery of his fellow fishermen ... He envied them no end.

His sigh as he gave the sea one last look was so heavy that his heart ached. When he closed his eyes, he thought he could feel the gentle waters lapping up to his forearms, which made him open his eyes again only to find himself on solid ground.

Champion believed the shipowner and visited him several times afterwards, but after a few days, the shipowner became curt and told him he was never being hired again. Champion thought he would lose his mind. He could not hold on to his pride when the little one was crying out for food. He took up a fishing rod and went to the sea all day, returning only late at night.

One evening, he came home to see Bawee asleep, holding on to his mother's skirt. 'Did he wait for me?'

'Yes.' His wife wiped her eyes on the long ribbon of her tunic. It broke Champion's heart, and he thought his wife would have been better off if he had let her go in the beginning when she ran away.

'I've caught some fish, let's fry them up.'

Bawee, in his sleep, smacked his lips as if he was eating something good. They could see saliva pooling in the back of his open mouth. The two parents teared up. The darkness in the corners of the room threatened to swallow their family whole.

Bawee suddenly sat up, awake. 'Mommy, I'm hungry!'

Wordlessly, Champion put Bawee on his back and left the house. He was going to beg for food somewhere.

He went to his blood brother Kim's house. Kim was living under someone else's roof, so while he understood Champion's position, there was little he could do to help him.

'Are you home, my brother?'

'Is it Little Brother?' Kim put down the hay he was braiding into rope and took Bawee from Champion, setting the boy down beside him. Kim's forehead shone with oil and he burped often.

'Daddy, I'm hungry, Daddy!'

Surprised, Kim looked at Champion. 'Is his mother sick?'

'Yes.' He thought of how much better it would be if his wife really were sick instead of them being impoverished.

'Too bad for little Bawee.'

Kim had suspected things were bad for Champion, but he had not known they were this dire. He went to the kitchen and came back with a bowl of rice and some kimchi.

Bawee grabbed the food as soon as he saw it and turned away from the two men.

'You should eat some, too.'

Kim could see the smell of food was making Champion's mouth water.

'Oh no, it's all right ...' Champion swallowed and turned his head. Tears flowed from his eyes. If Kim hadn't been there, he would have shoved Bawee aside and eaten the food himself. His heart pounded with desire for it.

Champion cursed his fate more and more as time went on, and his thirst for rebellion and revenge grew by the day. He had to endure for young Bawee's sake. He tried his hand at farming, but no one would lend him land because of the superstition that sailors were unlucky farmers.

He found himself with no choice but to become a bandit and wander at night with a cold knife concealed by his side. As he hid from valley to valley, he hoped and prayed, fervently, for the health of his boy and his wife.

One day, passing by a village, he saw a boy about Bawee's age and was so caught up in a desire to see his son that he turned on his heels and began running towards the seaside village that was his home. It was a hundred *li* away, and by the time he had arrived, having run day and night, his feet were swollen and bleeding.

Despite having rushed all this way, he had to wait until night fell before entering his own house.

'Mommy, let's go to sleep ...'

Bawee's voice! Champion could not wait anymore. He took a hard look around and opened the door to the house. His wife was so surprised she stood up. Recovering in the next moment, she quickly took his sack from him and hid it in the other room.

'My baby, Bawee!' Champion tried to embrace Bawee. The boy opened his eyes wide and hid behind his mother's skirts.

'It's your father!' said his mother. 'The father you've yearned to see every day!'

Bawee was tearful and refused to approach Champion. The father was saddened. He had run all this way, imagining Bawee would come running to him the moment he saw him. The strong man felt tears well up in his eyes.

'Would you like some dinner?' his wife asked.

'No, I won't eat. Turn off the light.'

He blew out the lamp and gripped his wife's hand. A wave of fear made her shudder from head to toe. But why? This was her husband, whom she should be glad to see!

After a while he said, 'Was Bawee sick?'

'He was fine.'

'And you?' he whispered. He absently stroked Bawee's leg as the child slept.

'Some police officers came today.' Bawee's mother immediately regretted saying this.

'Hmm. How many?'

Champion tried to sound casual, but he was devastated inside. He had the feeling that soon, he would not be able to see his wife and son so easily.

Bawee's mother guessed what he was feeling. She silently berated herself for being so careless with her words and making him worry. She felt like cutting off her own tongue.

After a silence, Champion said, 'Bring my blood brother to me.'

Bawee's mother quickly got up and left the house. Champion gently placed his cheek against Bawee's and held it there for a long time.

His wife finally returned with Kim in tow.

'Big Brother, how have you been?'

Kim received Champion's bow in the dark. 'Are you feeling stronger since I last saw you?'

'It's been a long time. Let's have a drink.' Champion knew Kim liked to drink.

But Kim was decidedly not in the mood. 'It's good just to see you like this.'

'Please.' Champion got up and grabbed Kim's hand. Kim had no choice but to be dragged out.

They reached the pub. Champion ordered wine and side dishes and sat across from Kim. It had been months since they had seen each other. Champion was glad to see him but at the same time did not know what he should say. He felt as if an invisible metal sheet had come between them, preventing him from saying everything that was weighing down his heart.

Kim did not know why, but he felt more and more anxious as they sat there.

'Big Brother! Have a bowl.'

'All right.'

Champion was sad that Kim's voice was the same as before, but his manner was hesitant, a fact that disappointed the younger man. He briefly remembered that an officer had visited his house that day, and the thought made his heart ache all the more.

He kept refilling his own bowl. 'Big Brother. Don't you feel sorry for my little Bawee?' he said, thinking of how he was headed for jail.

'Well, I suppose.' Kim could think of nothing more to say. Champion was acting too strange. He had to get out of there quickly, and to do so he had to avoid getting drunk. Kim spilt half his bowl on his knee before he brought it to his lips.

'Big Brother, take one more!' Champion was anguished at the sight of Kim's reluctance.

'See, well, I have to go. I belong to my master you know, I can't stay out for very long.'

'All right.'

Kim took the chance to bolt out of the pub. Champion followed him, which terrified Kim. Sweat flowed from his forehead.

A light rain began falling. Kim finally reached his house and leapt inside as if hiding from a demon.

'Big Brother! Big Brother!' Champion called through the crack in the door. He wanted to hear Kim's voice one more time before he was parted from his blood brother forever. But no one answered, and he turned away.

He plodded back to his house. He pulled at the door, but it was locked.

His senses were as sharp as the edge of a knife. After standing still for a time, he sat down on one of the protruding foundation stones of his house.

The raindrops grew larger. He felt loneliness with every fibre of his body. He had no wife, no child, and no friends. And what should appear next in his mind but the slothful face of that shipowner! He was responsible for all the hardships and loneliness in his life. Champion jumped up and down in the air like an angry tiger. Then, as if possessed, he ran towards the shipowner's house.

*

Bawee stopped thinking about the past and gathered his wits. He carefully looked around. The dew-drenched silo shone in the moonlight, and he could still hear the sound of Jeonjung's unending laughter.

He heard the chirping of insects at his feet. From somewhere came the rustling sound of leaves in the wind.

What had his father's rebellion resulted in? Only meaningless sacrifice. On top of that, Bawee was left with nothing but the curses of others for the rest of his life. The son of a bandit! The son of a murderer!

He shook these thoughts from his head. He hugged himself and hunched over, thinking of the moment he found himself jiggling the lock of the silo, and how the thought of the committee was the only thing that had prevented him from breaking it. The committee had saved him just in the nick of time, he thought, feeling a great warmth in his heart.

He recalled the words Hongcheol spoke often. 'Whatever we do, we must be prudent. Don't let yourself be overtaken by personal emotion ...'

Hongcheol had said this over and over again, shaking Bawee's hand for emphasis. The warmth of Hongcheol's hand that had spread to his! Bawee understood, for the first time, the true power of that warmth.

Bawee slowly moved away thinking that he was not alone. He had pledged himself to the committee. He must follow its precepts, and not be moved so easily!

The sound of the faraway waves grew louder with every step he took.

March 1933

MOTHER AND SON

This morning, despite the snow falling thick and fast, Seung-ho's mother bound her son to her body and set out from her father's house. As she passed the Chinese man's store, she thought of how she had nowhere to go. She had quit her maid position a few days before, and was now leaving her father's after an argument with her stepmother. She had not expected much from her stepmother, but her father! She had thought he would let them stay longer, maybe not for a year but for a few months, or at least until Seungho shook the hundred-day cough. She was no better than a stranger to her father now, she thought, tearfully.

Where could she go?

She stood on the sidewalk as pedestrians passed her without giving her a second glance. She stared at the sky and thought that her only option now was to bow her head and beg her mortal enemy, her brother-in-law, to take her in.

The mere thought of it made her feel like a cow headed for slaughter. She shuddered with disgust and her feet refused to move forward. But even if her husband had died, did she not still have Seungho? And did the little boy not have a better chance of being accepted by his paternal family than by her father? Surely a nephew who shared the family name was just like a son.

All right then, let's go! She managed to force her feet forward. Her brother-in-law had even opened a pharmacy recently. Getting accepted by the family would be the difficult part, but once they were in, she would be able to treat Seungho's cough. She gathered her courage and kept telling herself to endure whatever humiliation would be handed out to her, no matter what. But she kept slowing at the thought of the mean, beady eyes of her brother-in-law and his wife's piercing, fishhook stare.

Her brother-in-law had revered her scholar husband up until the Manchurian Incident, supporting their family with a stipend. But once the Japanese invaded China and the city of Longjing was turned upside down, her brother-in-law's affection for his younger brother changed into hate and constant humiliation, an attitude he did not spare towards her and her son. He had cut off his financial support, which was why she had to become a maid at someone else's house. More than anything else, her brother-in-law had the temerity to seem glad when her husband died overseas a year ago, prompting her to get into a screaming fight with him where she vowed never to see him again.

And yet, here she was, about to crawl back into his house, knowing full well that his family would not welcome her. There was, however, nothing else to be done.

Seungho, who had been quiet, raised his head and released another volley of heart-breaking coughs, so violent that he struggled to catch his breath. She moved him from her back to her front, rubbed her cheek against his, and shivered.

'Seungho! My baby!'

She put her lips against his and sucked, in the hope of sucking the sickness out of him and into herself. Sometimes after this, his coughing would cease for a while and she would think it had worked, but then it would start up again.

She continued on her way when his coughs had subsided somewhat. Soon, she turned a corner and the walls of her brother-in-law's house were in sight. She stopped. What was she going to do when her brother-in-law asked her what she was doing there? Tell him she had come to live in his house? Then what? Would he just stand there and let her do whatever she wanted? No, she would be made to tell him that she had quit her position. But what if they still refused her?

She felt as if she were standing on the edge of a chasm. She wanted to turn back. Better never to have gone there if she was only going to be humiliated. But where else would she go? She could impose on a friend for a night, perhaps, but then what? She thought of when she was thrown out of her employer's house. That could happen at any time, even within a single night, at any house that was not family. No one was going to welcome a sick baby. At least Seungho was a blood relation to her brother-in-law; it was worth a try. They would not really turn her away, would they?

She stepped forward. Her feet were heavy. She kept hesitating. What if Seungho were to cough when she was sitting with her brother-in-law? What if all was going well and suddenly her little boy coughed and her brother-in-law forbade her from bringing disease into the house? She decided to wait until her son's coughs had subsided. She stood until Seungho's coughing went away completely. She knew that the cold air was bad for him, but she could not help feeling nervous about their chances.

'Seungho,' she begged, patting the little boy's back, 'when we're with your uncle, you must hold in your cough. You simply must!'

Now she stood before her brother-in-law's door. The door had been newly painted since she had last been here. Her heart pounded. She hesitated.

Just then, the gate opened and out walked her brother-in-law's schoolteacher daughter, Jilnyuh. She seemed taken aback to find Seungho's mother standing outside.

'Auntie! It's been so long!' Her face was white as snow, framed by the feathery collar of her coat.

Seungho's mother was already bowing her head. 'How have you been ...?'

'Please come in. Is Seungho sleeping?' She leaned forward to look for a moment and stepped back again. 'Auntie, I have to go out now, but you're not allowed to leave until I come back!'

Jilnyuh's voice was bright and friendly. Should she beg Jilnyuh to intervene for her? But before she could think about it, Jilnyuh smiled at her and briskly walked away.

Seungho's mother had no choice but to enter the gate. Her footsteps must have alerted Jilnyuh's mother, whose fishhook stare appeared behind one of the windows. Her face was flushed, her demeanour hostile. She slid open the window and sneered.

'Well, look who's here! I never thought I'd see the day.'

Wordlessly, Seungho's mother went and sat down before her in the main room. The room smelled of medicine and humid warmth covered her cheeks like a blanket. Afraid Seungho would start coughing, she covered him up to his head with the wrap. Her heart felt like it had shrunk to the size of a bean.

Her brother-in-law's wife began packing tobacco into her long bamboo pipe. 'So, you were working? You must've made a lot of money by now ... And do you still think you were in the right that time?'

'I was at fault.'

Jilnyuh's mother seemed pleased enough with her apology. 'Good. Having a bad temper is one thing, but once you've calmed down, you must be able to apologize. And it will not do to stay away from your elders for over a year.'

Seungho's mother was so relieved, she could barely hold down her tears. What a selfish person she had been!

She could hear her brother-in-law's deep voice in the other room, as well as someone else speaking Chinese. Perhaps they were guests of the pharmacy. She decided to tell Jilnyuh's mother everything once it was clear she was forgiven. She tried to say something else but her throat was choked with tears. Just then, Seungho raised his head and coughed.

Seungho's mother could not hide her dismay.

Jilnyuh's mother narrowed her eyes. 'Does your son have the hundred-day cough?' She was beginning to guess the reason why Seungho's mother had come to them. 'There's no medicine for that. When did he get sick?'

Seungho's mother grew pale at the news that there was no medicine. That meant Seungho might die! Her mind went dark.

'You should've taken care of your child better. Did someone in the house you work for have it?'

'N-no.'

'Then wouldn't they want you to leave?'

'I have already left!'

Jilnyuh's mother had thought she was here for medicine, but now she realized she wanted to move in. This woman was trying to pull a fast one on her! Her calm pity flared into anger.

'Hah! You never so much as visited when things were well, but you come crawling now that your baby is dying? This is not our business. You marched out of here on your own two feet. You couldn't stay away for even a year! We're not going to tolerate this. Go back to your father's house or find a new husband. You cut off all ties with us back then!'

She was pounding her bamboo pipe on the ashtray for emphasis. Seungho's mother felt like the ashtray was her own face. She kept her mouth shut until the tirade was over and tried to beg her way in one more time.

'But there is nowhere else I can go! Please forgive me.'

'Huh? Forgive you? How much does forgiveness cost these days? Because we really don't know.'

The door to the other room slid open, and the brother-in-law's face popped in. He shouted, 'What's all this noise!'

'Well, your sister-in-law chose to ignore us all this time and happened to waltz in here when her child got sick.'

'Enough! Be quiet, both of you!' He slammed the door shut.

Her brother-in-law had been her last thread of hope. She quickly stood up.

'Have a good life.'

She ran out of the house.

*

She wandered the streets. The snow kept falling, heavy and silent. She could not help resenting her late husband, but then berated herself. What a stupid woman she was, resenting a man who rarely had a full night's sleep or a proper meal, who had been forced to live in hiding until he was caught and killed by the enemy.

What had her husband said to her before he went into the mountains? *No matter how hard we try to live, they will never let us live in peace.* She did not understand him at the time, but now she saw he could have been right. No … he *was* right.

We have to teach Seungho that this is life …

Her husband's last words before he left. What was she to do without her husband? When he was alive and by her side, she had hope at least, but what was left to her now? Nothing, only darkness.

She came to a halt. Her thoughts kept making her think of her husband's eyes, her husband's lips. It made her want to cry. She silently gazed at the falling snow and wondered if it would make good medicine for Seungho. She opened her mouth wide and caught a few flakes. Then she remembered the smell of medicine in her brother-in-law's house. The snowflakes on her tongue suddenly felt like blades. She remembered what her brother-in-law's wife had said, which made her widen her eyes in panic. Then she thought Seungho's cough would get worse with this wind blowing. She took off the towel covering her hair and covered his head with it.

She began to walk again. Where should she go? Anywhere, as long as it was out of Longjing. Everyone was so cruel here! Once they got out of Longjing, they would find people like themselves, people enduring the same struggle. They would not be mistreated then.

This made her think of the mountain that her husband had mentioned when he left her.

'But where are you going?' she had asked, full of sorrow.

Her husband had sat for a moment in silence before answering, 'I'm going to the mountain.'

'Which mountain?'

'Just know that it's a mountain ...'

Since then, she would gaze at any mountain in the distance. Her heart would skip whenever she heard anyone mention anything about mountains.

The mountains! He had already predicted that whatever mountain he ended up on, the enemy was sure to find him in the end and kill him. She looked up. She could barely see the mountains through the snow, but they were there, dream-like ... they seemed to call to both mother and son.

'Let's go, Seungho! Let's follow your father there!'

She was fired up now. She imagined she would find her dead husband's skull there, and when they died on the mountain, they would hear the last words he whispered before he died. A new vigour flowed through her. Snowflakes fell against her burning cheek.

After a long while, she looked around her; all she could see was snow-covered plains, stretching out into the distance. The only other thing was the mountain range that had given her such hope. But strangely, the more she walked, the further the mountains seemed. Her face hurt from the wind and snow smashing against it. The fervour that had burned in her had disappeared without a trace, and she wondered if she were chasing a ghost. She looked back with some regret. Longjing was already two or three *li* away.

She decided to go back, but she felt she would freeze before she got there. She turned around anyway. She would go as far as she could. If there were a house on the way, she would beg for a night's shelter, but in any case, she must try. She squinted into the distance to see if she could discern a house. The realization that it was getting darker made her even more anxious. She searched and searched for any sign of shelter. Seungho kept coughing. She could no longer pay attention to his coughs as she concentrated wholly on seeing through the falling snow.

This was not a completely unfamiliar road and she knew there was a village along it somewhere, but oddly enough, the village never appeared, no matter how long she walked. All she could see were fields buried in snow. She wandered for a while longer and thought she must have gone down the wrong path somewhere, but now she could not even tell where she had come from. The only thing she could feel and see was the fearsome wind that whipped at her head and the snow that shone so bright it made her dizzy. She stood still again. She tried to raise her arm to rub her eyes, but her arm felt like a block of wood and refused to move. This jolted her; was she dying? She pounded her feet against the ground and rubbed her hands together. She called for Seungho. She could not stand here like this, she needed to keep going forward. She saw something that looked like shelter in the distance. She ran to it. But it was not a house, it was only a few snow-covered pillars. This was strange to her. By the location, it looked like it had once been a rest stop for carriages. Now it was only a few pillars in the snow. She remembered hearing about the farming houses being burned down during the suppression, and the memory depressed her. What was she to do? She looked for the high earthen walls of the Chinese. She could not see any. She walked about a little, straining into the snow. Nothing, nothing.

The wind died down a little, but the snow continued to fall. The snow came up to her knees now. She stared at the pillars and wondered what to do, but then gritted her teeth and thought, *If I die, I die!*

She began to walk again. Her vision was getting darker, and she kept stumbling on her own feet. She had lost her shoes long ago and was walking in her socks, which the snow kept sticking to, making her footsteps heavier and heavier. The clinging snow refused to budge no matter how hard she shook her feet. Her hair and eyebrows were coated with white powder, as were the edges of her lips. She ran. Or she thought she ran, but in truth she was standing in place.

She suddenly felt weak and she slipped, getting snow in her nose and mouth. She could not breathe! By the time she realized she had fallen into a ditch or a stream, she was already thinking she was going to die. She flailed and tried to grab something. All that she could grab was dry snow. She screamed and grunted as she sank deep into the cold whiteness. Finally, at the bottom of wherever it was she fell, she managed to get to her feet.

She shook her head and pushed the snow away from her face to make an air pocket. The more she pushed at the snow, however, the more of it fell in from above. She suddenly feared that Seungho would suffocate, so she held him close with one arm and pushed the snow away from his head. The snow melted on her head and the water snaked down into her collar. Worried that this freezing water would touch her baby, she turned her head this way and that, trying to get the collar to absorb most of it. But the water kept flowing.

She was ready to give up. *This mother and son are going to die!*

She thought about her husband's death, her husband who had not died from any snow or drowning in the sea or slipping in a ditch or stream.

No matter how hard we try to live, they will never let us live in peace. We are all sure to be killed.

Her husband's words were right! How hard he had tried to live! She used to think that despite her husband's words, a person had to make a go of life anyway, but here she was, about to drown in the snow. The death of the mother and child was no better than the death of the father.

'Oh, Seungho ...'

She called her son's name and vowed she would never make him into a person like her. She would finish what her husband started through this son!

Her heart swelled, and her son's name escaped her lips. 'Seungho!'

This snow... this snow is nothing!

January 1935

TUITION

It was morning. In the playground of the town's school – the only school, despite the town having two thousand residences – the schoolchildren were running about playing games before class.

Except a little boy named Third, who was ten years old. He was sitting in the dim classroom where the curtains were drawn. The classroom had a stove for generating heat, and a kettle of water sat boiling on top of it.

The sound of children shouting and arguing could clearly be heard from outside. Then Third heard clapping and laughter. He lifted aside one of the curtains. The light stung his eyes.

A heavy snow was silently falling. It heaped on the branches of the bushy young pines and bare acacia trees planted along the fence on the far side of the playground.

A snowman stood in the middle of the playground, its horizontal twig for a mouth giving it a firm, serious expression. The children standing around it clapped and shrieked, their laughter escaping in wisps of steam from their lips.

A child put his hat on the snowman, and another made it a beard using more twigs. The children laughed even harder, stomping their feet. Third smiled, too. He wanted to go out and play with them, but just when he turned his head, he glimpsed the fearsome head of his teacher passing by the windows to the corridor.

The monthly tuition! He had forgotten about it for a moment.

The teacher told me that if I don't bring my monthly tuition today, he's going to kick me out of class ...

With this thought, an inexplicable feeling started welling up from his throat, and he had to bury his face in his hands.

But that snowman! Those eyes! That mouth! That beard! Third could not help giggling as he peeked out between his fingers.

'*Kimu Sansai!*'

Third jumped at the Japanese version of his name, thinking it was his teacher, and his eyes instantly filled with tears. But it was not his teacher; it was only Bongho, whom Third stared at wordlessly, relieved.

'Look at this money! Daddy told me to save it. He said he was going to buy me a coat, too. He's not going to give me his hand-me-downs, no sir!'

Bongho held up a silver coin for Third to see and tossed the coin into his desk, making a loud *plunk!* He then dashed outside. His arms and legs moved so fast that they were almost a blur. Third stared until Bongho was out of sight. He started biting his fingernails.

'Why doesn't Mother have any money?' he muttered through his fingers. His eyes stung, and tears flowed down his face. He wiped his cheeks with a fist. 'Mother said she would give me the monthly tuition tomorrow! She said she'd sell her potatoes and give me the money!'

But even as he mumbled these words into the emptiness, he could not help but remember his teacher's harsh scolding. He did not believe that his teacher would wait until the next day. Once the bell rang and the teacher stood at the lectern and called his name, all that was left for him was to be banished into the snow in tears. He would not get to learn Japanese, he would not get to learn Korean …

He suddenly remembered the silver coin Bongho had flashed before him. If he had that, he would get to stay with the other children and learn how to read! The thought had struck him like a bolt of lightning, making him dizzy with hope.

Third breathed fast as he stared at Bongho's desk. The day had been dark so far but here now was a strange light before his eyes! A joyful light! An urging light that was almost blinding.

The first bell of the day began to ring. At the sound of it, Third sprinted towards Bongho's desk, as if possessed.

February 1933

REAL AND UNREAL

Do you think such a thing might have really happened?

I still haven't found an answer to his question.

It all happened about a year ago. That night, I had just turned in, having washed up after another late dinner.

'Ma'am!' called out a deep voice. 'Are you home?'

I got up and opened the door a crack, but it was too dark for me to see who it was. I couldn't recognize the voice either.

'Are you at the right house?' I asked after some hesitation.

'It's me, ma'am. Boksoon's father.'

I flung opened the door and ran out to greet him. 'Boksoon's father! What a surprise! Please, come in.'

I sat him down inside and ran to the store to buy some cigarettes. I presented them to him with the ashtray and took a good look at him. His clothes were threadbare and his face was more melancholy than ever. The eyes beneath his prominent forehead were so deeply set that it was hard to read them. Their occasional glimmer of blackness, however, made my blood run cold, which held me back from being too glad to see him again, even after all this time. I was also feeling more and more apprehensive as to his reason for coming to our house.

We live in a two-storey house. Boksoon's father used to rent the room on the floor above us. He had no steady employment and lived as a day labourer. The family only got to eat when the father managed to find work, and starved when he didn't. I liked him and his wife well enough, and their little Boksoon was a dear girl, but their presence in our lives made me uncomfortable. It was hard to eat and drink merrily when we knew there was a family starving upstairs.

From time to time, I'd bring up for them whatever rice and stew we had left over. Even as I did so, there always remained a selfish corner of my heart that wished they would just move away.

On these occasions, their daughter Boksoon would come crawling towards me, knowing that I was bringing something to eat. She was so lovable that I pitied her and couldn't help taking her in my arms.

'And how old is Boksoon?'

The little girl was too young to speak. She was very clever, however, and she would stare into my face at this question before holding up two lean fingers.

'Two years old ... How can a baby who can't speak know how old she is?'

Her mother, who normally went about with a worried expression, would beam at her daughter at such moments. I couldn't tell if her smile was really a smile or more like another way of crying. Her eyes always seemed to be ready to cry. Whenever I sat with her, I wondered how a person with such a sad face could ever avoid hardship in life.

I visited their room often to play with little Boksoon, but I rarely saw Boksoon's father. Whenever we had an occasion to sit down together, I made sure to get up as soon as it was polite to do so. Sitting with him felt strangely disagreeable. I realized back then that the wife's sad face had been an unconscious response to her husband. Only Boksoon shone like a star between the two.

'Boksoon's father almost never speaks. It'll be the death of me,' the wife would often say.

Other times, she would mention, 'Boksoon's father goes somewhere every night, and when he returns, he's like that … His clothes soaked in sweat.'

Then she would realize she had said this out loud and bade me not to tell anyone.

I began to have dark suspicions of Boksoon's father and was not a little curious about him, so I asked his wife many questions whenever we sat together. I never got a straight answer from her about anything.

Then one day two years ago, I mixed some rice in tofu stew for little Boksoon, and carried it up the stairs, only to find the house a mess and no one home. I waited for a while, thinking they were only out to beg for rice somewhere. I eventually went to every house that they may have gone to visit, but no one knew where they were. In the end, they never came back. I was both sorry and relieved to see them go. At the same time, I felt a little angry with them. Even if they were so poor that they had to run away in the middle of the night, they could've at least said goodbye.

And a year after they vanished without a trace, as Boksoon's beautiful smile was starting to fade from my memory, here was Boksoon's father, come to see me in the night. As glad as I was, there was tension in the air. I wondered if he wanted something from me.

'And how are Boksoon and her mother?' I asked him.

I waited for his answer, but he only sat in silence. He looked so hungry that I got up and put on my apron. 'I'll make you some dinner. I don't have many side dishes, but I hope you'll eat some.'

He glanced at me and shifted in his seat. I couldn't read his expression. I understood that this was just his nature, but there was something about his face that seemed to say that his life had taken a turn for the worse since I last saw him. The darkness from his eyes was making me more and more afraid. Wishing my husband would hurry up and come home, I went out to the kitchen, which was so dark and scary that my feet could barely stay still as I prepared the meal. As soon as I laid it down, he sat right in front of the low meal table and began to eat before I could say anything. I could tell how hungry he had been by the speed with which he put it away.

'So why didn't you say anything when you left?' I said as soon as he laid down his spoon. Afraid that I'd offended him, I couldn't ask him any more questions in this vein. The very air in the room seemed to have grown heavier.

But thinking I glimpsed a bit of Boksoon in his face, I had to ask after her. 'Boksoon must be talking and walking now.'

I had said this before I could stop myself. He still had nothing to say. I bowed my head. A heavy silence surrounded us, whirling and spinning in the room. I was annoyed. If he had so little to say and he'd had his meal, why couldn't he just leave? If he wanted something else, why couldn't he just say it? I was anxious to know why he was here, and his silence was agitating me more with every moment, making me sweat and filling my small heart to the brim with worry. He looked as if he hadn't cut his hair or shaved his beard in weeks, a fact that only served to make me more nervous. At the same time, a small part of me was curious as to why he was here.

After a long silence, I felt as hostess that I needed to say something, even though I knew he wouldn't answer.

'So, tell me about what you've been up to this past year.'

Surprisingly, he laughed. It was a kind of laugh that I had never heard the likes of in my life, cold like the blade of a knife. A laugh heavy with frost. Intimidated, I bowed my head.

He coughed loudly. And then he said something completely unexpected.

'Ma'am! I don't know where Boksoon and her mother are!'

I was so surprised to get an answer at all, let alone such a strange one, that I raised my head and checked to see if his lips really were moving. And what strange, dream-like words! I wanted to ask him again what had happened, but I was afraid he would stop talking again. I kept quiet and waited for him to speak.

'What is the point of me saying such things? If I thought you were like the other women, I would not say anything. But I've heard, ma'am, that you are a writer ... I don't know what it is you write, but ...'

He glanced at me. I found his gaze uncomfortable, and his words, they almost sounded like a threat. But what had crossed my mind in that moment was: has anything of real life ever been produced from the flourishes of my pen? I had the feeling that the answer was 'not really', and this man's honest words stabbed barbs of guilt into my heart.

'I have nightmares every night. I've tried everything to avoid this dream but it's only getting worse. I can't tell anymore, whether it's a nightmare or my life is a dream. I'm afraid to go to sleep. In the dream, a group of monstrous men appear before me and drag me to a dark place. They are human, but they are not human like me. The place they take me to is in our world, but it is as dark as a cave.'

I had only thought of him as an uneducated labourer until now. His articulate way of speaking was surprising to me. The leaden weight of his words pressed down my heart.

'There are many people like me in that darkness. They were dragged there, too. It's a dream, so I can't be sure.

'I'll call the men who dragged me there the B's. Every night, the B's appear and take some of us from the darkness with them. The people taken out we never see again. We wonder what happened to them, and even though no one tells us, soon we all know their fate. We do not want to be summoned by the B's. So every night, we lie as silent and still as dead bodies.

'One night, I can hear the footsteps of the B's approach,

their shoe heels knocking against the concrete floor. A door opens with a clang. We all lie there, every hair standing up in fear. The B's call for someone. No one moves. The B's rush in, kicking us and whipping us. I hear one of us shout, *"Let's take it as far as we can!"* Others shout back, *"Let's go!"* The shout of people making their last stand. People who are not yet ready to die. We shivered as we heard them charge. But we didn't move a muscle.'

Boksoon's father breathed deeply and stared into the flame of the lamp. His eyes blazed. I felt as if my body had shrunk to the size of a fist. I trembled, ever so slightly.

'I dreamt that dream again. That night, the B's appeared. They called my name. I was numb as numb can be by then. I heard them call other names, but I stopped listening. I was just stroking the ground, looking for something – something I could grab hold of when they tried to drag me away. When I felt a whip crack against me, I realized then that I had no flesh on my body, only bone. We seemed to have been taken out some door. I stumbled at every step.

'The moon was bright. The snow that reflected the moonlight was also very bright. But that moon resembled a grinning skull. We reached a mountain path somehow, whether we walked there or were dragged there. I didn't think of pain or fainting or what was going to happen to me. I couldn't. All I did was what they made me do.

'I think I was holding on to the trunk of a pine tree. Then I heard a scream. When I looked, a B had pierced a baby with a knife and was holding the baby up with the blade. The baby's arms and legs flailed in the air. *"Mommy! Mommy!"* The baby kept calling for its mommy. The woman who was its mother just gazed at the scene. The baby began to choke. Even then I didn't think I would die. Even in that moment, I thought I would be spared somehow. I will live, I thought, whatever happens in this world.

'Then, somehow, from somewhere, a car appeared.

'"*Come here!*" someone shouted, and I looked around. One of the other prisoners beside me jumped up. I thought he must have had the same foolish thought that I had, that he was trying to escape to the car. I jumped up, too. "*Sit down!*" the voice commanded. I ignored it and tried to make a run for it. But I had heavy chains tied around my ankles. The B's had tied a chain around the other prisoner's neck. They hitched the end of the chain to the car. One of them said, "*If you can follow the car, we will spare your life!*"

'I realized what was happening; I tried to escape again. But they just laughed. "*Follow the car! Follow the car!*"

'The B's, who had got in the car, gestured towards us to follow. They turned on the engine. The car began to move. The other prisoner ran as fast as he could, his arms pumping so fast they were a blur. But soon, he collapsed. At the sound of him collapsing, the car disappeared in a cloud of dust.

'I was next. One of the B's attached a bayonet to a rifle and came up to me. I wondered, even, whether they were truly going to kill me. He brought the bayonet to my chest. My hopes, my life left me in that moment. But then, it happened. Ma'am, it happened then! I felt a strength at that very edge of my despair. I knew what I had to do. I knew that I was about to receive my death from someone else. I looked the B in the eye. He pierced my heart with the bayonet. I screamed. I woke up. That was the dream.'

Boksoon's father opened his eyes. His demeanour frightened me. I put a hand over my pounding heart as I stared at him. His face was taut with rage. His teeth were clenched together, his jaw trembling from the effort. I was so overwhelmed, I didn't know what to think. The lamp dispassionately illuminated his face.

After a long while, he turned to me.

'Do you think such a thing might have really happened?'

My eyes felt so hot that I had to look away from his gaze. I couldn't answer his question. My whole body shook. I heard the sound of raindrops pounding on the corrugated tin roof.

February 1934

BLACKIE

The sound of scuffing. The door to the classroom shakes as a dog's paws scratch at it. The claws peeking out of the tufts of black fur look as sharp as knives. The door swings open and in jumps a black dog with long, floppy ears. Its curly fur, shining eyes, prominent snout, and taut, slim body give it an air of well-bred dignity.

The children stare wide-eyed, some laughing. The teacher, who has been writing on the blackboard, turns at the sound of laughter and sees the dog. It approaches him, wagging its tail. As glad as Kim is to see the dog, he cannot help but flare in anger at the intrusion. He picks up a leash from his desk and throws it at the dog. The dog skips aside but does not back away from Kim. As it still tries to approach him, the hairs on the tip of its gently waving tail are as white as gourd flowers. Soon, though, it whines and barks as it rushes out of the classroom.

'All right, then. Don't forget your homework tomorrow.'

Kim's voice is a little shaky. His face is flushed a splotched red. The rise of flesh below one of his eyes is twitching.

The children whisper amongst themselves as they pack their bags.

'Was that the principal's dog?'

'No, it's Mr Kim's.'

'It was at the principal's house though ...'

Kim listens and realizes he has let his emotions get the best of him again. He silently berates himself for being small-minded; someone condemned, for the rest of his life, to the constant exposure of how pathetic he is. But, he almost shouts out loud, he does not envy the broadminded!

He does not envy them at all.

The children bow, and Kim leaves the building, his head throbbing and his legs shaking. Of course, he has not eaten for two days. The smell of new paint in the corridor almost makes him faint, and he lets his body ride the current of students leaving the school. The dusty air smells like chemicals, like shoe polish, and the sound of shoes rumbling on the floor is like the beating of drums. The red leaves of the poplars outside the window spin as they fall to the ground, and the distant blue sky peers in through the glass. A very familiar scene.

'Mr Kim, are you sick?'

Kim turns, and the effort blots out his vision. He blinks to clear it and sees a worried student standing in front of him, the very student who had been dragged away by the police as a suspect! He stares at the student's left cheek that is obscured as if by fog.

'It's you!'

But once the words are out of his mouth, he sees that it was not the student he thought but another, a current one. He leans on this student's arm as he is escorted to the staff room. Along the way, he wants to open his mouth and scream.

*

Kim feels better once they are at the door to the staff room.

'Send for a carriage,' he tells the student and goes inside

alone. The staff room is cloudy with cigarette smoke, and he does not want to look up to meet anyone's gaze. He keeps his head bowed on the way to his seat. Sitting down, he cradles his head in his hands and closes his eyes.

'Are you all right?' It is the music teacher's voice.

Suddenly, Kim imagines the face of Principal Choi, and the thought drains the life from his body. He scolds himself as weak, for being unable to come to a decision, and the despair overwhelms him. And these teachers, who have abused his weakness to do all sorts of underhanded things!

He stands up so quickly that the staff room seems to spin. He forces his legs to comply as he walks to the principal's office. Principal Choi is getting ready to leave but stands still when Kim enters. Choi's beard is as black as ink, his lips thick as sausages.

A mendacious smile reaches the principal's eyes behind the yellow of his dirty glasses. 'Did you want to talk to me about something?'

'Yes. I did.' Kim feels like he is about to suffocate.

Principal Choi's plump hand, lying on the blue desk, is white, unlike his face, and unlined like that of a young man. Choi stares at him as if to ask, *'Well, what of it?'* The eyes flashing behind his glasses look very deep.

'I went to your house last night,' Kim says, 'but you weren't there.'

'I see. Is that all?' Principal Choi asks, as if he is eager for their conversation to end.

Kim tries to calm his beating heart. He takes a deep breath. 'I don't think I can teach anymore. I don't feel well.'

'You don't?' Principal Choi frowns at this unexpected turn. 'What's wrong with you?'

Kim bites down on his lip, trying to suppress his discontent. His head hurts. There's a ringing in his ears. His rage has shattered and turned into something like sadness.

He remembers the dark underground. He remembers the

smell of the earth, the yellow light of the candles, the work they did day and night, that moment he simply had to rest his eyes. He had woken up by surprise, and then the very man standing before him now had said, 'Do rest,' and covered Kim's shoulders with his own jacket, smiling. Choi's hand that had brushed the earth from Kim's face, warm as his own mother's hand! Only ten years had passed since they had started working together, not knowing whether they would survive from one day to the next, but how things had changed now ...

Kim wants to embrace the principal and burst into tears. It is true that Kim knows the reason why things are the way they are. But this attitude the principal has, his ignoring Kim's suffering ... how can Kim call him a friend anymore? His position may have made him this way, and perhaps Choi has hidden depths that are difficult to read, or it could be that his greed has compromised his beliefs ... But was Choi not ready to give it all up, and was that not why he was dismissed as head of administration? Having thought himself into a corner, Kim tries to let go of his worries and calm himself. But the loneliness and empty feelings press down hard on his throat.

'If you say you can't teach ... well, then. There's nothing I can do.'

Principal Choi smiles! Kim feels like he has been struck across his face. He tries again to calm himself as the urge to grab Choi and convince him of his wrongdoing burns inside his chest. His eyes wet with tears. Choi's face grows dim. How can they be so cruel to each other over such a small misunderstanding, especially when circumstances were once so harsh that they could barely draw breath from one moment to the next?

'You must understand,' says Kim, 'that I do not want to leave the school. They insist I should be let go but is it not repulsive to scapegoat a teacher of clear conscience? Why should we have to do so!'

Choi's face is grim as he gets up from his seat. 'You're right. I'm taking care of this myself. You've failed to do so by the very words you've just uttered.'

'Principal Choi!' Kim grabs Choi's sleeve.

Choi takes up his cane. 'That's enough. We'll dismiss some other teacher.'

Choi has said his piece. He slams the door as he leaves. Kim is so grateful that tears drop from his eyes on to Choi's desk. He wipes them off and promises himself to talk through his pettier emotions someday with Choi. He is told the carriage is waiting when he comes out of the principal's office, so he tells the other teachers that he is not feeling well and goes home.

*

'Do you have any rice gruel?'

Kim gives his wife, who reeks of breast milk, a brief look as he lies down on the bedding she has spread for him. How could the thorny cushion of his situation seem so peaceful right now? All strength leaves his body as he stares up at the ceiling. He thinks, for the thousandth time, how hard it is to go against one's conscience. His wife is busy preparing rice gruel, and he hears the clamour of his two children somewhere in the house.

He opens the door and calls out, 'Come here, Kyounghee!'

His wife leads little Kyounghee by the hand, giving him a worried look. His wife's face looks dewy from the rice pot steam, her black hair thick and rich. Two trails of tears flow down Kyounghee's face. Kim closes his room door and hugs Kyounghee tight. The baby smell of Kyounghee's hair warms his fatherly heart. He can tell from Kyounghee's tears how he must have looked to the principal that afternoon. Choi probably thought no better of him than another child. He hugs Kyounghee close and listens to the sound of tinder being chopped and water sloshing in the kitchen.

*

He has always known that he does not have any particular strengths. If he were forced to name one, perhaps he would say it was the fact that he never lies. And that once he is convinced something is right, he never changes his mind. But this is also his biggest weakness. Sometimes, he wishes he was greedy like Principal Choi, but only for a moment, as the thought always turns his stomach in the end. No wonder he clashed with the principal so often.

Whenever he found something useful in his house, he would take it to school for his students, and this was the source of many arguments with his wife. He would try to ignore her. Meanwhile, the other teachers were so selfish that their eyes were practically bloodshot from looking out for things to steal. His earnest nature was isolating in such a place, but he tried to console himself by thinking it a strength and not a weakness. His colleagues, however, thought him foolish, and now he is sad that he is beginning to agree with them.

He really is a man with no strengths after all.

*

The door opens, and his wife enters with a steaming bowl of rice gruel. Kyounghee, whom he thought was asleep beside him, jumps up and clings to her skirt. Kim thinks of how her sparkling eyes are so much like his own. He can smell the not-unpleasant scent of cooking from his wife's skirts. Blue veins stand out near his wife's eyes, and her demeanour is heavy with fatigue. Was it because of the hardships he had put her through? Kim takes the bowl from his wife and pities her, a woman who was so unlucky as to have met a man like him.

'Stop that.' His wife extracts her skirts from Kyounghee's grasp and says to her husband, 'Please, eat up.'

Her eyebrows are knitted with worry. Kim thinks of the bowl of rice gruel that he had slapped from her offering hands this morning.

'Do give me one more bowl. And I will eat dinner tonight. Those bean sprouts you bought? I'll have them seasoned.'

A glad smile rises like a clear breeze in his wife's almost too-large eyes. She takes the empty bowl from him and goes out. How lovable are the very toes that peek out of the holes in her stockings? Kyounghee skips after her mother, crying out, 'Mama, Mama.'

'Dear! Blackie is here,' calls his wife.

Kim gets up and opens the door to the courtyard. Blackie comes running towards him, smelling of dog and fresh early autumn air. It thrusts its long snout at him and licks everything it can reach.

'Did I hurt you today, Blackie?'

Kim caresses Blackie's back and leans back to take a look at the dog. After what he did today, a man would hold resentment in his heart and not give him a second look, but the dog only licks him, friendly and trusting. The long hairs above its eyes and the ends of its whiskers flash with reflected light, and its thoughtful gaze and lovely chinless snout pull at Kim's heartstrings. He thinks of the dog's face as being much more heroic than the flat, featureless circle that is his own. He gave up the dog when the principal, whom he had believed in so much, asked for it. Despite this, his heart always yearned for the loyal dog he had trained since it was a pup, a dog that could now fetch groceries and even deliver letters.

Kim could not bring himself to walk away whenever he saw the dog chained up in the principal's yard. Blackie would jump up and down at the sight of him and keen like a person, which stopped Kim's heart and made him stand still for long periods of time in the middle of the street, unable to move on.

He had to press down on his anger whenever the principal made a derisive, throwaway comment about the dog. But Kim would not dream of actually saying anything to the man.

His wife reappeared, with little Kyoungseon in her arms, patting their son's back as she tried to stop his crying. 'Do stop it with the dog. The principal and his wife don't like how it tries to come here every chance it gets. We have to stop feeding it.'

Kim admired Kyoungseon's wide forehead over his wife's shoulder, so like that of his mother.

'It only seems like I always feed it because it's always coming here. But I've got to give it something now. The little bastard came into my classroom while I was teaching so I had to give it a whipping.' He felt Blackie's heart beating underneath its fur.

'In your classroom? Here, dog!' His wife holds out a bag of biscuits under its nose. The dog lies down and begins munching on them, its large teeth visible as it gnashes at the treats.

Later, Kim has to slap the dog's behind to urge it to leave, before laying the sleeping Kyoungseon next to him in his room. He feels drowsy.

Such cowardice. You can't even fight for what you want.

He abruptly wakes up when he feels his nose is blocked. Sweat sprouts from his forehead. The worries that had kept him up the night before are repeating themselves in his mind. His head pounds and his lips are parched. He asks his wife for a bowl of cold water and stares at the ceiling after drinking it. The room is filled with a smoke-like darkness. Only the crack above the door has a touch of moonlight seeping through. He hears the sound of his bowl being rinsed and Kyoungseon breathing somewhere in the darkness.

The principal said he would dismiss someone else, so surely he will keep his word. He'll dismiss Mr Oh. We'll know after tomorrow. Our actions this time might give them pause somewhat. The principal wants me to be the one who leaves, but that won't happen, will it? When someone else is being dismissed...

He knows from the stares and whispers of the staff that he, more than the principal, is being criticized. This was why he was thinking of leaving the school, but he also has to think about keeping his family fed, not to mention the matter of how hard it would be to give up something that he has held on to for so long. He could simply turn a blind eye, but not when his unsympathetic colleagues and even his trusted principal were all but begging him to step down.

*

Seven years ago, when Kim had left Seodaemun Prison, he had come to teach at that very school through an introduction made by a friend. There was a rumour of a second deployment to Jiandao at the time, which made even long-time teachers slip away in the middle of the night. The neophyte Kim was left all alone in the school.

Every day another student was arrested, with many others running away as they feared for their lives. Soon, only a little over ten students remained.

Kim was so busy with his teaching that he could barely fit in a meal during the day. Three years passed, and as the situation in the country stabilized, the students and teachers began increasing again. Principal Choi had also come then, and Kim had helped him get settled and operate the school. Seven years of rebuilding the school staff, term after term, had finally culminated in the institution now looking more or less like a proper school. It had communal toilets, plastered walls and paint, a foyer, widened playgrounds, and most recently, a proper gate. Kim could finally kick off his work shoes and wear a proper suit.

The glimmer of greed Professor Choi had always shown was now in full bloom with the new order taking over the country, and not every student felt comfortable about this. Kim kept giving up one thing after another to Principal Choi. This was due to the weakness in his personality, no doubt, but it was also because of his losing a sense of purpose in the new national situation.

After dinner, Kim goes to visit Principal Choi. The man's firm answer that afternoon had been a relief, but he wants to make sure that Choi will keep his word.

The early autumn air should be as refreshing as a cold splash of water, but its effects do not sink past Kim's skin. The crescent moon seems desperate, unable to decide whether to come or go, wandering alone in the great plain of the sky. It feels as if his food is stuck in his throat. He thinks about going down to the banks of the Hailan River for a while but decides against it.

When he passes the school, his footsteps turn towards the school grounds of their own accord. He grips the school gate. It feels smooth, and its paint smells fresh. He strokes it. Heat fills his palm. For seven years he had yearned to make this gate. Wherever he saw a grand gate, he would think of how the school would also one day have one. His dream had been realized only two months ago. Every free moment he had at school, he used to run out to the Chinese builder they had hired, supervising and nagging until the builder shook his head and said, 'I can't do this work anymore. I've done many jobs, but I've never met anyone like you!'

But Kim is not a brave man! Of course, the current state of the country is also to blame, but it is, in the end, his own weakness that is being exploited. His beloved school is being wrested from him. He looks down at himself, this pathetic slip of a man who will barely be able to afford a meal once he leaves this school. He lays his face against the railing of the gate before stepping on to the grounds. He can see the orange, prickly light of the night-watch office. The school grounds seem to undulate like vast, dark waves. The two-storey school building, rising in the darkness! He has touched every inch of it.

Five years ago, a morning when an endless spring rain had fallen, Kim had arrived to see the ceiling of his classroom leaking and his students standing sullenly in a corner. Kim gave a passionate speech about their education, trying to lift their spirits. Just then, the skies cleared, and he decided they should immediately fix the roof. He rolled up his sleeves and gave each of them a job to do.

They dug up some clay, propped a ladder against the roof, and Kim and the older students climbed up to the top while the younger students relayed the clay to them.

His foot between the roof tiles, Kim took each bit of clay and moulded it in between the tiles, directing the students from his vantage point. His eyes were afire with enthusiasm, and the head on his hair, which never in his life learned to lie flat, stretched up in all directions, his mouth unceasing in barking his orders. There was only one teacher, but it felt like there were several, and the class was so productive they finished by three. The roof tiles were laid in place once more, and the students sang the school song as they ran about in the rain. What days they used to have.

Now, the moonlight is so strong that it almost seems to make a metallic sound as it rolls off the galvanized iron roof. He sighs, relieved, for it occurs to him that no matter what others may say, at least he has accomplished this much in his life.

May 1938

BREAK THE STRINGS

The ship *Yeong Deokhwan* shuttling to Jinnampo Pier in Incheon leaves behind the lonely island of Girin as it sails, unspooling a long plume of black smoke. Extending like fingers through the tangles of clouds in the eastern sky, the red sunbeams roll back the ominous fog that screened off the faraway mountains, and the blue revealed above is enough to make the heaviest heart feel lighter. Like the heart of a slave freed from servitude ...

The white and red sails touching the sky beyond the watery horizon seem lost and alone like a pine tree clinging to a windy cliff. The waves relentlessly crash against the rocks. Again ... and again ... like humanity's very struggle for survival ...

*

Hyoungchul, who was going home for the summer holidays, leaned against the railing as he looked towards the horizon. The ship passed Mahap Island and turned its bow towards Bultasan Mountain, which peeked behind Gumipo Pier. A moment ago the ship had been quiet with its every passenger seemingly still asleep. Now he saw one or two early risers coming out on deck, toothbrushes in their mouths.

A few members of the crew were still curled asleep on the deck, caps drawn over their weary faces. Hyoungchul felt the surge of an unfamiliar emotion as he walked the deck and came down the stairs to third class. Hyegyoung, whom he was travelling with, had suffered seasickness all through the night but seemed to have adapted a little as she sat with her head leaning against the trunk they had brought on board. Hyoungchul sat by her and tried to read, but he could not concentrate. His gaze kept moving towards Hyegyoung. The strands of black hair scattered over her red cheeks and the voluptuous line of her body flowing from behind her dainty ears and past her narrow waist had an absolutely powerful effect that made men tremble.

The sound of the foghorn, loud enough to shake heaven and earth and Hyoungchul's very heart, gathered him from the dreamy maze he had been wandering in and reminded him of what he needed to do.

'Ah! We've reached Gumipo Harbour. We should be getting off here.' His shaky voice formed the words as he quickly stood up with Hyegyoung's luggage in hand.

'Really? Already?' Hyegyoung deftly wound the errant strands of her hair with her little finger and tucked them in with the help of a mirror. Hyoungchul moved the luggage across the deck.

The beach at Gumipo is one of the most beautiful in the East, with five to six hundred American missionaries visiting it every summer. Hyoungchul's family had built a house a little further up the mountain, in a town called Bongnae which had about two hundred new residences. They had a view of the endless Yellow Sea to the front and of the twisting Bultasan Mountain behind.

Hyoungchul and Hyegyoung got on a boat and left the

ship behind. An American flag flew high above the town of Bongnae as they made their way across the rough waters.

I am a pitiful son of Korea, you a pitiful daughter of Korea ... Filled with such thoughts, Hyoungchul gazed surreptitiously at Hyegyoung. His eyes welled up, blurring his sight.

*

One day, Hyoungchul stretched out on the beach after a swim and caught his breath. Whenever he came home for the holidays, he loved to breathe the fresh air coming in from across the water and feel the sunlight bouncing off the waves as he played in the sea. He could see the red roofs and grey walls of Western-style houses through the rich, green canopies of the well-tended trees, the perfect line of the horizon stretching to his right. A seagull flew by ... and another ... White sails disappeared behind an island. Hyoungchul felt as if his mind had left his body and become one with the universe. He himself knew not, in that moment, where he wandered in the cosmos ...

'Big Brother!'

He turned. Hyegyoung stood there holding hands with his younger sister Eunsook. Amused, Hyoungchul got up and walked towards them. Hyegyoung grinned as she coyly turned her waist. She manoeuvred her parasol to half-cover her body.

'Big Brother! Look at this flower!' Eunsook blinked her large eyes as she extended her small, pretty hand towards him. The sea breeze whipped through Eunsook's hair and threw ripples into Hyegyoung's skirt. Hyoungchul brought the flower up to his nose.

'Good weather we're having today,' he said to Hyegyoung.

'Yes! I was feeling a bit bored, so I brought Eunsook out to enjoy it.' Hyegyoung, as if she felt guilty about something, suddenly blushed.

'I'm glad you did. There isn't too much wind today, and the waves aren't too choppy. Let's go boating!'

He bravely bolted for the beach, looking back to see if they followed ...

Hyoungchul wore a bathing suit, and his face and arms were well-tanned. His chest was wide and solid enough to want to lean on. His occasional smile revealed white teeth between dark lips, the smile of a warrior, irrefutably masculine. Hyegyoung gave Eunsook a smile and slowly followed him – stepping on the very footsteps Hyoungchul had left in the sand – with her hand firmly holding the little girl's.

Hyoungchul's muscular arms, the roll of the boat on the waves ... They sailed out into the sea, a hull loaded with love and happiness. When the boat bounced on an occasional wave, they looked at each other and shared a smile. This was the happiest they had ever felt, a youthful joy that could never come again. *But we cannot forget that we can't enjoy even this bit of pleasure*, thought Hyoungchul. With this realization the bitterness and suffering of love cut through the surf and froth of its pleasures.

'Look at that bird!'

Eunsook, ever young and innocent, pointed at a bird flying close to the water. Hyoungchul adored and envied her guilelessness. He and Hyegyoung had never mentioned love to each other out loud, but both had thought of it as they proceeded with their studies in Seoul. With each passing day, their thoughts had deepened, and their feelings towards each other had grown warmer. The red sun had already left behind its redness in the sky as it dipped below the western mountains, colouring the clouds light pink and turning the ocean red. Their love burned as strong as ever, as unaltered as the fading islands were in the dying light. They tied up their boat to a pier and walked the path carpeted with pine needles towards a millet field. The evening smoke coming from a lone hut on the mountain path wound through the trees and into the valley. They heard the unexpected, tragic sound of a farmer's lament as he toiled in the fields.

Why were you born, why were you born
Why were you so frugally born
Dragging my hobo's shoes
I shall follow my longed-for lover

It was a peaceful song, sung by someone who had sweat blood over their fields all day long. The farmer's crops crept up into the sky; it would be a good harvest this year.

But this crop that the farmer had devoted their life to would be stolen come autumn, and there would hardly be a spoonful of millet for the family. They were like cows at a ranch. Like sheep. Like pigs. They lived to be exploited by the richer class. They lived to provide fur, milk, and meat. How were they different from cows, sheep, and pigs that lived to provide their owners with their work, fur, milk, and meat?

Hyoungchul said as much to Hyegyoung. He ended his speech with, 'And so, Miss Hyegyoung, I plan to quit college!'

'But why? Don't you think we need to learn more?' A determined glint came into Hyegyoung's pretty eyes, urging Hyoungchul to answer her question.

'We do. But how many of our folk have graduated college? How many of them are as ignorant as babies? I've come to realize that I cannot lead them with theories made by a small elite with heroic aspirations.' His voice got louder as he became more heated. 'What use is Marx and what use is Lenin? Our struggles have long surpassed their theories. The masses are twisting their intestines with their bare hands to stave off hunger. Their struggle should be our struggle. I feel the need to fight alongside them, more and more with each passing day.'

The three reached Songcheon as they conversed. A lonesome church bell sounded through the encroaching darkness.

Hyegyoung lowered her head and sent up a ritual prayer. The lights in the windows of the houses around them became more vivid with each moment.

They said their goodbyes and walked to their respective homes.

*

The summer holidays ended, and Hyoungchul and Hyegyoung went back to Seoul. The city was already cooling with the first hints of autumn; the chill of the evenings gave a clearer impression of the season. Hyoungchul struggled in his heart. After classes, he would wander towards the fields of Cheong-nyangni. He stared at the wild chrysanthemums by his feet, picked a few to give them a closer look, then crushed and tossed them away as if in anger. Then, he would walk again.

He was not thinking of Hyegyoung so much as worrying about what do to with his life. We each receive a speck of life somewhere on the edge of the vastness of the universe. Was each speck not the same as any other, be the person poor or deformed? What was he doing learning the law? Even if he could pass the bar exam and become a high official, what was so honourable or joyful about that? If anything, it would be a shame. What if he were to become an advocate? Defend the rights of a brave, condemned activist. What power would his advocacy truly have? He could become a rich businessman. This was impossible, but even if it were not, what then? He would only feel guilty towards his poor brethren.

He had to be brave for the sake of society. He had to use his life for meaning and beauty. That was the only way to be human. But ... wait a minute. Did he have the courage to live such a life? Or the necessary preparation for it? He was standing at a crossroads. Should he go right, or should he turn left? The setting sun urged him to make a decision.

Hyoungchul had no choice but to struggle with such thoughts. His head filled with ever more questions.

That night, he turned off his electric light to go to sleep. The soft moonlight found him as he lay his head on the pillow. For the past few nights he could not sleep because of his worries. They still tortured him every waking moment, so he was trying to sleep a bit earlier, to give his mind a rest. But all his nerves rebelled against peace. Sighing, he got up again. Shadows danced against his window in the autumn wind. Leaves fell. He took up his mandolin, usually a good friend in moments like these. His hands danced automatically up and down the strings. But not even this was enough to assuage the deep sadness in his heart. He pushed his mandolin into a corner and threw his blanket over his head. He tried counting ... one, two, three, four, five ... He eventually reached five thousand, but it did not help at all.

The next morning, his head felt heavy on his shoulders. His eyes were bloodshot in the mirror, and his face was paper white. He pushed away his breakfast and was about to step out of the house when a phalanx of Japanese troops, bayonets at the ready, marched by his path. Soldiering: the work of a true man. How brave they seemed! It must be training day. They streamed past him. Even the Japanese beggar digging through the trashcan at the end of the street smiled at them as they went by. That was it! He, too, could affix a bayonet to the end of a rifle and be another soldier, marching ... But that would only lead to being made fun of for his empty courage. How sad their lives were! Pedestrians glanced at Hyoungchul as they passed. Hyoungchul stood in the middle of the street, tilting his head this way and that, lost in thought. Then, as if coming to a conclusion, he nodded firmly and walked on. He almost seemed crazy.

Then one day, after school, he had come back to the boarding house to find an envelope on his desk. It was a letter from home. Glad for some news, he ripped the seal and began to read. He was in for a shock.

His family consisted of his parents, his sister Eunsook, and himself. They owned their own land and lived fairly well in their village. But his father had not expected his only son's education to cost so much. Their debt had mounted, and the worsening economy had hit crop prices hard. His father was no longer able to shoulder the debt. Being a man of a somewhat rushed disposition, he was determined to leave their old village and move in with a relative in Yeonggotap in Manchuria. The letter was to order Hyoungchul home before they left.

His father had spared him the prospect of their ruin until now because he had not wanted to distract Hyoungchul in his studies. Hyoungchul read the letter again and again, but it was unmistakable that he was being asked home.

He stood for a long time gripping the letter until his eyes began to shine with a determination close to rage.

'Good. I'm glad this happened. I can at last find my own way. I should've found it long ago ... I was weak, and I hadn't the courage to make my own way. Until now!'

His hands curled into fists as he shouted this into the air. He threw the letter down on the desk.

The wind rattling the windows tossed snow on the paper of the lattice. All that could be heard was the second hand of the clock ...

*

The street lamps shining on the wide lawn before the Shinto shrine by Namsan Mountain somehow made the winter seem more desolate. The snowflakes blowing into the spread of light from the lamps were like mayflies racing against each other towards their doom. Hyoungchul and Hyegyoung dragged their long shadows over the snow as they slowly walked down the stairs towards Namdaemun. The colourful, crowded angles of the modern buildings that surround the mountain attested to Seoul's position as a major metropolis. The massive white rock face of Bugaksan Mountain on the other side of the city showed its large form through the darkness. But around Bugaksan Mountain were only wide empty spaces, with occasional fires accentuating the melancholy emptiness.

Hyoungchul and Hyegyoung stopped in their tracks.

'Miss Hyegyoung! Thank you for coming all this way for me despite the cold. You must return to your dormitory before it gets too late.'

Hyegyoung only replied, 'No,' before bowing her head.

Hyoungchul looked at her and sighed. 'I cannot stay in our country any longer. But you must stay here and guard the future of our nation. Never let go of your duty. This is the final favour I ask of you.'

Hyoungchul stared into the cityscape and thought he saw the shape of the Korean peninsula wavering in the lights of Seoul. There was a brief silence, interrupted by the sound of taxis and trams.

Hyegyoung raised her head and said in a firm voice, 'I shall go with you.'

Hyoungchul could not believe his ears. All he could feel was a swell in his heart. Hyegyoung's tears made two tracks down her beautiful face. They kept flowing and flowing. He went towards her and gently, daringly, rested his hands on her shoulders.

'I see you were a woman all this time! You've only ever treated me as a friend! But I see ... I see now ...'

'Yes! I am your eternal friend. And I also wish to be your wife.'

'Is that so? I thought the fire of love burned only in my own heart!' Hyoungchul added in a trembling voice, 'But you must not marry someone of such misfortune.'

'What kind of fortune can people like us possibly have? And I am not the kind of person who chases after happiness.' Hyegyeong, having revealed her heart, did not hesitate in her answer.

'But not everything can be overcome by sheer will alone. I do not have the wherewithal to take you with me, and you do not have the wherewithal to follow. You must continue to concentrate on your studies and become a good mother and a diligent worker. I will take your words just now as a consolation in the face of our goodbyes.'

Their words turned into white mist in the cold. They started walking again and passed Namdaemun, eventually reaching Seoul Station. The express train coming up from the south slid along the rails before screeching to a stop by their platform.

Hyoungchul slid open the window decorated with blossoms of frost and leaned outward. Hyegyoung stood on the platform. They stared at each other, unable to speak save for the occasional sigh … A lamentation, no doubt, of the fact that they would never see each other again.

With the sound of a whistle, the wheels began moving. Hyoungchul and Hyegyoung grasped each other's hands before letting go.

'Goodbye!'

'Farewell!'

Through the window of the train flashed past a dozing man, a traveller eating something, another reading the paper, and someone looking out the station window, each scene accompanied by a whiff of something rotten puffing under Hyoungchul's nose.

Hyegyoung had gone after the train but then stood still. Hyoungchul's face disappeared into the dark, and soon, so did the rear lights of the last carriage. She felt all the blood in her body flow to her head. Her knees felt so weak she thought she would faint. Barely managing to stay on her feet, she only then realized that her face was red and that tears were blurring her vision. The streetlights had long tails and everyone that passed her looked like large, shapeless lumps … Seoul without Hyoungchul was a meaningless city to her.

Into her life, once golden with the summer of youth, now fell the first snow of winter.

Hyoungchul's family of four left for Manchuria. The snow that fell the night before blanketed the whole world white. Clumps of snow dropped from bare branches. Sunlight reflected on the white snow with an intensity that pierced the eye. A pair of crows living in the distant hills flew over their heads, looking for food.

It was 130 *li* from Songcheon to Sugyo Station, where their train departed. Ox-drawn barrows would take them there. They were too ashamed to leave in broad daylight, so they prepared to disappear in the night. There were two barrows, with one to carry some of their furniture and the other carrying the family with the rest of their luggage arranged into the shape of a house. Hyoungchul stared at the two barrows with bitterness in his heart. The image of Hyegyeong's face flitted past his mind's eye. Would he ever see the beautiful sight of his beloved homeland again? Hyoungchul played the mandolin as he looked towards the red sunset over the western mountains. Black smoke crept up from the chimneys of the nearby huts covered in white snow.

Hyoungchul's family got on the barrow and left two wheel tracks behind them, as well as Songcheon. The wind whipped up the fallen snow. Darkness surrounded them. The only thing they could see was the occasional lit window of a house, the cold stars that shone in the dark sky ... One of the stars disappeared, dragging a long train. The distant barking of a dog made it all the more bleak.

Hyoungchul lay sideways, trying to calm his complicated thoughts. His father smoked one cigarette after another. His mother and Eunsook sat in silence. They could only hear the clunky sound of the wheels turning, their bodies swaying left and right to the rhythm.

The roosters began crowing by the time the barrow rolled by Jangyeon Village. The houses along the road were deathly quiet. Not a soul was about. *They say the world is wide, but there is no place in it for my family to rest.* Hyoungchul's heart sank. They passed the village and went down another quiet road.

Hyoungchul, without realizing it, had taken out his mandolin. He turned to Eunsook.

'Eunsook, dear! Would you sing for us? A happy song. No sad songs ... Do sing us a happy tune!'

Eunsook, innocent and pure, opened her lovely mouth and began to sing. Hyoungchul's fingers danced across the mandolin strings.

> *Oh, my brother! Mother is crying*
> *She pats my head as she cries*
> *The money we gathered until our fingers bled*
> *The suited man stole it from us*
> *Oh, my brother! Mother is crying*
> *She pats my head as she cries*
> *The harvest we gathered eating bean paste and millet-rice*
> *The bearded old man stole it from us*

Before Eunsook could even finish singing, Hyoungchul threw his mandolin aside. It smashed to pieces. Eunsook, surprised, opened her eyes wide and huddled close to her mother.

'Why did I bring that damn thing with me!' he shouted as he shook his fist. 'What good can it do me now? This isn't the time for my hands to be dancing. All I have left is to go forward!'

The cold dawn wind sank into his bones. The red sun began rising in the east.

*

(Last summer, Hyoungchul was shot dead in XX and Hyegyoung, due to her involvement in the XX Incident, is currently serving time at XX Prison.)

January–February 1931

THE FIRING

The master flung open the door to the main room.

'Can't you hear me calling for you? Come!'

Kim jumped, almost dropping the rope he was twisting from millet stalks.

'Hurry!'

Kim scrambled to his feet. He wondered what the master was going to scold him for this time. His heart pounded as he anxiously made his way to his master's side of the courtyard. The lights in the main room were so bright that they stung his eyes.

'Sit there.'

Kim crouched down where he was told. His master stared for a moment at the bits of millet stalk in his hair and said, 'I summoned you to tell you that I've sold the field out front.'

The only words Kim understood immediately were 'the field out front.' He quickly looked up. The master did not look like he was joking.

'Don't go thinking that I really want to sell,' said the master, 'but we need the money, and I had no choice.'

Four years ago, the master had run for village mayor and

used that land as collateral to raise campaign funds. He thought he would easily get his land back once he won, but there were further expenses as mayor that he had not foreseen. The interest became too much, and he decided to sell the land before he fell in danger of losing it outright.

The explanation made sense, but Kim felt dizzy nonetheless, as if he were falling down a ravine that was a thousand *li* deep. He lowered his head.

*

Kim had lost his parents at an early age and gone begging from one village to the next until the master's father, the old master Park, had brought him into the house as a servant. He was put to work in the fields. Each harvest was better than the last, and Kim had cultivated the ever-expanding fields with more dedication and fervour, forgetting that the land did not belong to him. Soon, Park became the richest man in Shinhwa Village.

'You aren't my servant, you are my son. You are a foundation stone of my house. What would become of me without you? Once I have enough money, I'll get you a wife, a house, and a living.'

The old master Park would say this to him time and again, moving Kim to tears. Kim worked tirelessly for Park and now his son, never taking a day off the whole time he lived under their roof.

'I know you're disappointed,' said the young master in the present, his voice becoming thinner and thinner, 'but this is the situation, and there's nothing to be done.'

He hated having to take this pleading tone, hated Kim's dazed expression. He pretended he had not seen anything and brought his pipe to his lips, striking a pose that he fancied as dignified and mayoral.

'We can't farm like we used to,' he said, 'so you need to find other means of employment, I should think.'

Never let Kim go. If you do, our house will go to ruin.

His father's words, uttered on his deathbed, brought on a prickling of guilt in his heart. He glanced at Kim. A skull for a face! He would be nothing more than a corpse soon enough. Kim's coughs sounded like that of a dying man's. His hacking was so loud that it made the walls of the house shudder, much to his master's distaste. This abhorrent coughing was acutely embarrassing when he had visitors over from the larger district. It made him want to banish Kim on the spot.

For a moment, Kim was silent from the shock of this wholly unexpected news. There was a burnt spot on the woven cushion he sat on, perhaps from fallen pipe ash, and he rubbed it absently with his thumb. He had a pile of straw in his room that he needed to weave into cushions like this one. His head and hands were acting as if they were of different minds; he forced himself back into the present.

'Master!' he blurted out.

The master raised his head. Tears dropped from Kim's eyes.

'Well … say something!' urged the master after a long pause.

Kim realized that the man who sat before him was not the master of old he had called out to. This was only that master's son, the one who was pushing him out. Kim lowered his head again and rubbed the burnt spot. The hardened, cracked skin of his thumb showed clearly in the brightness of the oil lamp.

The master took out a five won bill from his wallet and pushed it before Kim.

'Look. Here is some money for your troubles. There's lots of work this time of year so you'd better hurry and find a good position before it's too late. That's all – I have guests coming.' The master, not wanting to sit with Kim for another minute, got to his feet. He was ecstatic at the thought of being freed from Kim's hacking cough.

Kim left the room in a daze and returned to his chamber. He fell upon the pile of straw.

A while later, he was surprised when the master's daughter, Okseon, slid open the door to his room.

'Kim! Mother wants you to come and light the fire. Hurry up!' She jumped up and down like a little bird and skipped into the room. 'Oh! Good heavens, you're slow. Come on, Kim, come on. What is this smell? Did you go to the bathroom in here?' She laughed and dramatically sniffed air a few times more before running out of the room.

Kim wearily got to his feet, took a handful of kindling from the firewood pile, and went into the kitchen. It was dimly lit, and the brass tableware piled up on a shelf gleamed and blinked like starlight. The smell of garlic wafted from every movement of the master's wife's apron as she moved busily about.

'Light the fire for me.'

Her head gave off a whiff of camellia oil. He crouched down before the furnace to light the fire and thought about what his master had just told him. Everything was too dreamlike, too unreal. His thoughts were too quick, much like the sparks that grew into a fire in the mouth of a furnace.

'Kim, what's wrong with you?' asked the master's wife. 'Are you ill?'

Kim realized the furnace was still dark and he had not put in any of the kindling.

'If you're sick, go lie down. The district errand boy will come soon, I'll ask him for help. Come on, get up.'

Kim got up and went out. The frosty wind cooled his head a little. He sank down in the corner of the yard. He had to leave? Could this really be happening? Or was the master drunk?

He heard the frantic clucking of hens. Which hen were they sacrificing for that night's party?

He knew each and every chicken they owned. In the morning, he brought out their meal in a gourd and sprinkled it on the flagstones as hens, roosters, and chicks came running towards him, necks stretched out. His heart would swell with pride to see them flock around him as they pecked at the feed. Were any of them hurt? Had any of them been snatched into the air by a black kite in the night? When he saw any were missing, he called out, '*Gururu, gururu*,' to summon the stragglers. But lately, the district errand boy kept having to kill hens for the master's frequent parties, and whenever Kim realized this had happened, he would break off his call and feel a jolt of sadness through him that settled into his very bones. The trusting eyes of the hens, his *gururu* sound that only they seemed to understand! The more the master killed for his parties, the more Kim hated him in a corner of his heart.

Kim got to eat chicken on special occasions when his old master was alive, but ever since his son had taken over, he had not received so much as a drumstick despite the large flock they owned. The new master was more than willing to kill two or three whenever there were guests, not to mention sending some off to people placed higher in the administration, and now the perch in the chicken coop was almost bare.

He began to shiver from the cold. He looked up and saw he had walked up to the shed while lost in his thoughts. There was a hoe in there that was dull, it needed to be sharpened or replaced before it could be used again. Sharpened or replaced. He had thought of asking the master for some money to replace it but had not quite got around to it.

But if he were really being dismissed, then this past summer would be the last time he would ever use the hoe.

'Sell the field?' he muttered. 'Who are you to sell the field?'

There was nowhere for him to plead his case despite his heart being ripped from his body. He could not stand still anymore. He paced. He heard a voice coming from the master bedroom.

'Heavenly Father, you who knows all and sees all, please bring good fortune on to the mayor's house. Please let the mayor see the error of his ways and be a true worker for God and let the whole household unite as one family under your name ...'

He surmised that the pastor was in the master bedroom with the master's wife, separate from the party. The master's wife was crazy with Jesus lately and frequently invited the pastor for large meals, whereupon the pastor would bestow prayers like this one. Kim hated the tone of the pastor's fervent pleading. He walked away.

This house will fall. The old master would have seen that. He missed the old master, who at least would have understood a tenth of what he felt.

He passed the kitchen and came to his room but did not feel like going in. He went out into the clearing outside the gate. The shadows of bare branches crisscrossed the clearing. Insects sang duets, the songs starting and stopping in pairs. He stood by a tree and crossed his arms.

Where am I supposed to go? Jiandao, where Dog Poo's father went? This master is a bastard. He thinks nothing of his father!

As if the master was in front of him, he shouted out, 'You bastard!'

The field! The stacks of straw from the rice and millet! The sight of the bound stacks was enough to make him cry, he could barely look at them. How difficult the crops had been that year!

'You bastard, this isn't right, I was the one who kept your household fed. You have lived to this day on the crops I raised with my own hands! The heavens will deal with you!'

He felt weighed down as if there were sacks of water around his neck. He paced the field and kicked over the stacks of straw. The savoury scent that rose from the overturned stacks! When he was gone, they would throw these stacks away or sell them as roof thatching. And what care he had taken to select only the good stalks to bind into stacks. He could have spent that winter weaving good sandals and cushions from them, soaking the straw in water so it would be soft and pliant in his hands.

His throat constricted as he called out, 'Master!'

The only answer was the rustling of the stacks. He grabbed a fistful of the straw and stood up. The field that spread before him, the field that seemed to embrace the moonlight in its sleep! He wanted to run to it. He had thought the field would always be waiting for him. The sound of the stream flowing by it, the two large rocks at the border ... His old master and he had sat many times on those rocks, talking of this and that, building trust and affection. How many times had they sat there eating lunch, how many times had they smoked as his master encouraged him in his work?

But looking back on it now, his old master had been lying to him the whole time. How many of his promises had he really kept?

This question was like a bolt of lightning in his head. He realized he had lived the past fifty years drunk on the old master's lies. What a waste of his own life!

'Fine, if you tell me to leave, I'll leave. I'll find some other place to live. Bastards!'

He thought of the words the old master had babbled from that hateful mouth. If he were right next to him, he would have slapped him and shouted, *'You worthless rubbish!'*

And what had the old master said when Kim was exhausted from clearing the field of rocks? He had lain next to the stream as the old master had encouraged him with false hopes of helping him make a family and giving him a house of his own. He had been so moved by what his master had promised that he had raised himself up again on his tired knees and continued to haul those rocks. He had run a fever that night and his knee had hurt so much he could hardly sleep, but he got up again the next morning and continued on with clearing that field. All day long, no less. Was that field not cleared by him and him alone?

He shouted into the night, 'You bastard, you talked and talked but you didn't give me so much as a handful of that land when you died! You rotten bastard, you're even worse than your son!'

He shook with rage. There was still a party going on in the main room. He could see by the shadows thrown against the paper screen of the doors that they were dancing inside. He could not stand to be in that house for another minute. He went to his room to pack his things. It was dark and filled with the scent of the dried straw scattered about the floor. He grabbed a box in the corner of the room, tied a bundle of his clothes with rope, tossed it in, and fastened the box to himself with the rope so that he could carry it on his back. He prodded around for his pipe and walked out of the house.

'Who is that!'

Kim turned around in the dark. He could just make out that the speaker was the errand boy, urinating by the field.

'Who is that! Show yourself, bastard!' the boy shouted again.

The cheek of him! Kim was fired up with all the rage in the world, which overwhelmed whatever sense he had left. 'How dare that bastard sell my field!'

He ran to the errand boy and slapped him hard across the face.

'Look at this bastard!' The errand boy jumped on him.

The merry party of drink and dancing continued in the main hall.

March 1935

VEGETABLE PATCH

Subang woke up to the sound of murmurs. She listened closely; her father and mother seemed to be worrying about the household finances. Her eyes slowly closed again, but they opened suddenly at the sound of the wind. She stared at the door.

That wind! What will it do to us?

She thought of the countless apples and peaches that must have fallen in the night. But this made her strangely happy. At least she would be able to have her fill of the fruit that was not ripe.

'All the fruit will fall from that wind ...' she heard her father say in the other room.

'That is exactly right,' said her mother. 'The money the fruit will bring in won't be enough, and the vegetables aren't any better. We need to dismiss some of our workers.'

'I thought of that, too. But cabbage season is coming. So ...'

'So, what? Use them for cabbage season, then dismiss them.'

'Should I?'

'Do it.'

Sleep fled from Subang altogether. Who were they going to

dismiss? Mr Meng? Mr Chu? Who would it be? She listened hard but all she could hear was the even breathing of them sleeping.

*

'Subang, come make breakfast!'

Subang woke with a start at her mother's summons. She found that she had fallen asleep with one hand on the door.

'That lazy girl! Does she need a good whipping if we're to see her face this morning?'

Now she simply had to get up. She rubbed her drowsy eyes and reluctantly pulled herself out of bed.

A fresh breeze shook the fringe of her hair. It made her wake up in earnest. She looked up at the sky.

When will I ever get to sleep as long as I want?

The sky was still dark except for a pewter light rising in the east. She stared at it for a minute and glanced at the kitchen door. Standing outside like this was not scary, but the kitchen frightened her this morning. She looked towards the workers' quarters and back to the kitchen door. She wished everyone would wake up soon.

She jumped at the sound of the gourd cup splashing in the well. A cigarette was also being lit in the dark.

'Who's there?'

'Me.'

It was Mr Meng's voice. She ran towards him.

'Mr Meng, light the fire in the kitchen for me.'

Mr Meng drank his water and went towards the kitchen. The door creaked open. Subang followed him up to the threshold and hesitated before the smoky darkness of the interior. What if there was something in there?

She heard a match being struck and saw Mr Meng's thick arm place the celadon lamp on its wooden stand.

He turned to her and smiled. 'All right, then. Now that I've done something for you, you must do something for me.'

She smiled back. 'That business again?'

'Yes, indeed.'

'The mistress has to say yes, first.' Then she remembered what she had overheard the night before. She stole a look in the direction of the master bedroom and bowed her head. 'Actually, Mr Meng ...'

Mr Meng sensed she was about to tell him a secret. He took a step closer to her. Instinctively, he knew she was about to say something about the mistress.

'Actually ... I'll tell you later.' Subang peeked up at him.

Mr Meng smiled more widely and left her in the kitchen. Subang watched him walk into the darkness and thought how it was not necessarily him who would be dismissed. It could always be someone else.

She heard the sound of the gourd cup splashing again. She turned her back to the sound of the accompanying murmurs and went to the opening of the furnace where a wisp of black smoke was escaping into the kitchen. She washed the iron rice pot that was installed above the furnace opening.

The mistress is a bad person ...

Only when the rice began to boil did her mother drowsily leave her room. Subang stood to attention and wondered what she would be scolded for this morning.

Her mother yawned loudly and trudged towards her. 'What vegetables did you do?'

'Leeks, ma'am.'

'Did you use too much oil?'

'I didn't.'

Her mother gave her a look. She turned and went out the door. Only then did Subang look up.

Her mother's glittering earrings! They flashed their menacing light with her every step. She could barely breathe until that telltale glitter was out of sight. Sighing, she touched her own earlobes where she, too, wore a pair of earrings, given to her by her mother. She hated them and made a face whenever she looked in the mirror. Once, when she was younger, she had taken them off. After the slap and the scolding she received for it, she dared not do it again.

She heard her mother yawning once more. Grey light tinted the grape vines outside the kitchen door. She put out the fire and stood up, wondering if any grapes had been knocked down as well. It was still too dark to tell.

She was too scared of her mother to venture out. She could not stop thinking of the grapes, though. A little while later, when there was more light, she saw that not a single grape had fallen from the vine. She comforted herself with the thought that maybe more of the apples and peaches would have fallen.

The sun began to rise once she had served breakfast and finished washing the dishes. She scraped together her own meal, picked up a basket, and went out to the vegetable patch. Her brother Wubang came bounding up towards her.

'Did any peaches fall?' Subang asked Wubang.

'None here. Maybe some did on the other side.'

Mr Meng, who was nearby, said, 'The mistress gathered them all up. She's going to sell them cheap to the servants.'

Wubang nodded and went to the house. Subang watched him go. Wubang would get to eat peaches, then. Subang felt her heart, which had been anxious for fruit all morning, sink into sadness and pain. Mr Meng held his hoe high up before plunging it into the earth. When he lifted it, a great haul of potatoes followed, tumbling out of the dirt.

Subang picked one of the potatoes up. 'Oh Mr Meng, look at these!'

'Aren't they beauties?'

Subang nodded. Mr Meng admired the fringe that came down to her long lashes and thought how good it would be to find a woman someday and get married.

A pungent smell made Subang turn to see Mr Chu and some other workers come out with buckets of manure to lay on the field. She blushed, thinking of the thing that she had tried to forget for a moment. But she still could not bring herself to talk to Mr Meng about it.

She also wondered what her mother or father would think if they knew she knew. Not sure of what to do, she hung her head.

The sound of cicadas echoed in the air. Then, she happened to spot Wubang as he was coming out of the house.

He wore a crisp suit and carried a book bag in one hand, a peach in the other. Subang watched him for a long time. When her envy made her look down in shame, she saw her old blue dress and felt disgusted with herself. Was this all she would get to wear? Wubang got to wear nice things, as did her mother and father, but she never got anything nice and new. She could feel the tears coming.

'Hey! Pick up some of these potatoes. Look at this one! It's as big as you are.'

Mr Meng pushed it with his hoe, and it rolled to Subang's feet. She quickly picked it up. Her tears suddenly changed to laughter. The potato ought to taste good steamed.

'Are you crying?' asked Mr Meng. He was looking directly at her.

His words almost sent Subang over the edge into tears. She bit her tongue.

Mr Meng remembered what she had said to him that morning and thought she must have received a beating again the night before.

'Did the mistress hit you again?'

She shook her head.

'Then what?'

Subang raised her head. 'Oh, Mr Meng!'

Her tone was so serious that Mr Meng could not reply. He waited, wide-eyed, for her to continue to speak.

'Subang! Pick some chillies!'

Subang jumped at the sound of her mother's voice. She

blushed. Mr Meng did not know what to say. He could only stare at her.

Subang quickly made her way to the chillies in another part of the patch. As she picked them, she kept asking herself whether she should tell him or not. She should not, of course, considering her mother and father. But the secret was a burden that kept making her sad.

What am I going to do about Mr Meng, Mr Chu, Mr Lee, and all the others, all the nice people who know nothing but work, the work that they share with me? How can such people be anything but good? People like my parents, who never get their hands dirty – can we really say they are good people? If all my mother does is lie about and be lazy, how do chillies grow from plants, how do potatoes grow in the earth? Maybe only the people who work are good. But for all this, we don't even get to wear nice clothes ...

Somehow, she had learned to associate good clothes with nobleness and intelligence.

She left the hot sun for the shade of a peach tree. She half-listened to the sound of Mr Meng's digging. When he stopped and did not continue after a long pause, she looked up in his direction.

Are the potatoes all out? Are there a lot of them?

Mr Meng put the potatoes in the basket and hoisted it on to one of his shoulders. He walked towards the house. Subang felt a warm feeling as she watched him. The pile of potatoes, especially, gave her a jolt of indescribable joy.

That's good money once they're sold at market. Father will buy rice and wood with that. And Wubang's suit, and Mother's clothes ... but not my clothes ... Father is a bad man ...

If that money were Mr Meng's or even any of the other workers', she was sure the first thing they would buy would be clothes for her.

She had a moment of doubt. Would they really? Who knew what they really felt?

Then, she remembered that Mr Meng had bought the pin in her hair from his cigarette money that one time. She touched the pin, stroking it gently.

They're not like Mother and Father at all.

Mr Meng walked towards her.

'Mr Meng!'

'You're touching the pin again.' He smiled.

She felt on her fingertips the tiny roundness of the red glass beads of the pin. Tears began to fall from her eyes.

'Mr Meng, you got me this pin. What are you going to get for me next time?'

Mr Meng could not bear the sight of this little girl being so moved over a little pin, one that had only cost a few coins. How she must suffer at the hands of her stepmother! He felt his own tears coming.

'Whatever you want!'

'Really?'

Her little chest heaved with waves of gratitude. Mr Meng saw Subang's eyes were bloodshot.

Then, she came towards him, looked around for a moment, and whispered into his ear. Mr Meng's eyes grew large and rage coloured his cheeks.

He stepped back and thought for a moment. Subang urged him to go away and begged him again and again that he must never tell her mother and father she had told him. She was grimacing, but another part of her felt relief.

The next morning, Mr Meng sat down with Subang's father, Mr Wang, and submitted the following conditions:

> *1. No matter what happens, we cannot be dismissed until spring.*
> *2. Each of us gets a new change of clothing.*

All the workers were ready to quit that day if these conditions were not met.

Mr Wang's eyes grew wide. How could they have known something he had only whispered in his bed? He forced himself to close his eyes and appear calm, but his eyelashes trembled with rage.

'We can't take you at your word,' said Mr Meng, 'so we had this written out for you to press your seal on.'

Mr Meng slid a piece of paper towards him. No matter how hard Mr Wang tried, he could not think of another way other than hiring new people. That would be even more expensive, however, as they were so close to harvest season.

He pressed his seal on the paper.

*

A few days later, Subang was found dead. The pin still glittered in her hair.

September 1933

THE TOURNAMENT

Seungho had fallen asleep before he knew it, but he was soon jolted awake. Was it time? He opened a window and looked out.

The usually busy avenue was calm, and only the electric street lamps shone their long beams through the trees. Seungho rubbed his eyes and ran out of the house.

He walked for a while rubbing his cold cheeks until he realized he was not wearing a hat. He doubled back, put on his hat, and set off again.

When he reached the park, with its poplar trees that grew so tall they pierced the sky, he was worried that Heesook would have been waiting for him a long time. But she was not there, and he felt glad and disappointed at the same time.

He leaned against one of the railings of the pagoda-roofed gazebo and kept looking around him as he did not know from which direction Heesook would appear. He was also nervous that someone might be taking an evening stroll in the park.

The chilly wind blew into the gazebo and made the leaves on the floor tumble about. It made him shiver and think strange, fearful thoughts.

It was already autumn here. They would still be wearing single layers down south, but here the cold penetrated the thick suit jacket he was wearing, down to his trousers. He crossed his arms and wondered how much time he had left as he glanced at his watch. He was suddenly reminded of the watch he had put up at the pawnshop a year ago.

Back then, when schools were turned upside down for questioning, several of his fellow students had been taken to the consular office to be detained. But the days were getting colder and they had entered custody wearing thin clothes, so he managed to get together some money from friends and pawned his watch to buy cotton-padded clothing to send them.

He thought about his schoolmates who were still being held. Were they sleeping in their dark cells right now? Or were they sleepless as they thought of their comrades on the outside? He felt a fire in his heart.

Sighing, he looked down over the railing of the gazebo. The pond shone like glass in the moonlight.

'A moonlit night!' he exclaimed as he looked up.

The few lights that could be glimpsed through the trees reminded him of his classmates scattered throughout the city. But those lights would conquer this park soon. He paced around the gazebo, wondering why Heesook was not showing up.

He heard the faraway sound of a passing carriage, hoofs clopping and bells ringing, and the sound of footsteps a little afterwards. Seungho ducked and looked towards the sound. The figure approaching looked like Heesook. Relieved, he stepped forward.

Heesook paused until she heard Seungho clear his throat. She walked up to him in the gazebo.

'Have you waited long?'

'No.'

Seungho relaxed as he listened to the sound of Heesook's light breathing. They leaned against the railing together.

'Comrade,' said Seungho, 'the reason I asked you to come out here ...'

Heesook raised her head and looked him straight in the eye.

'... is that I thought it would be good to enter our school in the football tournament being sponsored by the XX Committee.'

Heesook seemed to think for a moment before answering, 'But comrade! It's supposedly sponsored by the XX Committee, but in truth, it's supported by all kinds of X in this city.'

'Absolutely!' Seungho replied quickly. 'But even if we play in the tournament, we won't be compromised as long as we are careful. I feel we must participate this time... Since the incident with the arrests last year, the morale in our school has hit rock bottom. Our participation shall not be about winning but to show the world that we are still alive and ready to fight!' Seungho coughed before continuing. 'In these reactionary times, the masses will despair in the face of active suppression by the ruling class. We cannot decrease our activities when the masses need us more than ever.'

Heesook glanced at the moon. How bright that damned moon had been that night, too, when she had to hide so many of her friends during the sweeping arrests! She suddenly thought they were being watched, so she took a quick glance around her.

'You'll need funds to enter. Where will you get the money?'

'Well ... that's the hard part. As you know, the school would never pay for it ... We'll have to take up a collection. We thought of an idea. Some of us will work as day labourers on the Gilhwe Line for the railway corporation!'

Heesook was so moved that she felt her heart would burst. She quickly thought of what she and her comrades could do to raise some money. 'We would like to do something as well.'

'Well. What about ... They say there will be a horse race held along with the football. At the racecourse right next to the football field.'

'And?' Heesook took a step closer, waiting to hear of this opportunity to raise more funds.

'We saw some ads posted about jobs for women clerks. Have you seen them?'

Heesook thought of the racecourse and felt her face blush at the thought. But if her male comrades were willing to become day labourers on the Gilhwe Line, what work could she possibly find to be beneath her!

She looked directly at Seungho again. 'Are you sure of it? If it's true, we female comrades will gladly work there! What exactly do they mean by women clerks?' She giggled, thinking of how they were going to pose as employees in front of all those people. The prospect was both funny and alarming.

Seungho was so grateful that he wanted to squeeze her hand. In that moment, she exuded a strong sense of camaraderie that transcended the fact that he was a man and she a woman.

'It won't be too strenuous. I imagine it's something like making tea and guiding visitors. Tomorrow at the student meeting, let's formally decide on what we're going to do.'

Seungho stood up. Heesook noticed his broad shoulders and felt the strength of his solid determination flowing through him.

'I wonder what time it is?' she wondered aloud, standing up. 'It's probably very late.'

They left the gazebo and entered the dark wood together.

*

A few days later, Heesook and her comrades were hired as temporary women clerks and were put to work in the 'barracks' right on the racecourse selling tickets and serving tea.

They had managed to begin working there with great courage, but carrying a tray of tea things in front of guests was so embarrassing that they blushed so severely they could hardly hold up their heads. They also felt that everyone was looking at them. It was reassuring that the barracks had no windows and one could not see the racecourse. All they had to do was deal with the guests who actually entered.

It was a rare warm spell. It smelled a little of dust and horse dung, carried in from the outside on the shoes of the guests. There were so many people talking at the same time that a large cloud of voices seemed to hover over them. The only distinguishable sound was the occasional crying of a baby, which carried over the other voices like a willow pipe.

The buzzer rang. The guests crowded each other as they tried to buy tickets.

Heesook and her comrades briskly carried their tea trays and went about their work, but their hearts were set on the football field nearby. Did the games begin? Which team were they up against? Had they already suffered a goal scored by the other side? They occasionally tapped their feet, anxious to hear some news.

It was loud outside with the sound of people running back and forth. To Heesook, it sounded like the running of their players on the field. Her heart would skip, and she would stare at the walls for a long time, trying to calm herself down.

She was glad whenever a new customer entered; they might have news of the football. But of the myriad of people who came into the room, not a single person brought up the tournament.

The entrance where they were selling betting tickets was crowded, and the hands of the ticket sellers moved rapidly as the money came pouring in. At the sight of the bills, Heesook felt a greed she had never felt before. Just one of those bundles was enough to buy good football boots and white rice for the entire team! It could mean the difference between winning and losing. Instead, she had seen the pitiful sight of her comrades going to play in worn shoes and on a breakfast of millet. How could they even kick the ball in such a state!

She could almost see for herself the ball being taken from

their possession by stronger players wearing good football boots. She felt ashamed of her own inability to make a difference. She wanted to grab a bill bundle and make a run for it, but that was just a silly fantasy. She sighed.

The buzzer rang again. The sound of hoofs was followed by thunderous cheering. For a moment, it sounded like cheering coming from her comrades on the football field, and her heart soared, her back breaking into a sweat.

'How could they …!'

Heesook looked up at her comrade's exclamation of disgust. Their eyes met for a second and then they each looked away. Tears glistened in their eyes.

The shouting in that room, the bets, the odds, the money that they kept screaming about! It shook the room. Somewhere above them, a ten won bill floated over the crowd. They stared at this scene with hate flaring up inside them.

On the football field, their comrades were trying to bring hope to a world that seemed like it was about to end, a world where the ball, kicked high in the air, eclipsed the very sun, but these people would rather be in here! How little they cared about that ball! They felt like they were a different race. No, they *were* a different race!

Heesook and her comrades spent the day performing anxious, tedious labour, before running out to the field at the end of the day.

They saw an older woman pass by and stopped her.

'What happened at the football tournament? Did the D— school do well?'

The woman looked around them and said, 'They lost! They put up a good fight but kept falling on the field. They probably hadn't had enough to eat. It was too sad to watch. The other team was better fed. They were even eating on the field. But the students, all they had was water. One had a bleeding leg, one had a gash on his forehead …'

The woman frowned and shook her head. She began to cry.

The young students felt the energy drain from them. They stood still, unable to say anything at all.

'You must have relatives in the school. I have no relatives there, but ...' The woman did not finish her sentence. She seemed to be thinking of the bleeding students again. 'You better go, then. Go and comfort them.'

The students were crying so hard that for a while they did not realize that the woman had walked away. When they turned to look back at her, they noticed for the first time how worn her clothes were.

They felt a sudden surge of strength and ran to the football field. Their comrades had already left and formed a parade, headed downtown. They could hear a march being played. Heesook could see Seungho leading the way, carrying a banner. A real parade! The students being followed by the masses!

The D— school banner was blood red in the setting afternoon sun.

December 1933

THE UNDERGROUND VILLAGE

The sun smoulders over the line of the mountains in the west.

Chilsung unsteadily walks past the village, his begging sack slung over his shoulder like always. His shoddy straw hat stings his forehead. It does not stop his flowing sweat or block the dust that rises like unbearable smoke beneath his nose.

'Hey, he's back!'

'Hey!'

Here come the village children with their taunts. *Not these bastards again.* Chilsung quickens his pace, but soon they are tugging at the tails of his tunic.

'Hey, you gonna cry?'

'What did you get this time? Let's see.'

One of them snatches away Chilsung's begging sack as the others clap with glee. Chilsung stands silent and stares at the biggest child in the gang. He knows if he tries to move away or curse aloud, it would only provoke them.

'Look at the fool, all calm and nice!'

The one with the pointy head comes at him with a fresh cowpat at the end of a stick. The others cackle as they scramble to get their own cowpats on sticks to threaten him with. It is too much. Chilsung makes a run for it.

He raises his arms and takes a step, shaking all the while, his head jerking side to side uncontrollably. The children follow him, imitating him. They skip behind him and run in front, blocking his progress and smearing the cowpats on his face.

Chilsung opens his eyes as wide as he can. His lips twitch as they struggle to form words.

'Y-you bastards!'

The children roll on the ground in gales of laughter as they imitate him. 'You bastards! You bastards!'

Chilsung spits as a child brings a cowpat against his lips. He opens his eyes wide again, trying to look as scary as possible.

'Hey, idiot, stop looking at me like that!'

It seems to work. The children retreat. Chilsung rubs his lips with his arm and looks back as they run away. He feels angry and lonely, abandoned by the whole world.

With the children gone, the road stretches on into the gloom before curving a little at a millet field. This will lead to the cool shade of the reeds ... He walks. He shakes off the dung, but some still clings to him and stains his clothes. He stares into the empty horizon as he makes his way. Soon, he reaches the foot of a hill and plops down for a rest.

A breeze meanders through the tall grass. The sound of insects makes him think a stream is nearby. He scratches his matted hair, lost in thought. Long rays of sunlight filter through the woods near the road, and the chirping of birds rings in his ears. *Why was I born a cripple so that even the most worthless of those bastards think they can mock me?* He pulls at a reed growing next to him. A sharp pain jolts through his wrist.

But what about Big Girl? She's blind, but she doesn't complain! And I'm better off than she is. He thinks of Big Girl as he gazes at the delicate hairs on the grains of the grass, soft as a puppy's fur. He slowly remembers her face. *Such lovely closed eyes, I can't stand it!* He squirms with pleasure. He looks at the begging sack next to him. *I better give Big Girl the best thing I got today. But how? Hand it over the fence at night? Big Girl has to come out and stand near it. But someone has to tell her to come out to the yard. Right, I can send in Chilwoon. No, then Big Girl's mother will know, and my mother will know. I'll go during the day when the others are out weeding the fields and hand it over the fence.* Excited, he finds himself standing up again, ready to go.

The sun that almost flayed his skin during the day is now behind the mountains, and the chill of the wind that sweeps through the undulating grass seeps into his bones. He pats his begging sack before slinging it over his shoulder and taking a shaky step.

The vast sky meets the ocean in the distance, and the red remnants of sunset float leisurely across the horizon. Chilsung presses his straw hat down on his head and leaves the bottom of the hill. The smell of cow dung wafts upwards with every step he takes.

After he goes around the hill and comes to his village, his little brother Chilwoon runs out of the village entrance, carrying a baby on his back. 'It's you, Big Brother, I was waiting for you!'

Chilwoon is all smiles as he comes up to Chilsung and grabs at his begging sack, eager to see what he has. 'Did you get some biscuits again?'

'N-no.' Chilsung grips the sack to his chest and takes a step back.

Chilwoon presses up to him. 'Can't I have just one? Please, Big Brother!'

Chilwoon's mouth waters as he holds out a filthy hand towards Chilsung. The baby on his back imitates Chilwoon, stretching out her palms towards Chilsung and looking at him with wide, innocent eyes.

'Hey, s-stop it!' Chilsung turns his back on them.

Chilwoon almost trips as he runs in front of Chilsung. 'Big Brother, Big Brother, just one! Give me one!'

Chilsung gives him his scariest look. Tears glisten in Chilwoon's eyes. 'I'm telling Mother when she gets here! She told me that if I watched the baby while she was out in the fields, you would get candy for me! I'm telling her, I'm telling her what you did!'

Chilwoon wipes his tears with a fist. The baby, not knowing what is going on, opens her mouth and lets out a loud cry. The darkness unfolds around them as Chilwoon, sobbing, runs towards the hill where their mother is working. 'Mother! Mother!'

Chilwoon's shouting prompts the baby to shout along. 'Momma! Momma!'

The echoes from the mountain sound as if their mother really is answering them with a shout of, '*What?*' Chilsung is glad to be rid of Chilwoon and Young-ae for a moment. He continues on his way.

The neighbourhood is so dark that he can barely see in front of him, save the old cypress tree reaching up to the sky as if to touch the stars. He thinks only of how he will see Big Girl, and how he will give her the biscuits he received that day.

'Is that my Chilsung?'

It is his mother's voice. He looks back. He cannot see her face as she approaches him, her back weighed down with kindling, but he can still feel his head being weighed down with shame. He stands up straight.

'Why were you so late today?' She had strained her eyes looking for her son on the way up the mountain from the field. Had he stumbled somewhere and was struggling to get up? Did those horrible children throw stones and kick him again? She had been about to go looking for him. His mother's questions make Chilsung recall being smeared with cowpats. His nose begins to tickle.

The scent of wood hits him as his mother draws closer. She carries the baby around her neck in addition to the burden on her back.

'Mother, he won't give me any biscuits!'

Chilwoon grabs on to her skirt, and she almost falls backwards from the force. She pats the top of his head.

'Th-that little bastard, I'll k-kill you!' Chilsung tries to kick Chilwoon. His mother almost stumbles again as she blocks him.

'Don't be like that. He's had to take care of the little one all day. He's got a nasty heat rash on his waist from carrying her.'

At the end of her lament, his mother sighs. A whiff of cowpat assaults Chilsung's nose, which makes him burst out in anger.

'I-I wasn't just sit-sitting on my ass, either!'

'Chilsung, that wasn't what I meant!' His mother is too overcome with fatigue to continue. They walk on in silence.

When they reach home, they collapse on top of the stack of kindling to rest. Chilsung's mother tries to say something to make her son feel better.

'So many skin rashes this year ... Your hands are shaking.'

She resists the urge to grab those hands as she caresses the baby she is holding and takes out a breast for her to suckle. Little Chilwoon keeps kicking the wood stack, huffing and puffing in anger. Chilsung cannot stand his younger siblings anymore. He stands up. His eyes sweep over the darkness as he thinks, *Big Girl must be over there somewhere.* He goes into the single room of the house in which Chilsung's family all live, sits down on his toe that smarts from having kicked a rock, and empties the contents of his sack. The sound of scattering matches and grain makes his hair stand on end. He quickly runs his hands over the goods. He remembers the money, takes it out, and stares at it in his hand. He can see almost nothing in the dark room, but feels the presence of eyes embedded in the walls.

He divides the matches, rice, and biscuits, and thinks again of Big Girl. *What do I give her? One of these?* He grabs a sweet, and tosses it in his mouth. There is a crunching sound and a sweet burst of saliva. He smacks his lips and freezes again in case Chilwoon is listening.

His hand hurts from gripping the money so hard. He spreads it out and counts it and thinks about how Big Girl would love to have a measure of fabric with this money. His heart races. *Why won't she come to our house? If only she would, I could give her money and these biscuits and anything she asked for. Yes, I would.* The thought makes him sad. He wraps the matches and biscuits and pushes them underneath the folded bedding, adds the money to the stash, and puts only the rice out for his mother. Then he goes up to the back door of the room and peers out at the fence separating his home and Big Girl's.

Bees buzz over the squash vines that twist along the fence. How to meet her? He grabs his toe without thinking and it hurts. The cool wind flows down his cheek. He feels a pain somewhere that is deeper than the hurt in his toe.

'Aren't you going to eat?'

Chilsung gives a start. He realizes his mother is just outside the other door. He feels an inexplicable emptiness in his heart.

'Why did you lock the latch?'

His mother keeps rattling the door. As though asking for biscuits or money. A wave of resentment overtakes him.

'I-I'm not hungry!' His whole body shakes.

'Did you eat something in the market?' Her voice seems far away. She always sounds listless whenever Chilsung is angry at her. 'Eat some more.'

'N-no!' he barks.

His mother mumbles something as she leaves him alone, and it is calm again. Chilsung sits in the dark and keeps thinking about the biscuits he hid underneath the bedding. His hand flips over a corner of the bedding, rewarding him with puffs of stale dust and the sour smell of bedbugs. He turns his back on it, but his hand keeps sweeping over the spot where the biscuits are hidden. *No! I'm giving the biscuits to Big Girl.* He whips his hand away and grips the door handle.

The breeze cools the sweat pouring from his forehead. He throws off his shirt and hugs the wind. He feels so itchy he rubs his body against a wall, which excites him and makes him rub more frantically until he is out of breath and the skin is almost scratched off his back. He stands up.

Now that he is moving, he feels pain in every single part of his body. It feels like his fingertips have been pierced by splinters. His elbows ache, and the toe he hurt earlier throbs more than ever. He tries to ignore the pain as he begins to walk.

Little white flowers blink like starlight on the fence. Their scent excites him as if a girl were standing nearby. He creeps up against the fence.

The scent from a fire burning to repel mosquitoes comes through from Big Girl's side, and he imagines the flickering lights of the little fire as he draws his ear near, the fuzz of the squash vines tickling his cheek. The thought that Big Girl might be doing the same thing on the other side of the fence makes him blush. He stands so long that his clothes are damp with dew, and his eyes are so used to the dark that the white flowers on the fence shout out their white light.

But after a long while, the mosquito fire dies down, and insects buzz incessantly about his head. He goes back inside in frustration.

*

The fields are already full of sunlight when he wakes up the next morning.

He looks to see if his mother or Chilwoon is still home, but they are out. He sits by the back door and stares out at Big Girl's fence again. *Big Girl's parents are in the fields, and she'll be home alone ... The village leader won't visit today, I have to see her today...* He looks down at his arm. The wrist protruding from his worn burlap sleeve is skin and bone, nothing but a wan yellow shading into blue. He sighs with sadness. It is a good thing Big Girl is blind, else her eyes would have widened at the sight of this hand, and she would have run ten *li* in a heartbeat just to get away from him. But if Big Girl were to hold his hand and say, *'Why do you have no strength, what would you do with such a hand ...'* He cannot bear the thought! He tries to calm his breathing. *Isn't there a medicine I can try? There must be* ... Dewdrops dangle fatly on the cobwebs draped over Big Girl's fence. *That might be medicine.* He gets up.

He carefully pulls at the cobwebs. His arm has no strength and trembles too much to get a good grip. He only manages to shake the fence, and the dew falls off the cobwebs like rain. He tries to catch some but fails to palm a single one.

'Damn it all!'

He has a habit of shouting this at the sky when things do not go his way. He is at it when he hears the sound of footsteps. He quickly looks through the fence. His eyes water as soon as his eyelashes rub against the fuzz of the squash vines. *Big Girl!* He forces himself to open his eyes wide despite the tickling.

Big Girl carries a large bucket of washing and lowers it to the ground with a thud. Her eyes are closed as if she were sleeping. She must have just finished the washing as her cheeks are flushed from the effort, and her sharp chin makes him think that she has been sick these past few days. Big Girl starts to unfurl each item of washing and hang them on the fence to dry, her hands feeling for the vines.

Chilsung can scarcely breathe. He holds his breath. His lungs are fit to burst, and his stomach flips. He lowers his head, wipes away his tears, and continues to stare. He cannot think of anything. He is full of Big Girl's movements. Big Girl slowly makes her way towards where he stands. Chilsung wants to reach through the fence and grab her hand, but he slowly walks backwards instead, his entire body shaking uncontrollably.

As the sound of wet clothes being slapped over the fence rings in his ears, a bird seems to fly about inside his chest and his eyes become dark. He hears Big Girl's footsteps as she walks away and finds himself able to move again. He lifts a vine leaf and looks in. Big Girl is carrying an empty bucket and walking towards the kitchen door. He wants to shout out to her so she will halt, but he cannot bear to say anything. He glimpses her bare legs through the holes in her worn skirt. He stares at the dark kitchen doorway, hoping she will reappear, but she does not. He sighs and steps back. The sunlight shines down and stings his skin. *I should've given her some biscuits ... or some money. Or I could gather the money and buy her a new skirt.* He looks through the fence again. The creaking fence is the only thing making a sound, and the white of Big Girl's washing shines as bright as the sun. He turns around. *If I don't get Big Girl a skirt, she'll have to wear those torn rags forever.*

'Big Brother, give me some biscuits ...?'

Chilwoon appears out of the kitchen with the baby on his back. Chilsung quickly steps back from the fence, surprised like a thief caught in the act. Chilwoon thinks his older brother is trying to hit him, so he quickly retreats, but then he peeks out of the kitchen doorway again.

'Please, please, can't I have just one ...?'

He holds out his hand.

The baby tilts her head and holds out her hand as well. There are always boils on the baby's head, bursting with pus. Thin, sickly yellow hairs grow here and there on her head, and a halo of flies refuses to leave her alone. The baby keeps pulling at her thin hairs with her skinny fingers, picking at the scabs of her pustules and nibbling on them.

The baby now holds out that hand to Chilsung. She does not know how to curl her fingers, but she knows how to beg.

Chilsung scares them with his eyes again and tries to enter the room. Chilwoon blocks the door and huffs and puffs in frustration.

'Big Brother, please, just one little bite?' He noisily sucks in a drip from his nose.

'G-go away!'

Chilwoon has no proper clothes, just some makeshift trousers, the sunburned skin flaking off his back. The baby does not even have that and is naked. The sight of his younger siblings inflames Chilsung with rage, his eyes almost turning into balls of fire. He turns away towards the wall and is reminded of the layers of fabric he saw in a store in town. His hand involuntarily rises to slap Chilwoon, but his arm drops listlessly to his side.

'Then I'm not going to watch the baby!' Chilwoon puts down his sister and runs away. The baby immediately begins to cry with all her might. Chilsung does not give her the time of day as he sits with his back to her.

A swarm of flies catches his eye. It is the little meal table. His mother would prepare him a meal before going out to the fields, the food covered with a bit of cloth. He creeps up to the table and tosses the cloth aside. There are drowned flies floating in the stew, and the thicket of flies covering the rice bowl spring into the air in surprise. Chilsung picks out the flies in the stew and shoves a big spoonful of rice into his mouth. They call it rice, but it is mostly acorns with some rice mixed in. The rice he does manage to taste is extremely soft and sticky, the taste so sweet he almost coughs. But that taste is brief, and he soon chews another slippery bit of acorn, turning the sweet taste into bitterness. The acorns are hard to chew, and if he does not do a thorough job, he cannot swallow them, so he is left with a constant bitter taste at the tip of his tongue.

He looks up after a time. The baby has stopped crying and has crawled towards him. Her eyes are fixed on his rice bowl, with only occasional glances at his face. Chilsung, grateful that she has stopped her detestable crying, picks out a bite from his bowl. The baby grips his offering in her hands and eats it, lying on her stomach, licking the rice off the acorns. She only fondles the acorns in her hands and does not eat them.

'Y-you won't eat them?'

It enrages him that the ungrateful baby can tell the difference between rice and acorns. His shouting makes the baby cry loudly again.

'Y-you're crying!'

Chilsung kicks the baby. The baby closes her eyes and falls on her back. The swarm of flies briefly alight from her body and settle down again. As Chilsung makes to kick her once more, the baby's crying fades to whimpers. Tears gather in her eyes. Chilsung ignores her and sits down again with his back to her. He hears a tiny cough, and he turns around.

The baby must have tried to swallow the acorn. She is coughing up its rough slices, which have not been chewed at all, slimed with saliva and what looks like blood. The baby's face is red, and the tendons stick out on her neck.

The sight turns the acorns in Chilsung's mouth into sand, and their bitter taste hits his nose like a blow. He drops his spoon, picks up the baby, and puts her down outside the door. He slaps the baby's gaunt cheek to make her colour return. She starts to cry. He kicks his bowl, which clangs against the floor and rolls away. The baby's cries make him shiver in disgust. He cannot be still. He remembers the biscuits under his bedding, so he fetches all of them and tosses them in front of her. He runs out to the backyard, walks a few circles, and spits.

When he goes back inside, the room is as silent as the inside of a kiln.

He fidgets, sitting and standing and tilting his head, until he sees the baby sleeping on the step outside the room, her hands for a pillow. She is teeming with flies, especially around her open mouth. Surprised, he looks for the biscuits. Not a crumb. The baby could not have eaten all of them, so Chilwoon must have been here. He should have left some for his little sister! Chilsung should not have given all of them away! He wants to find Chilwoon and beat him up. He runs out the room, kicking the baby on the way. It was the ugliness of her emaciated arms and legs that made him do it, along with the pitiful sight of her sleeping on her side.

Leaving her cries behind, he looks for Chilwoon. There are children gathered underneath the willow tree over there. He's there! Chilsung huffs as he makes his way to them.

He had wanted to sneak up on him, but Chilwoon sees his older brother coming and runs away. The other children chew on millet stalks as they stare at him and grin. One of them imitates Chilsung's walk.

Chilwoon must have run into the millet field. Chilsung trips on some weeds, and the children following him laugh. Chilsung gets up with great effort and glares at them. He was afraid they would gang up on him, but the children seem intimidated as they step away. They are more like a crazy pack of monkeys than children, always on the prowl for food. He watches them run off and thinks of how the children in these villages are all hateful creatures. His forehead hurts and his toe stings, and now the millet stalks on the ground prick the bottom of his feet. The children look back as they run. Chilwoon will probably join them, he thinks, and he rests underneath the willow tree.

Its shade is littered with millet stalks. It must be where cows are occasionally tethered because there are cowpats everywhere. Chilsung leans against the tree, his gaze automatically at Big Girl's house. How is he going to see her? *I can go now, but if someone is there ...* He feels a stinging pain on his skin. Large ants are walking up his leg. He brushes them off and gazes at Big Girl's house again.

He sees the white of her hung laundry as the corners flutter in the breeze like the wings of birds taking flight. *What 'someone'? No one is there, they're all out in the fields …*

He hears the sound of slippers dragging. Dog Poo's mother passes by, breathing heavily, carrying a woman on her back.

Ordinarily, Dog Poo's mother would have brightly greeted him joking, *'Hey, you got a lot of matches lately? Give me some!'* But today she only walks by with a grimace on her face. Her forehead beads with sweat, her legs shake, and she is about to breathe in the whole sky. The woman on her back is like a dead body. Long hair loose, foaming at the mouth, bloodied clothes … *Big Girl's Mother!* Chilsung is taken aback. He wants to ask her what happened, but Dog Poo's mother quickly passes the willow tree. Did Big Girl's mother fall? Did she get into a fight? Curiosity gets the better of him as he begins to follow them. If only he could move faster, he would catch up and ask what is going on, but he only stumbles and falls. He struggles for a while and picks himself up.

Smoke comes out of Big Girl's house. What could be wrong with her mother? He reaches their yard, and his feet keep trying to make him go in. He hesitates, listening, but eventually goes back to his house.

There is a cloud of flies in their yard. The baby squats in the midst of it, trying to pass a stool. She is trying with all her might, but no stool appears, only red drops of blood. Her eyes bulge, and the tendons of her neck stand out like blades. Her little forehead is dripping with sweat. Chilsung turns his head in disgust and goes into the house. If he could, he would squash the baby like a bug or throw her out somewhere far away. That would rid him of this nuisance.

Chilsung picks up an acorn rolling around on the floor and chews on it. The sound of the baby straining is too much. He bolts out to the backyard. He is reminded of Big Girl's mother. He creeps up to the fence again.

'Ah, ah …'

This is not the sound of Young-ae, their own baby, crying;

he realizes it is a newborn. Big Girl's mother must have given birth to another baby. He is a little reassured, but just the thought of another baby makes him sick. It seems better to squash the baby to death now than to have it squatting in the yard passing bloody stools like some sick cat.

Did she give birth to another one like Big Girl, another blind one ...? He lets out a bitter laugh. He wonders why the women of the village only give birth to cripples. *Well, Big Girl wasn't blind at birth, and even I wasn't a cripple until I got measles when I was three and then convulsions after.* His mother always said that.

His mother had carried his sick body to a clinic in the town, over snow so heavy the paths were buried. The doctor would not see her as she waited in the unheated corridor for hours. Desperate, she had slid open the door to his office, but the doctor had only given her an angry look, so she went back to waiting in the corridor until sundown. Then, a child who ran errands came to her with a bottle the size of a little finger and told her to be on her way.

His mother always got swept up in a rage when she told this story. She cursed doctors and cursed this world. Chilsung would shout at her and try to stop her from talking whenever this happened. The story sickened him.

If only I had some medicine, and Big Girl, too ... No, we're already cripples, medicine won't make us better. But maybe it will. Maybe if I had good medicine, I'd have normal legs and arms like other people, and I wouldn't have to go begging and I could work in the fields and go to the mountains and chop-chop for wood and those little bastards wouldn't tease me ... His heart soared. He opened his eyes from his imagining. *I could go to the hospital and ask ... But those bastards care about nothing except money. Mother always says so.* The thought makes him listless again.

Big Girl's house is silent. The baby has stopped crying. He begins to feel hungry. He looks up at where the sun was and imagines his mother coming in for lunch, her sweat-soaked hair escaping her bun and worries twisting her face. *Why aren't you out begging? What are we going to eat if you don't?*

His eyes go to the cypress tree growing nearby. He sniffs its cool scent. *Maybe this cypress tree will be good for my sickness?* He goes up to it and rips off a mouthful. He chews on it, gagging at the taste, but makes himself swallow. It hurts all the way down, and saliva runs down the corners of his mouth. He thinks this saliva might be medicine, too, so he tries to swallow it. Tears run down his cheeks.

He looks at the sky and begs. *Please, at least let my hands be better, so I can gather kindling for mother.* He had never thought this before and normally did not think much of his mother coming home carrying a stack of kindling on her back, but somehow this time, the prayer comes to mind.

He is still. Slowly, he raises his hand. His heart races at the thought that it has worked. Then, his hand curls up again. Suddenly, he vomits, and his head hits the ground with a thud. He is crying.

His mother comes back when it is very dark. She had to go to the mountains for wood again.

'Are you sick?'

Her mere shadow suggests how tired she is. Chilsung is lying in the room and does not say a word. A strong smell of grass and something like garlic emanates from the folds of her skirt.

'Chilsung, why aren't you answering?' The twig-like hand that caresses her son is not without warmth.

Chilsung slaps her hand away and turns on his side. His mother steps back and mutters something to herself. 'If you're sick just tell me, you worthless ...'

She leaves him alone. A long while later, she returns with some rice mixed into a stew with greens. She sits him up with the usual difficulty. Chilsung takes up the proffered spoon with a shaking hand.

'You sick?' His mother smells of soot now, and the savoury scent of the stew makes his heavy body feel lighter.

'N-no.'

This reassures her. She watches her son eat. 'Big Girl's mother had a baby while she was out in the field. What use are more babies to someone so poor?'

This reminds him of seeing Big Girl's mother as he stood underneath the willow tree, the cries of the newborn baby, and the pathetic sight of Young-ae. He makes a face.

'Why have another baby? Sick of babies.'

His mother says this with a sigh and leaves with the empty bowl. It is too warm in the room, and Chilsung is also curious about what is going on at Big Girl's, so he gets up and leaves.

The stack of kindling in the corner of the yard gives off a deep scent of mountain greenery, and the stars against the black sky blink like the pretty eyes of babies.

Chilsung waves away the buzzing mosquitoes and plops himself down on the kindling. The dried branches and leaves make a crackling sound, and his legs are warmed by a gust of hot air that is pushed out by the impact. His mother approaches.

'Chilsung? Why are you out?'

She sits down next to him. She smells of dried sweat and Young-ae's stool. Chilsung turns his head away.

His mother takes out a breast, latches Young-ae's mouth on it, and sighs. Chilsung keeps expecting her to say something, but all she does is caress her sickly daughter.

She must be tired from working in the fields all day and gathering kindling in the mountain in the evening, but now she has to take care of her baby. She often says she feels as though if she slept now she would never wake up. Something about his tired mother not taking care of herself makes Chilsung resentful of her.

'Doesn't that stupid girl ever sleep!'

At his shouting, Young-ae starts to cry with the breast in her mouth.

His mother almost scolds him. *Of course she's not sleepy. She's sick and she's starved all day, and now my milk won't come.* She clamps down on these words with a pain that brings tears to her eyes. 'Don't listen to him, he's not talking to you, keep feeding.'

The tears overflow. If only these tears would be enough to sooth the baby's thirst, then the mother would not feel so bitter in her heart.

After a while, she speaks again.

'If that baby wasn't going to live anyway, it shouldn't have almost killed the mother. I just saw them. The baby's dead, but the mother is alive ... Poor thing. She must've wandered the tilled fields, the baby's head had dirt all over it. The baby probably would've turned out a cripple, too, with all that earth filling her eyes and ears. It's good that she died, good!'

His mother was vehement in her grumbling. Chilsung also took a deep breath in frustration. If he had died when he was a baby, he would not have turned out to be a cripple either.

'And wouldn't you know? Big Girl's mother wants to go out into the fields tomorrow. She should rest for a day, but there is so much work to be done. She can't afford to rest. Why should the poor have babies at all? Why?'

She remembers the awful period when she gave birth to Young-ae and the very next day went to help with the barley. The sky was yellow and spinning, the grains of barley tiny. As she flailed the barley stalks, she felt something creep out beneath her and hang from her. There were others with her, so she did nothing about it until she went to relieve herself, and found that her thigh was wet with blood, and a fist-like lump of flesh drooped from her privates. It frightened her, but she felt too shy to ask anyone about it and left it alone. To this day, the lump of flesh hung from her and refused to retract itself, and a strange liquid flowed from it.

In the summer the thing stank and made her feel hotter, and in the winter it made her shiver as if she was about to catch the flu. It felt like fire when she had to walk a long way and sometimes swelled up so badly she could barely walk at all. It eventually erupted in pustules, which were unbelievably painful as they burst one by one. But despite how awful the pain was, it was not the kind of disease she could tell anyone about.

She feels the lump again and sighs deeply. The dried kindling crackles. Young-ae bites down on her nipple.

She wants to shout out in pain, but she does not want to set Chilsung off again. She bites her lip. She silently presses down on Young-ae's head, signalling that she hurt her. Then, thinking she pressed down too hard, she rubs the child's head.

'And with all that trouble at that house, they had a guest who waited for her but had to be turned away without seeing her.'

Chilsung raises his head. He can smell a mosquito fire burning somewhere.

'He's from that house they mentioned before. Maybe you don't know about it. They own a shop in town. They've got some money, it looks like. But no children. Enough concubines, but they still have no children. She'll be better off there.'

His mother looks down at Young-ae. Chilsung is annoyed at how his mother keeps thinking of the baby even when she is talking. But he sits silently because he wants to hear the rest of the story.

'So, they got word of Big Girl, and the man seemed all excited to meet her. He visited today, and they were supposed to discuss a match. Big Girl's luck is turning! She's such a lovely girl. She may be blind, but is there anything she can't do? Hard work or sitting work, she does it better than any person who can see. And now she'll be married to that house and give birth to a son and spend her days in comfort. She deserves it ...'

'She's going to do what!'

Chilsung's shouting is unexpected. His heart fills with jealousy, and he is ready to kill anyone who dares to harm Big Girl. His head is hot enough to explode, and his legs and arms are shaking.

'S-so she's going t-to marry?'

His mother sees his distress and is reluctant to answer. She pities his affection for the girl, and at the same time, the future of her son looks dark as night.

'She isn't yet but ...'

These words seem to calm him a little. Saddened, she stands up. 'Go inside and sleep. I have to go into town early tomorrow. What can we do?'

Chilsung screams out in a rage and drags his feet out into the night.

His footsteps take him away from the scent of the mosquito fire and into the fresh air of the mountain. The sound of the breeze rubbing against the fields of grain is soothing, the breeze itself coiling around his body. His clothes become damp with dew, and the many songs of insects rise from near his feet ...

He stands still. He is blocked by complete darkness, with only the outline of Bultasan Mountain delineating a jagged border between earth and stars. The stars sparkle and prickle his eyes, making him want to cry out into the night. That mountain, that sky seems so cruel to him ...

He can hear the tired calling of his mother.

'Son, come back!'

'Wh-why are you following me!' The resentment in his heart rears its head again.

'Please come back. What are you going to do out here?'

His mother grabs his hand. He tries to shake it off, but he does not have the strength. The tall grasses of the path brush against their clothes and make a hissing sound. His mother begs him, almost in tears. As his mother leads him back home by the hand, he thinks about what he will do.

All right, tomorrow I'll see her and ask if she's getting married and if she'll marry me.

His heart begins to thump, and he feels a distant, thread-like hope.

'Think of me and think of your brother and sister ...'

His mother tries comforting him with these words. Chilsung says nothing as they return home.

*

The next day, Chilsung deliberately wakes up late. He is determined to meet Big Girl and say something. *If she really is to be married ...* Darkness falls in his mind. *Then I'm going to kill myself, I'm going to die.*

He goes towards the fence. Big Girl's house is quiet, and there is only the buzzing of flies from the bucket of water left over from washing the rice. *This is it!*

He steps away from the fence and goes back into the room. He is out of breath from excitement. *I can't wear this to see her,* he thinks, looking down at himself. His clothes are smeared with cowpat, ripped here and there, but she is blind anyway. *What do I say?* He looks up at the ceiling, thinking. He sucks back the saliva flowing down his chin a few times, but nothing comes to mind. His thoughts are as dim, as if he had never spoken a word in his life.

Does she know I'm a cripple? The thought depresses him. He can almost hear Big Girl saying, '*I can't marry a thing like you!*' Defeated, he looks outside.

He gazes at the squash and gourd vines, the stalks of corn beside them, the apricot tree, and the big and small cypress trees, their leaves fluttering in the slight breeze. They seem freer than he could ever be. He sighs.

A long while later, he makes up his mind and leaves his yard, hesitating before the low gate leading into Big Girl's yard. He pushes it, and leaps in.

The door to their house is closed, and there is only a stack of kindling in the corner of the yard. The door creaks open, and a meowing cat runs out. He is so surprised that his heart almost jumps to the sky. He steps up on to the porch and, after more hesitating, opens the door to the house. Stale air pushes out the doorway, but there is no one there. *Big Girl is not here. Is she already married?* He goes to the kitchen and the backyard, but there is nobody anywhere. Just when he is about to leave, he hears the low gate open. He quickly hides behind a pillar in the kitchen, next to a rolled-up straw mat. Big Girl comes through the kitchen door, holding a bucket full of washing. His eyes grow dark. He feels faint. It looks like Big Girl recognizes him and is approaching him, that she has not been blind this whole time and is staring at him with the eyes he would gaze at through the slats of the fence. He can barely breathe. He tries to creep around the straw mat, but his breathing becomes rougher, and the smell from the mat is about to make him faint.

Big Girl goes out to the backyard. He listens to the dragging of her slippers and peers out when she seems far enough away. His body is twisting so much he can barely take a step. He thinks this is too much and he should go back home. His body feels like stone, but the sound of Big Girl slapping the laundry up on the fence to dry reminds him of why he is here. *Big Girl is marrying in town!* He takes a step.

Big Girl whirls around, almost stumbling. Chilsung cannot bring himself to look in her direction and simply stands.

'Who is it?'

Chilsung is silent.

'Who is there!'

Her voice shakes. Chilsung wants to say something, anything, but his jaw is locked in place. He takes a step forward.

'Wh-who am I, I?'

Big Girl backs up against the fence, her head bowed. Her delicately-closed eyelids tremble. Chilsung realizes she recognizes him and this gives him courage. Now he is more worried about someone walking by, and he keeps looking towards the gate.

'Get out, Mother is coming.'

Big Girl's voice is firm. It is as high-pitched as a little girl's.

'Y-you're getting married. Good for you!'

'Bastard, what's it to you? Get out!'

Big Girl nervously grips the washing and breathes lightly. Her white breasts rise through the tatters of her tunic. Chilsung unconsciously takes a step towards her.

'Go away!' Big Girl shouts as she grips the fence. Her shout frightens Chilsung, who takes a step back and thinks he should leave. The world seems to be going dark and spinning out of control.

'Mother is coming!'

Chilsung briefly closes his eyes and opens them again at her shaking voice. He can smell the scent of her long hair, woven into a long braid down her back. He steps on her foot. Big Girl's face turns red as she extricates her foot and moves away. The wet clothes she is holding flop down into the dirt.

Chilsung is afraid she is going to pick up a rock. She gropes the fence, her braid tossing wildly about. Her courageous words have abandoned her, and all she does is helplessly grab the fence.

'I'll give you biscuits, I'll give you cloth, don't get married!'

Big Girl calms down a little. She raises her head.

'You ... have biscuits ...?' She grins. Chilsung grins with her.

'Yes, so don't get married, alright?'

'That's not up to me. That's up to Father.'

Chilsung is stumped. He stands there, not saying anything.

'Get out. Come on. Go away.'

Big Girl turns her head towards him. Little beads of sweat are dotted above the black curves of her eyebrows.

'Th-then you're getting married!'

Big Girl drops her head and rolls a stone about with one foot. Chilsung is so sad he is about to cry.

'D-don't, don't marry! All right?'

Big Girl only answers this with a sigh and turns away from him. Suddenly, he hears the sound of a baby crying. Chilsung gives a start and runs back home.

The baby is rolling about on the kitchen floor with Chilwoon trying to tie her up. The baby struggles and screams. Chilwoon treats her roughly, as if he is trussing a piece of meat, and knocks his knuckles painfully against her skull.

'This stupid girl, will you sleep or not! I'll kill you!'

His nose running, he waves his fists at her. The baby shudders. Tears run from her eyes.

'Sleep, you stupid girl!'

Chilwoon falls next to her and pinches his side. 'It hurts here, I can't watch the baby anymore ...'

Licking at the snot running from his nose, he mumbles these complaints before falling into an exhausted sleep.

Chilsung dispassionately takes in this scene and turns to go into the main room.

'Mama?'

The baby he thought was asleep has opened her eyes wide and is staring at her brother. Chilsung's hair stands on end. He raises his leg as if to give a kick, but when he looks, the baby has pursed her tiny lips and closed her eyes.

'Mama! Mama!'

The baby begins to cry. Chilsung goes back to the room and paces around. He goes out to the backyard in the hopes of seeing Big Girl, but there's only the washing drying on the fence.

He goes back to the room and stares at his begging sack. He thinks of how he can get her fabric. *Then Big Girl and her mother and father might prefer me to him, who knows?* He grabs his sack and puts on his straw hat and goes out the door.

From the corner of his eye, he sees the baby drinking something off the floor. He takes a closer look. She had wriggled out of her bonds, crawled towards the furnace opening and urinated next to it. She is lapping up the urine.

'Y-you stupid girl!' Chilsung shouts at her and goes out the gate.

It is so hot that he feels as if he is submerged in soup. Once on the road, he adjusts his clothes and his hat and tries to be as grown-up and calm as possible. Somehow, he thinks this is how he should act from now on. He gives a dignified cough. He tries to walk in a more leisurely manner. Children would then not attack him, and the adults would not make fun of him either. He thinks of Big Girl. When he turns around, his village is far off in the distance, hidden behind the rise of the millet field. The field gives off a fresh scent, and his back is hot and sweaty from the sun. He takes a couple of steps more and looks out.

The blue wall of Bultasan Mountain looms above the millet field, so close it looks mere steps away. He sometimes lays down on the millet and stares up at the mountain. No matter how scattered his thoughts are, he can always centre himself by gazing at the mountain's grandeur, and sometimes remember one or two things he has forgotten.

One spring day long ago, he had woken up and opened the window, and looked out at the children with their carrying racks on their backs as they went to the mountain to collect kindling. He had thought, *When I'm an adult, I'm going to that mountain and chopping down the biggest tree there and carrying it down …*

He scoffs at his younger self. His heart aches at the memory. He shakes his head and carries on along his way. The only thing that matters now is Big Girl.

*

Two days later, Chilsung is standing six *li* from the village, at the entrance of the small town of Songhwa. The begging has not been good outside the town, which has brought him all the way out here. He has just about managed to get a length of rayon for Big Girl and is about to go home.

But home is far away. He is not sure where he is going to spend the night, but he wants to give the cloth to Big Girl as soon as possible, and he is worried that she still wants to marry. He starts walking homewards.

The night has no stars and is black as animal fur. But somehow, his heart is light and his eyes are filled with hope. He can sense the blue of the mountain and water, and the little stones by the path are perfect for kicking around when he gets bored. The road at night is peaceful because there are no people to harass him or cars churning up clouds of dust. He walks, forgetting the pain in his legs.

When he rests, he can fill his lungs with the sweet mountain air and hear the babble of the streams. The fields give off their smell, and the calls of birds echo back and forth. The lights of the villages shine in the distance and seem to be floating in the darkness.

He carries the roll of rayon fabric underneath his tunic, right on his chest, and it is as silky as a young woman's skin. The sensation makes his injured toe jolt. He smiles with his mouth open as he imagines what it will be like when he sees Big Girl. She will be so overjoyed her smile will reach the very curls of her eyelashes. He can feel his heart beating fast.

The eastern sky is beginning to light up above him, wide as an ocean, when raindrops begin to fall. He begins to walk faster, but the rain starts to come down harder, disturbing the sparrows. He hesitates. There's a hamlet nearby. If it were not for Big Girl's fabric getting wet, he would simply walk through the rain. But now he heads for shelter.

When he looks back, he can clearly see the road toward

home. His eagerness to return home makes his steps away from the road reluctant.

Once he reaches the hamlet, the smell of hay and manure crawls up to his nose. He ducks underneath the overhang of a roof of a house nearby. When he closes his eyes, he sees visions of Big Girl and the locust tree at the entrance of his village ...

He opens his eyes. It is daylight now but still raining. He sees a mountain far away and groups of rooftops in the distance. He also hears the loud sound of falling water. He gathers his courage and looks around him.

He seems to be standing next to a rich man's house. The walls are built with cement and the roof with black tiles, the main gate made of thick planks and large nails. His spirits lift.

The family name is engraved on a white stone that hangs by the gate. Chilsung stares at this white stone, lost in thought, until his eyebrows are studded with rain.

Ha, today is my lucky day. I'm going to get breakfast from this house and an armful of money or rice. Should I close my eyes and pretend to be blind, too? They might take pity on me and give me extra.

He tries to keep his eyes closed but the insides of his eyelids tickle too much, and his eyelashes keep trembling. *Oh no, my clothes are too clean, as well.* He rushes to a puddle and sits down in it. He comes up to the gate again. He is colder now, and his lips are shivering. He leans forward, trying to see between the two doors of the gate when he hears plodding footsteps. He jumps back.

The gate creaks loudly as it swings open. As he has done countless times before, Chilsung bows his head low and feels the uncomfortable gaze of a stranger.

'What do you want?'

A heavy voice. Chilsung looks up and sees a man with narrowed eyes. He wears the black clothes of a servant.

'Can you spare a spoonful?'

'At this early hour?'

The man turns away and goes back inside. How generous this house is; most other houses would ask him to leave. Chilsung feels hopeful, and he takes a look inside.

He glimpses what must be a guest room straight ahead across the courtyard, a door leading elsewhere besides it, and part of the main hall. To the left of the guest room is something that must be a storage room. There's a large stack of rice stalks before it. Raindrops drip from the slightly yellowed stalks.

The courtyard is wide, and rivulets of rainwater flow by.

He has to make it in there for food. He sees the door to the inner compound and makes his way towards it. Once he enters, a dog comes running out from the kitchen. It growls at him as he clucks his tongue, trying to pacify it. The dog shows its teeth and then lunges at his begging sack. Chilsung shouts and goes out the door, hoping that someone from the guest room will see him and call the dog off, but all is quiet in the house. The dog jumps up at him. Chilsung holds his begging sack in his mouth and tries to fight off the dog, but he gives up and moves towards the main gate. When he hesitates, the dog lunges at him once more and takes a bite of his trouser leg. He screams and runs outside. The servant from before comes out from the house.

'Come here, dog ...'

The dog ignores him and keeps barking at Chilsung. Chilsung is furious and looks back at it, wondering if there is a way to kill it. The servant gestures to the dog to come inside. The dog finally complies but keeps looking back at Chilsung.

Chilsung walks. A sudden feeling of terror makes him look back, but there is no dog behind him, only the hateful sight of the closed door. He considers going back, but the mere thought of the dog disgusts him. He gives up and continues to walk.

The rain mixed with the wind whips him mercilessly. The sound of the trees shaking and water roaring through the irrigation canals assaults his ears. Leaves shaped like blue birds float and spin along with clumps of straw on the waters of the canal.

His drenched clothes are plastered to his skin, and he can barely breathe because of the wind. He looks about for shelter, but every house has its door firmly closed with only morning smoke coming out of their chimneys. He looks for an empty house or rice mill, but none are in sight. He keeps thinking that the dog is running up behind him. His trouser leg is tattered from the dog's attack, his yellow leg clearly visible, and the rainwater gathering on his straw hat is dripping down to his lips like teardrops. The sudden thought of Big Girl's fabric getting soaked makes him want to bawl.

He stops in his tracks. The rain is so thick he cannot tell mountains from falling water, and through the dancing crops, he hears a deep, loud sound like that of a growling beast.

His heart wants to go forward more than anything, but his feet refuse to move.

He is two or three houses away from leaving the hamlet altogether. He turns around but keeps looking back at the fields beyond, reluctant.

This is not the first time he has been chased by a dog, and often enough he had to bear the abuse and insults of people, but for some reason this time he is enraged.

'Hello, friend. What are you doing over there?'

Surprised, Chilsung looks towards the little shed that he is standing next to and discovers it is actually a millstone hut. The man looking out at him seems about forty or fifty. *He's a cripple like me*, thinks Chilsung. The man smiles. Chilsung has searched for shelter for a long time, but the sight of the man makes him hesitate. In the end, he goes in. It smells of rice husks and horse manure.

'Hurry in, your clothes are wet.'

The man gets up with the help of a walking stick, straightens out the mat he is sitting on, and sits on the edge, bidding

Chilsung to take his place. Chilsung stares at the white strands in the man's beard and hair. He is scared that the man wants to steal what he has begged.

'You're going to catch a cold. I can lend you my old clothes so you can let yours dry.' The man digs through the bag at his side. 'Here we go. Come here.'

Chilsung stays where he is. It is a black suit, worn in places. *What luck he must've had, getting that suit, I wish I had a suit like that.* Chilsung feels strange, and he looks into the eyes of the man. He does not look like the kind of person who would steal his begging sack. Chilsung bows his head and looks at the raindrops dripping from his sleeve. The man gets up again and moves closer to him with the help of his walking stick.

'Why are you standing there? Here, put this on. You don't want it?'

Chilsung takes a step back and eyes the suit jacket. He does not know why, but his heart beats fast at the sight of this thing he has never worn in his life.

'My! Such stubbornness, my friend. Then sit down, at least.'

The man takes him by the hand and sits him down on the mat by the millstone. Chilsung takes care not to stare at the man's lame leg.

'Did you have breakfast?'

Chilsung wonders if the man thinks he has just begged food from somewhere. He looks at his sack, which is soaked and dripping.

'No?' The man is silent for a moment. 'Poor thing. You ought to eat something.'

He seems to think for a while before rummaging through his bag again. 'Here. It's not much but take it.'

The man opens a small package wrapped in newspaper and holds it out to Chilsung. It is a few mouthfuls of stale rice and millet.

At the sight of the food, Chilsung's appetite comes back in

a wave. He reaches out for it, but his hands do not listen to him. They shake uncontrollably in the air. The man understands and holds up the package nearer to his mouth.

'I'm sorry it's not much.'

The man's kind apology makes Chilsung feel ashamed of himself. He lowers his gaze, tries to breathe in his snot, and places the package on his knees. He licks off the rice. He can smell the newsprint and the savoury taste of the old rice, more savoury the more he chews. The more he eats, the more he cannot help thinking it is not enough. He feels the gaze of the man on him and looks up.

'Slow down!'

Chilsung detaches his mouth from the paper and gives an open-mouthed smile. The man smiles back, but then he notices Chilsung's leg.

'You're bleeding!'

He bends to take a closer look. Chilsung is made aware of the pain and looks himself. The end of his trouser leg is drenched in blood. Bright red flows from a wound near his ankle. He suddenly feels unwell. He curls his leg and lifts his head. There's a faint smell of wet dog.

'A dog did that, right? You must've gone to that house with the black roof tiles ... Those bastards keep a horrible dog! Huh! Those rich bastards are all alike. Come on, give it here, it looks bad.'

The man pulls Chilsung's leg towards him. Chilsung quickly retracts his leg, but even as he does so, a vague anger runs up his back and makes him tear up. The man sighs and pats his back. 'Friend, don't cry. Come on, no tears. Look at my leg. Whole when I entered the factory; now bitten in half by a machine.'

Chilsung stares at the man, his eyes full of rage. He looks down at his wound, and it makes him feel a tightening in his chest. He lowers his head again and grabs a fistful of soft dust and smears it on his wound.

'Oh! You mustn't do that!' The man grabs Chilsung's hand. Chilsung smiles like a child and speaks.

'W-will this help?'

'No, it won't! Don't ever do that again. If you have no medicine, it's better to do without. It can get worse, and you can get sicker.'

Chilsung, somewhat rebuffed, curls his leg towards him and looks out. The man is also lost in thought.

The rain blows into the hut and the countless broken spider webs dance in the rafters like smoke. The branches of a willow tree sway, and a stream of red, muddy water babbles by. Chilsung glances over his shoulder to see the large wooden handle of the millstone, silent and solid amidst the cacophony around them.

'Were you born a cripple?'

Chilsung lowers his head at the man's question and hesitates before answering. 'N-no.'

'Then it must've been a sickness. Did you try any medicine?'

Chilsung hesitates again as if finding it difficult to speak. 'N-no, I d-didn't.'

'My! I suppose they're breaking healthy legs now, much less giving medicine for babies ...' The man laughs at nothing in particular. Chilsung shivers at the sound of his laughter and secretly gives him a look. The man's eyes are wide open and scary, and a blue vein stands out on his forehead.

'Damn it all. Why was I so foolish? If I had the chance again, I'd do it even if it killed me. Why was I such a fool? Damn!'

Chilsung pays close attention to what the man is mumbling, but he has no idea what the words mean. The man turns to Chilsung. The bags under his eyes remind Chilsung of his dead father.

'Look, friend, I used to have a family of my own. I was a master mechanic in a factory. Yes, a master mechanic ... Since that machine bit my leg and I was fired from the factory without any compensation, my wife ran away, my children are hungry and crying, and my parents have passed away ... My, but what use is there in talking about it? Who do you think is responsible for our suffering? The heavens? Or ourselves?'

The man gives Chilsung a hard look. Chilsung doesn't know why his heart is suddenly beating faster and why he can't look him in the eye. He looks down at the man's broken leg instead and the silent earth beneath it.

'It isn't our fault. We have to know who did this to us ... The bastard who broke my leg, the bastard that made you a cripple, who do you think it is? Do you understand me? Friend, do you understand?'

His words are like jolts of pain at the ends of Chilsung's bones. Chilsung has only blamed himself his whole life, but now the man's words seem to flicker in that darkness of his self-loathing. It is too much, and he feels dizzy. He raises his head to ask a question, but no words come forth from his mouth. Dispirited, he looks up at the sky.

The mountains in the distance seem to be holding back tears, their peaks soaring jaggedly in the distance, and the cries of frogs that had been drowned out by the sound of rain remind Chilsung of home. He can almost see Big Girl's silhouette underneath the locust tree. He gets up.

'I-I'm going home.'

The man gets up, too. 'You have a home? You must go then.'

Chilsung raises his head, and the man firmly readjusts Chilsung's hat. The man smiles. Chilsung feels like he has met someone he could lean on somehow, like his mother.

'Good luck. If fate is in our favour, we'll meet again.'

Chilsung answers with a smile and begins to walk. He looks back after a while; the man is standing there. Chilsung rubs his eyes with his fist and looks back again.

The millet and sorghum fields are flooded with water, half their stalks fallen and submerged. The frogs' noisy cry is indifferent to the destruction. Their calls have the weight of human voices.

Light rain continues to fall. Chilsung's clothes are soaked once more, and the raindrops lingering on the ends of his eyebrows seem to blot his very soul with unanswerable questions.

When he reaches his village, the rain grows heavy again, and the wind begins to blow. The locust tree, usually looking cool underneath the sun, seems gloomy beneath the grimacing sky, and the low hills that surround the village are also veiled in rain. But the thought of Big Girl going down to the well near the hill carrying her water jar on her head makes his own steps lighter, as he sees the fences around the houses and the longer fences around the garden plots.

His mother greets him tearfully at their home.

'You naughty boy! Didn't you think about how worried I would be!'

His mother takes his begging sack from him and sobs loudly. Chilsung goes into the room, where half the floor is taken up by bowls collecting rainwater leaking through the roof, the drops plinking in rhythm. Chilsung stands at the door, not knowing what to do. He feels colder than he was before.

Chilwoon and the baby are lying on the warmest spot of the floor, and the baby's head is wrapped in cloth. Raindrops occasionally fall on their little bodies, too.

'Just sit anywhere, there's nothing to be done ... I went to town last night and searched everywhere for you. I even knocked on the doors of the drinking houses! Why didn't you tell me where you were going?'

She is crying more loudly now. Having long lost her husband, she loves her poor son and relies on him to keep her grounded. Her crying wakes Chilwoon.

'Big Brother is here!'

He rubs his eyes and jumps to his feet, making the crowd

of flies about him jump too. The baby starts to cry. Chilwoon keeps rubbing his eyes and looking at his brother.

'Stop it, you little brat. You're making yourself sicker. See, this is what has happened to your siblings since you left. They keep getting sick. And now his eye is sick. The whole village has this eye disease. Adults, children, none of them can keep their eyes open!'

Chilsung isn't listening to a word she is saying. He only wants to lie down where there is no rain leaking and take a long nap. Chilwoon seems to think of something and goes to the back door and urinates out of it. He rubs some of the urine in his eye.

'Get it right in there. Not just your eyelids but the inside of your eye ... Your little brother is so happy to see you, he's trying to open his eyes for you. He kept calling for you yesterday.'

His mother begins to cry again. Chilsung tries to shift away from a dripping spot that wets his back, but instead a different drip hits his nose and goes down his lips. He slaps at his own nose and grunts in rage.

Chilsung's mother pleads to the sky with both arms raised, 'And why is it raining so? The wind shouldn't blow, that wind! All the millet we grew will fall and rot. What's going to happen to us? Dear God!'

Her soaked hair is plastered to her skull, and the corners of her bloodshot eyes are crusty. The water from the roof drips down on her dirty clothes.

Chilsung sits down on the threshold and closes his eyes. He is tired, and some of his eyelashes pierce his eye like thorns. He rolls his eyes twice and thinks of the millhouse.

'Dog Poo's dyke burst yesterday – their crops were washed away. What a wind! I'm so frightened. What about our field?'

His mother runs outside. Chilwoon cries as he follows but trips on the threshold and screams. Chilsung opens his eyes.

'Y-you stupid bastard, I'll k-kill you!'

His mother picks Chilwoon up and carries him on her

back as she paces in and out of the room. Chilwoon cries for a while before drifting off to sleep.

Chilsung cannot stand it. He closes his eyes to it all. When he opens them again, he sees the baby lying on the warm spot, sobbing silently. She rubs her head against the bedding, but finding this inadequate, reaches up and scratches at the cloth wrapped around her head. The sound alone makes his stomach turn.

Chilsung tries not to look, but he keeps opening his eyes and seeing the baby's yellow fingers ripping at her hair. *Why can't that stupid girl just die*, he thinks as he closes his eyes again. He hears the branches of the apricot tree snap off and the pillars of the house creak as they lean in the wind. Chilwoon comes back into the room and lies down.

'Big Brother, tomorrow get me some eye medicine. Dog Poo's father went into town and got him eye medicine, and that made him better. Will you?'

Chilsung does not say anything but thinks of the fabric hidden near his chest. He briefly regrets getting it instead of eye medicine, but then thinks of ways to get the gift to Big Girl.

He hears the scratch of a match being struck in the kitchen. His mother enters the room.

'The furnace is filled with water, what am I to do ...? Those poor things haven't eaten anything ... You must be hungry, too ...'

She leaves the room but soon rushes back in.

'Big Girl's field has also flooded! Their strong dykes, useless!'

Chilsung's eyes grow wide.

'Go to sleep, you wretched girl, why do you keep ripping out your hair? She hasn't slept for days. Dog Poo's mother told me rat skin was just the thing, so I caught a rat and put it on her, but she keeps picking at it. It must be itchy.'

Chilsung agrees with her, just to calm her down. Chilsung had opened his eyes at the news of Big Girl, but he didn't want to hear his mother's lamentations about anything else. He swallows his irritation and speaks.

'S-so. Big Girl's field...?'

'It's ruined! Oh, why won't my milk come?'

His mother stares at the child, massaging her breasts. They sag like old silk pouches.

The baby's breathing quickens, and she does not seem to have the strength to reach for the bandage anymore. Her arm falls by her side. His mother listens to the wind for a while before speaking again.

'Our millet is useless now! If Big Girl's field is ruined, so is ours ... How lucky that Big Girl is getting married now, and she can get away from this!'

'Big Girl!' Chilsung screams. The roll of fabric he has for her feels as heavy as a rock. His mother is surprised at his reaction.

Chilwoon jumps up and starts crying. 'Mother! Look!'

Chilsung and his mother are so surprised they look round in unison.

The baby has somehow torn off her bandage, and white maggots like rice grains are crawling out of it.

'Oh, what has happened, what has happened!'

The mother jumps to her baby and turns the bandage over. The rat skin falls off, and bloody maggots spill out everywhere.

'Baby, open your eyes! Open your eyes, my baby!'

Chilsung lets out a short scream at his mother's wailing and stumbles outside.

The rain pours down, and the wind blows mercilessly, and now the sky is being torn in half by the sound of thunder.

Chilsung wordlessly gazes at the sky.

March–April 1936

TRANSLATOR'S NOTE

I was told this story about my mother by one of my aunts:

When my aunt was in the sixth grade and my mother was in second, my aunt came home crying after being bullied by a group of girls in her class.

My mother, furious, stormed out of the house, found this gang, and *beat the crap out of them.*

'They were older girls,' explained my aunt, 'and they were a group. Your mother was alone. But it didn't matter to her. And when she came home, she was still angry. She was angry at *me.* She said, "Why do you let other people push you around!"'

*

I came to translate Kang Kyeong-ae partly because she reminded me of my mother: fierce, independent, empathic, and descended from people in what is now North Korea (my maternal grandparents fled from the communists to the South just before the Korean War). Kang's stories, like my mother, have a remarkable lack of self-consciousness; they are all about the story's characters and their inner lives and struggles. They don't say much about the author herself. When a character *is* a writer, she's either an object of light satire ('The Authoress') or a simple framing device ('Real and Unreal').

The closest thing we get to a glimpse of the writer herself is perhaps 'Manuscript Money,' but the character's profession as a writer is ultimately inconsequential to the story. The point of her conflict isn't the fact that she's a writer, it's the fact that she has material desires. In fact, the point of that story is the parasols.

Those goddamn parasols! I don't find communism particularly relatable even after translating all these stories, and I can safely say I still deplore every seminar-eating Marxist windbag I met in graduate school, but I completely, utterly understood the obsession with parasols. In fact, my familial connections to North Korean cadence aside, the parasols in

'Manuscript Money' were what really made me want to translate Kang Kyeong-ae in the first place.

I'll leave the close-reading of this story's interrogation of capitalist desire – a theme in virtually every story in this book – to the aforementioned Marxist windbags. Meanwhile, my own totally bourgeois sensibilities were focused on the oddly seductive language of things that pervaded that story, the act of revelling in these objects – fluffy yarn, gold fillings, furs, linen textiles as light as dragonfly wings – and outwardly condemning them at the same time.

Other stories feature lush natural descriptions, virile male body hair and muscles, ghosts, ominous medical equipment, and straw woven into rope and sandals. Kang's language is highly tactile in a way that I've arguably failed to really convey into English (Korean is much richer in onomatopoeia than English is, sorry!), and to me it is clear that Kang is enjoying her talent at making objects appear at the tip of her pen, enjoying the pleasure of creating a tableau of words.

It's not just actual objects that are depicted as objects; the thoughts and emotions of her characters are as concrete as any treasured parasol. The emotions in her stories physically move, have textures, temperatures, and are indicated with corporeal markers more than abstractions (I quickly ran out of different ways to describe tears welling and bursting). Her stories are so simple in plot and her endings are so perfunctory that the appeal for her in writing these sketches must have lain in characterization and description.

And, of course, in the constant urging to wake up, smell the class struggle, and do something about it: 'Why do you let other people push you around!'

*

Special thanks to Anthony and Taylor at Honford Star for their vision and hard work, and to English PEN for their invaluable support in the form of the PEN Translates award.

Extra special thanks to all the amazing and fierce Korean women who made this translation what it is: the laser-sharp Sophie "Sohee" Bowman for her essential edits, my fantastic translation professors – Hayun Jung, Suh Ji-moon, and Sora Kim-Russell – who taught me everything I know about translation, my formidable graduate advisor Nancy Jiwon Cho who gave literature back to me, and, of course, my mother, Myoung-Sook Ham. This translation is dedicated to her.

*

The stories in this volume were translated from manuscripts provided by the Korean Copyright Commission (www.copyright.or.kr), apart from 'The Authoress' and 'The Underground Village' which were translated from *Gang Gyeong-ae Jeonjib* (*Complete Works of Kang Kyeong-ae*), ed. Lee Sang-kyung (Somyeong Publishers, 1999). The translation of 'Salt' incorporates the originally unpublished ending as reported in Han Man-soo's 'Gang Gyeong-ae so-geum-ui bokja bog-won-gwa geom-yeol-u-hoe-ro-seo-oe "na-nwo-sseu-gi"' ('Restoration process of brush-stroke bokja/fuseji in Kang Kyeong-Ae's "Salt" and the strategies used to avoid censorship'), published in *Han-gukmunhak-yeongu* (*Korean Literature Research*), 31, pp.169-191.

Anton Hur
Translator